ONCE UPON A COURTESAN

THE COMERFORD COURTESANS

BOOK ONE

JESS MICHAELS

For Michael. Even after so many years and so many book dedications, I'll never run out of ways to say how much I love and appreciate you and your support.

PROLOGUE

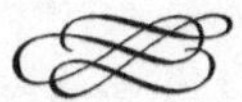

1807

Arabella Comerford didn't know everything at seventeen, but she knew one thing: she didn't want to marry.

Well, that wasn't entirely true. She didn't hate the *idea* of marriage. She understood there were benefits, such as a sense of security and getting to participate in the very naughty things she'd found out about in book stolen from her father's private library. The ones that made her achy and hot.

But she *didn't* want to marry the way her father wished her to do. He'd been on the hunt for her husband since she was sixteen, parading her in front of old men of a certain rank and monetary situation, talking about her like she was a horse at market. Once, when she'd left the room for a moment, she'd overheard one of the men having a conversation with him about her maidenhead being intact. How much the potential suitor looked forward to having it.

And her father had encouraged such talk, so long as it got him what he wanted: increased position and access.

He hadn't forced her hand yet. To marry her off at sixteen would be looked upon with arched brows and whispers. No, he had to bide his time, and so she did so, as well. What she'd do, she had no idea, but the desperation to save herself and her two younger sisters was only just beginning to burn the edges. Ever more so since her seventeenth birthday when her father had packed her up and hauled her off to London.

Arabella loved London with all its loudness and boldness and brightness. She loved catching glimpses of things she wasn't allowed to see as a gentleman's daughter, real slices of the lives being led behind closed doors. She wanted to throw those doors open and look inside. She wanted to spin and dance and laugh too loudly and truly experience the world around her.

Her father would never allow it, of course. She was honestly surprised that he had agreed to the trip they were currently on to Vauxhall Garden with her aunt, Caroline Ashfield. Her aunt was her father's younger sister, who had also been married off many years ago. Luckily for her, her husband was now dead and she was free.

"You are distracted," Aunt Caroline said as she leaned over to take her arm while they filtered toward the front gate of the garden, metal tickets in hand. "I thought you'd been waiting for ages to finally see the garden."

Arabella jolted from her worries. "I have been. And oh, I can hear the music and I *am* excited. I just..."

"Can't stop thinking about this afternoon?"

Arabella nodded. "How can he be serious about lining up gentlemen for me to pick from already? About buying wedding trousseaus? I haven't even had a Season. I've never even been able to attend a dance, never been able to mingle amongst friends and young men and feel the rush of the chase. Ugh, he'll have me in the bed of one of those ogres before the year is out and my life will be over."

Her aunt flinched, probably at her blunt assessment, but she didn't correct Arabella. "I am sorry, my dear. I've tried to discuss this with him. I've tried to convince him to turn his course, but he has little respect for women as a whole and even less for me."

"I know." Arabella squeezed her aunt's arm gently. "I appreciate you trying."

"There *is* one benefit to being forced to marry an old man," Caroline said after a pause.

"He can barely perform his husbandly duties so you don't have to bear his pawing for long?" Arabella asked.

Caroline's eyes went wide. "Goodness, you should be careful what you say."

Arabella shifted, heat flooding her cheeks, and looked around to see if anyone had heard her. Those in the line shuffling toward the entrance all seemed too tangled up in their own conversations and excitements to be listening to her and her father was bellowing to some person a few people farther up in line. A man his age, of course. And occasionally they looked at her like she was something on sale in a shop window.

She supposed that was an apt comparison. Still, she lowered her voice when she spoke to her aunt again. "Then what *is* the benefit?"

"They die when you're still young enough to have a future." Caroline stared off into the distance a moment, but there was no mistaking her sadness.

"I'm glad you still have a future," Arabella said softly. "I wish I could see mine, *control* mine on any level. Even tonight, when I should be thrilling at every bright beauty of the garden, I know my father will be watching me. Judging me. Trotting me out to any man with the right rank and pocketbook."

"Hmmm. Yes. Well, *I* am your chaperone tonight," Caroline said. "And *he* can be distracted. Perhaps you'll be separated from our party. Briefly, of course. *Safely.* And you'll get a moment to truly enjoy yourself where you don't feel him breathing down your neck."

Arabella's lips parted. "You...you would allow that?"

"*I could do nothing about the crowd, Albert,*" her aunt said, using

Arabella's father's first name while she blinked in what was very believable false innocence. *"The poor girl must be terrified to be lost from us. But give it a moment and I'm certain she'll reappear. How far could she have gone?"*

"And when I return I will *be* terrified," Arabella mused. *"Oh, Father, I'm so sorry. A horrid man…oh, a juggler. He hates jugglers. A horrid juggler stepped in my path and by the time I got around him you were both out of my sight.* Then I'll sniffle and you'll comfort me…"

Caroline nodded as their tickets were examined by brightly liveried servants and then they stepped through the gates. Arabella's breath caught as she forgot their wicked little plan and really looked around her. She had been obsessed with Vauxhall Garden for years, reading everything ever written about it and its entertainments in any paper or book she could get her hands on.

It had the wide, stone-lined paths and tall trees and well-manicured bushes and flower displays of a regular public park. But it was far more than that. Vauxhall Garden was a spectacle. There were lanterns strung along the path in dazzling closeness so that it was almost as bright as day even though the sun had gone down over an hour before. There was music playing from the large, open concert hall in the middle of the garden and a woman sang opera with a clear, perfect tone above the murmurs of the crowd. Everyone was in their finest, with royalty mingling with even the lowliest patron.

There was laughter, occasional gasps of excitement at the presentation of a scantily clad tightrope walker making her way across wires that were stretched over one segment of the crowd. Later there would be fireworks, a fine display that Arabella had heard told could shake a person down to their bones. It was all a singular delight and her worries faded a fraction.

In that moment, of course, her father reached for her, tugging her forward and away from Caroline. "Stop gaping up, you silly girl."

Arabella's natural reaction was to snap back at him. She did that at home plenty, a way to draw his ire to her so it wouldn't fall on her younger sisters, Evelina and Julia. But tonight she didn't want him to find a way to punish her. To drag her off from all the joy and pleasure she wanted to savor in this magical fairyland that was all she had ever hoped for.

"I apologize, Papa," she said, all sweetness and light. "I'm simply washed away by all the magic."

"Magic," he snorted. "Foolhardy waste of time and money, I say. If it weren't one of *the* places for a woman of your position to be seen, I wouldn't have bothered to make the expense."

"Yes, Papa," she said, sending her aunt a small look. Caroline dashed her gaze away. It seemed that even as a widowed and self-sufficient woman, she didn't dare go against her brother. Perhaps stand up to *any* man with more power. That was the way of the world, after all.

"Now later I'll introduce you to a few gentlemen. I saw more than one eyeing you while we were in the line. You'll do well to impress them tonight. You'll want to have choices, I think, or you might not like where you end up. I have other daughters, so if you fail I'll have to put my efforts to Evelina. She may not be yet sixteen, but arrangements can still be made."

Arabella's stomach turned, but she was saved from having to act sweet and obedient because her aunt did step up then, catching her father's arm, drawing him away to point at something in the distance. As she did so, she shot Arabella a hard look.

It was time, it seemed, despite the fact they had barely arrived in the garden. Caroline clearly didn't think she'd be allowed another chance to be free, to enjoy herself…perhaps ever.

And with that thick, cold fact choking her, she turned away and slipped into the milling crowd, away from her family and her father's cruel intentions. For a few moments as she walked, all she could do was mull his wretched plans and the destruction that would follow in their wake. All she could do was mourn what she would lose and fear for the sisters she would no longer be able to protect.

But then she shook those thoughts away. She was not going to have much time. She wanted to use it well. So she shoved her shoulders back, drew a shaky breath and slowly picked her way through the crowd, eyes turned up to all the sights and sounds.

The opera singer was pouring another tune into the magical air and the lanterns flickered, almost in time to the music. A peel of laughter came from a group of beautifully dressed women who were huddled together and just past them a few couples had begun to dance. Even farther away she saw tables by the pavilion and perfectly liveried servants brought out a feast to those who observed from the distance. She knew she should go back now, time was slipping by, but she continued moving instead, farther into the crowd.

A man twirled past her, torch in hand, and then startled Arabella by leaning forward and spitting fire like a dragon across the walkway, just between the groups of people, including herself. She let out a little screech and turned away, down a narrow trail that was somewhat quieter. Her heart pounded as she made her way along the paths scented by honeysuckle and jasmine, sweetness mixed with something richer, more sensual.

For a moment she gathered herself. There was a nagging sense that she should return to her father and aunt. That she was pressing the bounds of explaining her absence as a mere accidental separation. But the garden was so lovely, and she realized, as she stood there, that she was just on the edge of the area on the maps she'd studied that contained the alcoves in the gardens. Little places for attendees to have a moment's peace or a refreshment, or even a romantic assignation. She crept closer and peeked into the first alcove. It was empty, though the richly painted fresco on the vine-lined wall was beautiful, indeed.

She moved along, finding quietly talking groups or couples until she reached the last alcove, farthest down the line and barely touched by the light. As she neared it, she heard the most curious sound.

Moaning. Her heart leapt, for she wondered if someone was ill or hurt. But as she peeked into the protected area, she stopped, blood rushing away from her face. There was a couple in the alcove and they were not sharing what she'd have pictured as a *romantic* interlude. No, it was far too animal to be considered that. The woman was perched on the edge of the wall, skirt tugged up around her waist, one leg wrapped around the thickly muscled thigh of a man. He was arched up against her, rotating his hips, his partially uncovered and shockingly toned backside moving as he thrust into her.

Arabella covered her mouth with one hand. Everything that had been trained into her over her entire life about propriety and sin rushed up and told her to run away from such a lewd display.

But the parts of her that felt the tingle of desire in the night, the parts that had stolen her father's naughty books and sometimes peered over them as she touched herself beneath the covers…

Well, those parts kept her firmly in place, watching the couple, her body becoming hot and wet as she stared.

The woman against the wall was shaking now, her hands digging against the jacketed shoulders of the man as she whimpered, "Yes, Silas. Oh fuck, yes."

He leaned away, watching his partner. The moonlight and lamplight hit his face just so when he did and Arabella couldn't breathe anymore. He was beautiful. With thick, finger tousled hair and bright green eyes that held on his lover, with full lips that he licked as she arched beneath him and her cries became louder still as her body jerked out of control.

He chuckled, a low sound almost lost in the cacophony of her pleasure, and then he reared back to thrust again. As he did so, he glanced over and before Arabella could react, he speared her with those stunning eyes. They stared at each other, gazes locked, and then his grew hotter. He thrust harder, never parting his stare from hers, and somehow she couldn't run away. Time stood still, no longer had meaning, as she became part of the scene before her.

It was only when he dipped his head back with a grunt that the spell was broken and she pivoted to race back toward the crowd, away from the magic of that moment in the alcove.

Her hands shook as she careened up the walkway. She should have been shocked, horrified, afraid even. She was none of those things. She was entranced. She'd been aware of her own physical needs for years and explored the ways she could touch herself that made her feel good. But this...*this* was a culmination of every ill-informed fantasy and breathless reading of forbidden books. This was passion and pleasure and surrender to everything a person truly was, without apology, without censure.

She came out into the area near the concert hall once more and immediately she found her aunt and father. Caroline was lifting up on her tiptoes, searching the crowd while her purple-faced father looked the other way. When her aunt met her eyes, there was no mistaking the relief on her expression.

"There she is, Albert," she said as Arabella rushed to them, hoping the truth of what she'd seen wasn't clear on her face. Hoping they wouldn't see that watching that man, that *amazing* man with his lover had changed her. Cracked open a part of her she'd been trying to pretend didn't exist. Now that part was alive. She couldn't be ignored anymore.

"I'm so sorry," she managed to croak out. "This horrible juggler pushed into my path, Papa, and the next thing I knew I couldn't find you."

"Hmmph," her father said with a glare. "You were gone long enough. Wait here with your aunt, I see one of the men who wishes to meet you. I'll have to convince him to join us for the first round of fireworks."

Arabella should have been troubled by those words, but she was too wrapped up in what she'd just seen to truly register her father's continuing drive.

When he had left them, Caroline took her arm. "You were gone too long, dearest. I was truly worried."

"I'm sorry," Arabella gasped out. "I was lost in the moment, I fear."

She looked toward the alcoves and saw, to her shock, the very woman she'd watched being taken a moment ago. Arabella recognized the mauve silk of her beautiful gown. The lady was lovely, probably somewhere between Arabella's age and her aunt's, with dark hair. Her lover was nowhere to found, much to Arabella's disappointment.

"Who is that woman?" Arabella asked, motioning.

Her aunt followed her gesture and caught her breath as she turned Arabella away. "That is Simone Stanhope and you should steer clear of her."

"Why?" Arabella asked, glancing over her shoulder toward the woman again. "What's wrong with her?"

She had already guessed some of the answer. After all, ladies didn't go around having passionate encounters in the middle of public gardens, did they? *Did they?*

"She's a courtesan," her aunt whispered. "An infamous one. Ladies like you shouldn't involve yourself in such things. Shouldn't ask about women like that. Your father would be enraged."

Arabella nodded slowly. She'd heard vaguely of courtesans and lightskirts. Almost always in negative and desperate terms. Their lives were used as threats. If she didn't come to heel she'd end up making her living on her back like a whore. The very man who threatened her with that end was the same one who would sell her to further himself.

Even now he was coming back across the crowd, false smile bright on his expression, a man at his side. Arabella didn't know who her father's companion was, it didn't really matter. They were all the same. Selfish men like her father. Men who wanted to buy her virginity and her youth and her assumed ability to breed them sons so they could continue their lines. Men who were three times her age and leered at her outwardly.

Her father stopped before her and introduced her to the man in question. Arabella nodded and smiled and pretended to give a damn, even though she didn't truly pay attention. How could she when thoughts of that man and woman in the alcove haunted her.

Despite being pinned against a wall, Simone Stanhope hadn't seemed trapped. She hadn't seemed miserable. She hadn't seemed to be out of control. She'd been free to throw her head back and moan so passionately that her pleasure couldn't have been mistaken by a great many people around her, not just Arabella.

And Arabella was chided not to laugh too loudly.

She gave her head a tiny shake and then jumped when fireworks began to pop overhead. Their group turned to look at them, admire their beauty, Arabella felt their concussive explosions shaking her to her very soul. It seemed the night for such things, for realizations that once made couldn't be unmade.

The biggest of those was that she didn't *want* the life her father had planned for her. Well, that wasn't entirely true. She'd known that from the beginning, hadn't she? No, what she knew for the first time was what she wanted instead. Not to find some other gentleman who was more palatable to marry and who would ultimately control her just as the men her father chose would do. Not to give away her passions to someone who would put all his effort into breaking her so she would be a more proper lady.

She wanted what she'd seen tonight in the alcove. To live her life with freedom, to make her money off her own choices. To be able to laugh and moan too loudly for proper ears and to dance until dawn in the morning with as many men as she wished.

She glanced again at Simone Stanhope, who was watching the fireworks with a small group of her own. The man who had taken her was not with them. Simone stared up at the night, her face clear and bright and lined with a power that Arabella had never seen any woman in her life be allowed to possess. This woman wasn't a broodmare whose entire existence was meant to make a man happy and comfortable.

She was a goddess.

No, Arabella Comerford was not going to marry some old man to please her father. She would *never* work to please him again. She would instead forge her own future, release her wild heart and damn the consequences of it all.

CHAPTER 1

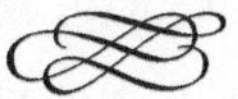

1813

Six Years Later

Silas Windham hadn't been to the Donville Masquerade in six years, yet he found it much the same as he remembered it with its unapologetic celebration of pleasure and sin. He'd been in America all that time—running, his siblings would call it. And he would snort and deny it, but in his heart he knew it was true. He *had* been running for almost every day since he'd left London.

Of course, none of that mattered. He'd returned to the city a week ago now, and had been trying to find some way to ease back into his old life and finding it ill-fitting. Like he'd changed too much and his old clothes no longer fell around him as they should. Perhaps he had at that. When he looked around the great hall at the people flirting and teasing and often fucking, he felt little stir of longing. Once that had been his currency.

"Is that Silas? *My* Silas?"

He turned at the female voice calling out to him and couldn't help but smile as his tangled emotions faded a fraction. "Simone," he said as his former lover reached him and leaned in to kiss first one cheek then the other. He took both her hands and shook his head. "You haven't aged a day."

It wasn't a pretty lie. Somehow she hadn't. Although Simone was more than half a decade older than his thirty years, her dark hair and eyes were just as bright, there was not an additional wrinkle to her cheek. It seemed her life of joyful excess suited her.

"You are a flatterer, my dear," she said, and slid her arm through his.

From any other woman, especially a courtesan like this one, he would have thought this was her trying to make a physical connection to perhaps land him again now that he was back in London. But Simone had always been as good a friend as she was a lover.

"How long has it been?" she asked.

"Six years," he said, and refused to add that he could actually mark the time down to the day, the hour almost. Not because Simone had been so very important to him, but because just hours after his last heated encounter with her something had happened to him that had been life changing.

"Too long," she said. "How are you, then? Are you home to see your brother?"

He tensed a little and pulled away from her grip. She let him go and no reaction to that rejection registered on her lovely face. "Yes," he said, short but hopefully not cruel. He simply had no interest in getting into that topic with anyone. "But how are you?"

"Very well, thank you," she said. "I'm currently affiliated with the Marquess of Harding and he treats me well. Not as…passionate as some of my lovers, you included, but every chapter of a book like mine is different, isn't it?"

He nodded. "You have always written a fascinating tale, Simone. No one could deny it."

"How long will you be in London, then?" she asked. "Are you back permanently?"

He hesitated. There was the question, wasn't it? He'd come

"home" to a place that had never felt home. But the place he'd run to hadn't felt that way either. Would he stay here? Would he run back? Would he go somewhere else?

"I'm not certain," he finally admitted. "A month, maybe more if this all doesn't become unbearable."

"Hardly enough time!" Simone said with a false pout that turned into a wicked smile. "You know someone in my acquaintance is going to be *thrilled* to have you here."

He blinked at that surprising and entirely confident declaration. "What?"

Her expression became teasing, playful, as it was often wont to do, and she laughed. "Oh, nothing."

"It doesn't sound like nothing, you cheeky little minx." He was laughing but his interest was truly piqued, and that was something. "Are you saying I have a secret admirer?"

Her laughter boomed out over the crowd and caused a few to look their way. "Oh, I wouldn't ruin it for you. It is so lovely to have you back, darling. Will I see you at Vivien's later this week?"

Vivien Manning, another infamous courtesan, was hosting a fete in a few days' time and somehow she had been aware of his return, as well. Of course, the courtesans always knew everything, Silas had always admired them for the information they shared to protect themselves and each other.

"Yes, the invitation hit my tray before my trunks were even unpacked."

"Well, it's not every day we see such a welcome return," Simone said. She squeezed his hand. "I'll see you then."

He watched as she darted off into the crowd, back to her protector or some other lover or to who knew what entertainments. Once she was gone, he sighed. No, he really didn't know if his was who he was anymore, where he fit. And that was like a weight around his neck.

~

The courtesans of London were a network of sorts. Staying connected, sharing information, it made everyone safer, but also gave insider facts so that a woman might make a quicker connection, get a better settlement or avoid an entanglement that would ask her to perform acts she didn't like.

Once monthly, the courtesans gathered at a rotating residence, to drink tea and compare notes and coo over clothing and jewels that had been gifted by grateful protectors.

Arabella loved these nights of friendship and connection and tonight she stood with her two sisters, Evelina and Julia, and they watched the milling crowd of women with smiles on their faces.

"Georgina looks well," Julia said. "She seems to like her new arrangement with Lord Leughton."

"Her old one was so ghastly," Evelina reflected with a shiver. "It's one thing to agree to those kinds of things, it's another to have a man want to force them."

Arabella nodded. "Well, he's on the list now, isn't he? Not a one of us will grace us with our attention. He's shunned. He can go back to his wife."

"Well, considering *she's* having an affair with Lucy *and* Lucy's protector, Mr. Horace, I doubt he'll be having much luck with her either," Julia giggled.

Arabella pivoted to face her. "*What?* I hadn't heard that."

"It's all very new, apparently," Julia said. "I bumped into Lucy at the opera two nights ago and she was with them both. Couldn't stop smiling."

Arabella smiled herself. It was always lovely to see a person come into their own. To do what they wished and what pleased them. Of course, she worried if their friend was so happy, she might have developed feelings for one or both of her lovers. That could lead to hurt, but every courtesan had to learn that lesson for themselves if they couldn't see it from those around them.

She had never risked her heart with any of her lovers. It was part of her charm that she was a dancing sprite who pleased and laughed and charmed and then flitted away without so much as a look backward as she counted her settlement.

At present, of course, she was between protectors. She had parted ways with the lovely second son of an earl just a week before. She'd taught him things that had made his eyes go delightfully wide and then sent him on his way as soon as he'd started talking about a young lady he was properly courting. He liked her, would probably love her eventually, and he would be happy in his choice. He'd allowed Arabella to keep all the jewels he'd given her over the few months they'd been lovers and added nicely to her coffers with a monthly annuity to last for the next year. Perhaps she'd wallpaper the breakfast room. It could use some freshening up and she liked to make it pretty since it was one of the spaces in her home where she and her sisters were the only ones who came. A private place not for lovers.

"*Arabella!*"

She jolted as Evelina said her name with some force. When she glanced at her sisters, they were both staring expectantly.

"Oh, was I woolgathering? My apologies. Just wondering if I should do green or blue in the breakfast room if I redecorate."

Julia laughed, her face brightening with pleasure. "Oh, green! A lovely spring green would be so happy."

"For you?" Arabella reached out to boop a fingertip on her sister's nose. "Anything."

"I was asking you who you were considering for your next protector," Evelina said. "While you stared off into space thinking about paint and wall hangings."

"Yes, you never go long without one," Julia said, and her face fell a fraction.

She had been without a protector for over a month. Arabella's younger sister was far more selective than she was. Or at least had fewer resources to catch herself a new gentleman within hours of her last. Sometimes Arabella worried about her. She was such a romantic at heart and that was the way courtesans ended badly. Not that Julia would ever be unprotected. She and Evelina had been ensuring that all their lives.

"Well, I like having someone rich and powerful on my arm," Arabella said. "I let them think I'm the decoration for them, but it's the opposite. As for picking a new one, I know my worth. I've watched *them* sniff around me and place their wagers and claim that they would have me since the moment Geoffrey stepped out my door. There will be a frenzy in a few more days. I'll have my pick."

"And what do *you* want?" Evelina asked as she wrinkled her brow. She had been with the same lover for nearly two years now, the Duke of Southwater, who they all cheekily called Harry after his given name, Harold.

"Whoever pays the best settlement and benefits, I suppose," Arabella said with a wink, though for a moment she had a flash of a memory that was *not* new. The man in the garden all those years ago, his green eyes meeting hers and holding there in the heights of his pleasure. She pushed the thought away. She could savor it later, as she often did when she entered the realm of fantasy.

"Is that all?" Julia asked. "You'll only look for some man's pocketbook?"

"Well, fun is also nice," Arabella said. "And satisfaction if it's possible."

"Someone who will appreciate your wild," Evelina said quietly.

For a moment, Arabella was struck silent by the sting of her sister's words. What she and her sisters called her "wild" was a topic of great contention amongst the men who had bedded and kept her over the years. Almost as much contention as it had been with her father, though she had far more power in those relationships than she ever had in the one with him.

"They all appreciate my wild until they have it," Arabella said. "Then it becomes about who can stifle it. Bridle it and keep it just between the sheets. Until they realize I won't give it away and it all ends." She shrugged. "*C'est la vie.*"

"Oh, Arabella," Julia breathed softly.

Arabella caught her sister's hands and spun her around in the circle with a laugh. "Don't you take that tone with me, Miss Comerford! I am not pitiable and I shall not be pitied."

Julia giggled as they came to a stop and she rebalanced herself. "Of course not."

"Oh look, here comes Simone," Evelina said, waving off toward the crowd.

Arabella looked in the direction that she indicated and her smile widened as her old friend and mentor started across the room toward them. She was wearing a gorgeous dark blue silk that brought out the absolute perfection of her skin. Arabella could only hope she would age so well and still be so sought after at the long end of her thirties.

"Simone," she said, and hugged her friend. Her sisters did the same and then stepped away to talk with another friend and give the two of them privacy. They were all close to Simone, but her sisters knew that Arabella and Simone were the closest. "My God, you are a vision. I'm desperately jealous."

Simone barked out a burst of laughter and linked arms with her. For a moment they looked out over the group of courtesans.

"We might need to offer a little assistance to Beatrice Holms," Simone said. "She's not had much luck with her choice of protectors and her last didn't settle her well."

"Oh, poor Bea, she's so new," Arabella said with a sigh. "Yes, I'll be on the lookout for her."

"What about yourself?" Simone asked, repeating the question Arabella's sisters had just posted, but with far more experience behind the words. "Who will you pick, do you think?"

"Oh, it's early days yet," Arabella said with a knowing smile. "I'm not allowing anyone near."

Unlike her sisters, who had seemed troubled by the answer, Simone nodded knowingly. "Ah, so you let them work themselves into a froth for you. Fight over the honor of your attention. You increase your value."

"I learned from the best," Arabella said.

"Hmmm," Simone replied. "That's a lovely compliment, but I think you've surpassed me in your reputation and accomplishments in these last five years. You are the ultimate courtesan and one we all strive to emulate."

"You shall make me blush," Arabella said with a shake of her head. "I didn't think I still knew how to do that."

Simone laughed and then squeezed Arabella's arm gently. "I do have some information for you that might just change your thought process on your next lover."

Arabella's eyebrows lifted. "Really? And what is that?"

"Silas is back."

It felt as though the room around Arabella faded into a blur, the music stopping, the buzz of the women dissipating into the wind. There was nothing but her and Simone then, and the name that hung between them.

"Silas Windham?" she managed to choke out.

Simone nodded. "The very one."

Simone was watching her closely now. But of course she would. Silas and that night at the Vauxhall Gardens had brought Arabella to her and to this life. She'd never made her desire for him a secret over the years because she had decided never to make what she wanted a secret ever again. She pursued her passions, whether it be men, the occasional woman, orgasms or the finest silk for a gown.

"Back from America," Arabella mused.

"Yes, I saw him at the Donville Masquerade two nights ago."

"Oh," Arabella said slowly. "Does that mean he's yours?"

"Mine?" Simone cackled. "My dear, he was never mine. That moment in the garden altered your life, I know, but it was, as I've told you many times over the years, nothing but a bit of fun for me. Silas has never *belonged* to anyone, I don't think."

There was far too much pleasure in the idea that the man was fair game. Arabella had to fight for breath as she murmured, "Hmmmm."

"So he's yours to claim if you'd like him."

She tossed a lock of hair off her shoulder with a shrug that was far more nonchalant than she actually felt. "We shall see. Who even knows what kind of man he'd be after his long disappearance? What brought him back anyway?"

A little shadow crossed Simone's expression, but then she shrugged. "I have my theories, but he didn't say. Silas has always blown by his own wind. Rather like someone else I know."

"Sounds like it could be explosive," Arabella said.

"I fear it might be. But I may see him at Vivien's party tomorrow. Are you going?"

"No. My aunt is having us over for our monthly supper at her home."

"Oh, sweetest Caroline. Give her my regards," Simone said.

Arabella laughed, for her proper aunt had only encountered Simone once, but any mention of the courtesan always made her blush.

"And should I make an overture to Silas on your behalf?" Simone continued. "Set the groundwork for you?"

A shiver worked through Arabella at that thought and yet she still shrugged as if it didn't matter. "I suppose."

"Then I shall. And now I must go. Harding is expecting me soon and one mustn't disappoint."

"Goodbye, dearest," Arabella said, kissing her cheek. Her sisters floated toward Simone, as well, saying their goodbyes, too.

But as Arabella stood there, still watching the room but no longer seeing it, she couldn't deny the thrill that worked through her body and soul. The man she had dreamed of, obsessed over, fantasized about as back. And she was going to make him hers.

There was already no doubt about it.

CHAPTER 2

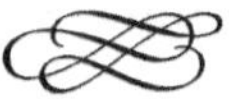

The house of the Marquess of Pentaghast was just the same as
Silas remembered it from growing up here. It was cold, for
one, sophisticated without ever allowing tenderness inside. His
memories here were mostly unpleasant. There was the loneliness,
the isolation, the fear, the pain and the absolute knowledge that as
the marquess's illegitimate son, he didn't belong. He almost felt like
that child again as he stood in the front parlor, nursing a whisky
he'd poured for himself while he waited. It didn't take the edge off
nearly enough.

"Mr. Windham?"

Silas turned toward the butler watching him from the door. The
same one who had served his father, it seemed. Hateful creature
who had always treated him as what he was…or perhaps what he
wasn't. "What is it, Russell?"

"Lord Pentaghast will see you," Russell said, and then shifted
with what seemed to be discomfort. "However, he is abed, sir, and
you will have to meet with him in his chamber."

Silas blinked at that revelation. His brother had never been so
informal. "Is it…is it that bad?"

For a moment, true worry crossed the butler's expression. "I-I cannot say, sir."

Silas wasn't certain if he meant he wasn't allowed to share, he didn't know, or he feared too much to repeat. Whatever the answer, it was disquieting. Silas smoothed his jacket and said, "I see. Well, if Charles will see me in the chamber, I'll meet him there."

"I'll escort you," Russell said.

Silas tilted his head. "I know where the chamber is."

There was a moment of quiet, of memory for them both. Then the butler surprised him by executing a small bow. "Of course."

He exited the room, freeing Silas to do as he would. He wanted to move, wanted to go up and get this over with, but his feet didn't seem to be capable of going forward at present. He finished his drink, took a shaky breath and forced them to do so.

Just as the parlor was the same, the rest of the house also remained unchanged. He made his way down the winding halls and up the large staircase to the private chambers. The family rooms were to the left at the top. His had been to the right. A guest in the home he'd been raised in after his father dragged him from his mother. What did that room look like now? Was any remnant of him left here or had his brother erased them all in the last six years?

He blinked and made himself turn left, past the doors to his siblings' rooms. Portia's first, then Reggie's and finally the room Charles had inhabited when he lived here and eventually when he came to visit after he'd reached his majority.

At the end of the hall was the big room. That was what Silas had called it as a boy. The prick's chamber was what he'd called it later. He flinched and lifted his hand to the carved double door and finally managed to force himself to knock.

There was a hesitation and then the door opened to reveal a servant. Charles' valet, perhaps. Like Russell, he appeared pale and worried.

"Mr. Windham," he said softly. "The marquess is ready for you."

He motioned to the open door on the left side of the antechamber. Silas nodded at the man and then made his way across the room where he'd received so many punishments over the years and into the bedchamber that had once been his father's.

It also looked the same. It seemed even after all these years, Charles was too afraid or meek to change anything in the house, down to the bedclothes. But that wasn't the main thing that Silas noticed. It was the man himself who drew all his attention.

Charles was fifteen years older than Silas. That was bound to happen when one was the bastard half-brother stolen from his mother as a child and raised amongst the *real* children. When Silas had last seen him, he'd been in his late thirties, the morning he'd become marquess.

He'd aged far more than half a decade since. He looked like he was in his sixties now, not his mid-forties. In fact, he looked just like their late father. He also was pale and frail, too thin and stretched by whatever illness plagued him.

"Silas," he said softly, Charles's gaze flicking over him from head to toe. It was not the same green as Silas's. No, he'd inherited that from his mother. Charles had their father's eyes, as did the rest of his siblings, though the result of that gaze was somehow softer. Kinder? Silas wasn't certain. "You are here."

Silas cleared his throat and inclined his head. "I was called here, my lord."

Charles stiffened a little and an almost imperceptible twitch rippled across his cheek. "Is that the only reason?"

Silas bent his head. "What is it you want me to say, Charles? Should I pretend away the past for you? When we last saw each other, we had a falling out. I left as you asked me to. I now return as you ask me to. I am, apparently, your servant." He cleared his throat. "But I'm also still not what you wish me to be. And I'm still a bastard. So here we are."

Charles didn't respond, but darted his gaze away. He cleared his throat and then began to cough, something raw and painful-sounding.

Silas found himself taking a step closer to this brother. "Can I do anything?"

When the fit ended, Charles shook his head.

"How are you?"

His brother spit into a handkerchief before he said, "They tell me the worst is over, but I've felt better a few times before and the illness returned."

Despite his complicated feelings for this man and the title he now held, anxiety still worked through Silas at that statement. Charles had been out of the house by the time Silas had been brought in. He'd not had a relationship with him like he'd had with Reggie, who'd lived at home for a year after Silas made his appearance. Or Portia, whom he was closest to. But when his mother died, Charles had been kind about it. At least until their father ordered him to stop speaking about the topic.

Silas blinked. "I'm not certain why you wished me to come here."

"Wasn't it Portia who asked you?"

"Yes." Silas gritted his teeth. "She told me it was on your behest. If you're telling me I sailed thousands of miles for nothing, that will be of great irritation to me."

"God forbid you be irritated," Charles muttered.

Silas folded his arms. "If you're about to imply that *I* was the spoiled one of the four of us, I would remind you that I never had the advantages of your name, only the disadvantage of being despised by almost everyone in this house."

Charles jerked his head up and the two brothers locked gazes for a long moment. Years of hurt flowed there, too sharp for Silas, drawing him back to long stretches when he'd had no power. He didn't want to return to those days.

He smoothed his jacket. "Charlie, I'm here. You're obviously unwell and I shouldn't make it worse by arguing. Why don't you think about exactly what it is you want me to do and I'll return in a few days to check on you? I'm letting a place on Camberley Park, I'll leave the address with Russell if you have need of me."

He moved to the door but not quickly, allowing his brother time to call him back if he wished to do so. He didn't. So Silas sighed and turned without being asked.

"I do hate that you're ill, Charlie," he said. "For whatever that's worth. Good night."

"Good night, Silas," Charles said softly, and let him go.

But as Silas made his way back through the house of his nightmares, his hands shook. How he hated what this place and these people made him feel. And he knew one way to take the edge off it all.

When Arabella had marched herself to Simone Stanhope's fine London townhouse and demanded she be trained in the arts of a courtesan, she had walked away from everything in her old life. Her father had cut her off in a rage so deep it still terrified her. Her sisters had been, albeit briefly, torn away from her. She'd lost her clothes and her money and everything but her own wits and charms.

Except for, that was, Aunt Caroline. Although Caroline had cautioned her against what she'd done, although she hadn't ever been able to support her financially or risk the consequences of a public connection, she had never withheld her love of Arabella. Nor of Evelina and Julia when they'd joined Arabella in London and on her chosen path.

These suppers, like the one Arabella was currently attending, were a monthly occurrence between the women. A little glimpse back at the life they'd all departed and a way to keep in contact with the aunt they all treasured.

"Aunt Caroline," Julia was saying. "Did you ever determine why your book kept getting moved from its place in the library?"

Caroline laughed. "It was my maid, Peg. She thought I had finished that one because the title was so similar to the next by the author. She thought another servant must be sneaking a read of it and kept putting it away. It's all resolved now."

"It's disappointing it wasn't a ghost after all," Evelina said with a sigh.

"You were the only one who ever considered that possibility," Arabella said. "And it's because you read far too many gothic novels yourself."

"You sound like Harry now," Evelina said. "He keeps trying to convince me to stop reading them. He even threatens to empty my library."

"He says he'll take your books?" Arabella asked, unable to keep the sharpness from her tone.

Julia shot her a look and then burst out, "Did either of you tell Aunt Caroline that Simone gave her regards?"

All three sisters glanced toward their aunt, giggling at her red-cheeked response to that statement. She always blushed when the topic of Simone came up. She'd been positively plum the one and only time the two women had met. Caroline was polite—of course, their aunt was too kind to be cruel or dismissive. But the two women were from vastly different worlds and it was fun to watch her stammer and go pink whenever someone said Simone's name.

"You will have to return my own," Caroline finally managed to choke out. "I caught a glimpse of her at the opera the other week, you know. She was in her box with…isn't she currently with the Marquess of Harding?"

"You know a great deal about a courtesan's movements," Arabella teased. "Yes, she's with Harding. Lord, that man hardly deserves to shine her boots, but there it is."

"Miss Stanhope is a friend to you girls," their aunt said, turning away to set her glass on the sideboard. "Of course I notice her."

Arabella opened her mouth to say more, but the parlor door opened and Caroline's butler was there. "Supper is served, Mrs. Ashfield, ladies."

"Thank you, Dennis," Caroline said, and looked genuinely

relieved as they all made their way to the supper table. She was just too easy to tease.

They were seated and a wonderful meal began. They spoke of theatre and music, of old acquaintances and new scandals in Society. At least she and her sisters had more insider information on those than their aunt often did, for they all saw Society from a very different angle now.

"And when will Southwater go to his country estate this year?" her aunt asked as the desserts were brought.

Evelina's smile softened a fraction, as it always did when Southwater was mentioned. Over the last two years, and despite Arabella's annoyance at the idea that he might try to manage what her sister read, he was normally a good protector. He seemed to care for Evelina and it was evident she felt far more than just attraction for him.

"Harry will stay until the final session of the House of Lords," she said. "He always takes his duty very seriously. Then he'll be out in Southwater for a month or so."

"Will you join him?" Julia asked.

Evelina nodded. "I always do, at least for some of the time. I do love it there. The estate is lovely."

Julia leaned on the table with an almost gooey-eyed expression. Unlike Arabella, her sisters still had a good dose of the romantic in them. Evelina had often spoke about how she thought Southwater would be her last protector. He'd made promises, it seemed, to keep her almost as his wife. To put off marrying for as long as he could and to make a political match and nothing more when he did. Those promises worried Arabella, for she'd often seen courtesans burned by such things.

As for Julia, she had idealized that kind of connection almost from the first moment she took on the life of a courtesan. She was still hopeful she would find a long-term arrangement, perhaps even one day marry.

Arabella felt a twinge of guilt at those desires of both her sisters. She always felt that more keenly when they were with their aunt. When she saw the life Evelina and Julia had left to become courtesans like she was. That had been the only choice, of course, the only mode of escape that Arabella could offer them, but that didn't change the fact that their dreams of being gentlewomen had gone.

"Have you heard from your father lately?" Aunt Caroline asked softly.

Arabella jerked her head up and snagged her aunt's gaze. She felt her sisters staring at her and cleared her throat before she answered as carefully as she could manage. "I have. Just his usual monthly screed against me."

Evelina's breath caught. "Still?" she gasped. "I thought that ended last year."

"Oh no," Arabella said. "He has never missed a one in all the time I've been gone from his home."

"Why didn't you tell us he has continued?" Julia asked, reaching across the table to take Arabella's hand. There was fear in her youngest sister's eyes. The emotion Arabella had tried to protect her from for decades, not just recently.

She shrugged. "It simply doesn't matter. You don't need to know what he says to me. He isn't very creative, it's the same as it ever was."

Evelina pursed her lips and it was evident she was truly irritated by that response. "I'm not eight years old anymore, Arabella!" she snapped. "You don't need to protect me or Julia anymore."

"I'm not certain that's true," Arabella said softly.

Evelina pushed back from the table and shot their aunt an apologetic look. "We have this round and round conversation too often for it to be productive and I have somewhere to be, as Southwater expects me soon. Julia, may I drop you off back at Arabella's?"

Julia looked from one sister to the other, clearly struggling with who to choose in this quiet argument that occasionally blew up into something louder.

"Go with Evelina," Arabella said gently. "I'll stay with Aunt Caroline for a while and then I also have somewhere to be."

Julia nodded and got up. Caroline led them to the foyer where there were kisses goodbye and promises to meet again soon.

"I'll see you later tonight," Julia said to Arabella, and shot Evelina a look before she headed out to the carriage that had been brought around.

Arabella met her sister's gaze and then Evelina huffed out a breath and kissed her cheek. "You're impossible and I adore you," she whispered.

Arabella smiled as Evelina followed Julia into the carriage and she and Caroline waved them away. It was over now, the argument wouldn't carry on. They would pretend it hadn't even come up.

"I apologize," Caroline said as they re-entered the house. She motioned them to the parlor where they'd began the night and Arabella followed her with a shake of her head.

"Do you? I think you wanted that truth to come out and you knew it would cause a scene."

Caroline shrugged. "Perhaps I did have ulterior motives. Your father's continued anger…*rage* toward you has always been frightening, Arabella. You stole his hopes for the future. Not just the ones that moved through you, but through your sisters."

"If he hadn't been willing to sell us all, I would never have rushed to save them. Anyway, what's the point of them knowing? It only hurts them."

"It allows them the opportunity to protect you as much as you strive to protect them," Caroline said and took her hand. "I'd like to hope that my brother would never move against his own child, but *believe* that he wouldn't? That's harder to do. Especially when you're between protectors at present."

Arabella sighed. "I know what you're saying. But I'll settle for one soon enough and then his title and money will likely be enough to keep Father from pushing too hard." She squeezed her aunt's hand. "Now I'll take my leave, too."

"Not to go home though."

"You have a lot of questions for a woman who doesn't approve of my path," Arabella said with a laugh. "If you must know, I'm going to the Donville Masquerade. And my invitation for you to go there one night always stands."

Caroline blushed to the roots of her hair and swatted at Arabella playfully. "Go on with you then! Good night!"

"Good night," Arabella answered, and then slipped out onto the drive and to the carriage that awaited her there. The carriage that would take her to distractions that she hoped might erase the sour taste which remained in her mouth thanks to thoughts of her father's deep and abiding hatred.

CHAPTER 3

Most who held membership at the infamous Donville Masquerade wore masks when they attended the hell's gatherings. After all, a great many of them had something to lose when it came to the games of passion and pleasure that were always encouraged within.

But Silas had never worn a mask here. He was the bastard son of a man of title. In some ways, he was expected to ruin himself in whatever way he chose. Living up to that reputation had been his pleasure. Or at least it had reduced his pain.

Tonight, though, still stinging from the encounter with his brother, the pain was not as dulled by the erotic images around him as it would normally be. He felt disconnected, like he was watching the writhing bodies and hearing the moans through deep water. It wasn't that he didn't feel the eyes on him, those who would seek his touch, it was that he found he didn't really care. There was no spark when all he wanted was that fire of desire to burn over him and make him forget everything else.

Just as he had the previous night he'd come here, it left a bad taste in his mouth. A fear that perhaps he no longer belonged in any corner of what was once his world. Perhaps he never would again.

With those maudlin thoughts cascading through his mind, he began to make his way through the pulsing crowd toward the bar in the back of the main hall. A few drinks and this would pass.

He was trying to believe that when he turned his head and everything else faded away. A woman stood at the wall near the end of the bar. She wore no mask, which was shocking enough at the masquerade. Women almost always wore one, though some of the courtesans and lightskirts didn't.

This woman wore a pretty blue gown that was the height of fashion and clung to seductive curves. She had dark hair and even darker eyes, though from the distance he couldn't make out their color.

She was gorgeous, the kind of woman that drew every eye of any room she entered. This one was no different, for she had admirers staring at her from every direction. She, on the other hand, was entirely focused on him. Their gazes met and he realized who she was in a rush of heated memories.

The woman at Vauxhall Gardens all those years ago. The night before everything changed when he'd fucked Simone Stanhope in the alcove and looked up to find a fallen angel watching him with a hooded, heated stare. With her focused attention on him, he'd come so hard he'd seen stars.

Under normal circumstances, he might have pursued her after that. Discovered her name, found her location, pursued until he could make *her* shake with pleasure. But his father had died that same night. He'd been called to the house the next morning and then he'd departed from the country. Left everything in this life behind as he stewed in his anger and pain and loss.

But now she was here, almost like a phantom drawn forward from the past and she was watching him just as she had that night. Her expression was almost as stunned as he feared his own was, too.

But then she shook it off and that shrewd playfulness that many of the courtesans he'd known in his life came over that lovely face. She started toward him, hips twitching just so as she licked her lips like he was a feast she was about to devour. Normally he had his own reactions to such things, but at present he felt a little stunned.

"There you are," she breathed as she reached him, standing a little too close to be proper, not that it mattered in this room where couples were actually copulating against walls.

"Here I am," he agreed, wondering at the fact that his voice had any heft when he could scarcely breathe. "And how did I manage to grab the attention of the most beautiful woman in this room?"

She placed a palm flat on his chest and laughed, the sound as gorgeous as the music around them. "Aren't you a flatterer."

"Somehow I think you know that I'm telling the truth."

"Hmmm." She looked around. "There are women of great power and beauty here. I suppose I *am* one of them. A lady must know her strengths in order to exploit them."

"A very clever lady must, at any rate," he said. He couldn't stop staring at her, taking in every new detail now that she was practically climbing his chest. God, her eyes were a beautiful midnight blue. He'd never seen anything like it. She had a little freckle on the corner of her lip that looked infinitely kissable.

But it was more than her beauty that captured his attention and wiped away every other distraction and thought that had been plaguing him. There was something electric about her. Immediately attracting and made a man unable to look away.

"I think you must know something about exploiting your strengths, don't you, Silas?" she asked.

He started. She knew his name, so she obviously recognized him just as he did her. The way she said it felt like a caress, as intimate as if they were picking up some conversation they'd started all those years ago. "I think people like us must."

She nodded slowly. "Is one of your strengths the ability to dance? I think I know the answer to that, but I thought I should ask."

"I would very much like to dance with you," he said, and took her hand.

Just as when she'd placed her palm to his chest, the shock of her touch worked through him with a rushing, electric power. Every hair on his body felt like it was standing on end and the heating of his blood was powerful and instant.

She led him to the dancefloor and he almost laughed. Dancing at the Donville Masquerade was practically a euphemism, especially as the night drew on. Couples ground together, they kissed with abandon, they made it clear what they would do when they were alone… or perhaps just in a corner with a place to lean.

But hardly any of it could be called dancing.

Still he pulled her close and cupped her hip, loving her tiny intake of breath and the way her pupils dilated in response. She never took her eyes from his, and it was intensely intimate to feel so absolutely drawn into another person.

"You know me," he said after they'd taken a turn to the music, somehow dodging the couples who weren't paying attention to anything but each other. "You said my name."

"Yes, I know you, Silas Windham," she said softly, a tiny smile tilting the corner of her full lips.

"And I know you," he said.

She blinked, the only crack in the sensual mask that wasn't of the cloth or leather kind. "Oh, do you?"

"I think you know what I mean. You and I shared a moment during a night a very long time ago. A lifetime ago."

There was a moment when he thought she might deny it. Her gaze dipped down, her steps slowed, but then she lifted her eyes back to his and nodded. "There is no point in denying it. I saw you at Vauxhall Gardens with Simone Stanhope almost six years ago now."

"You're the one she was talking about," he breathed.

She tilted her head. "You mean tonight when you were at Vivien's together?"

He blinked. It seemed she'd been asking about him. Or at least aware of him being back in London. "No, I didn't end up going," he said. "When I saw her a few days ago, she teased me that someone would be happy I was back."

"Simone, Simone," the woman breathed. "Well, I admit I *am* happy. I've had a great many thoughts of you since that night."

He leaned closer and drew a deep breath of her scent. Jasmine and vanilla, a sensual combination that spread increasing warmth through his entire body. "What is *your* name?" he whispered.

She licked her lips and he almost went mad with the desire that was increasing with every moment with her. When was the last time he'd felt so out of control with need? He couldn't even remember.

"Arabella Comerford," she said softly.

"Arabella," he repeated, letting the pretty name roll on his tongue. "Is that your real name or just the one you give here?"

"It's my real name," she said. "I've no reason to have a false one, even here. I think we both know what I am, don't we? You could guess it from my not wearing a mask, from how bold I am."

"I have experienced many a lady of many a rank who was bold."

"Yes, I assume you bring that out in women," she said, almost thoughtfully. "You draw them to the edge of what they believe is reason and then make them jump. What a fall, though."

"It's a lovely name," he said. "I think it would be lovely to moan while you shatter around my cock."

Her smile became mischievous. "There he is. *There's* the man who I first saw all those years ago, watching Simone as she came, holding my stare while he did the same. That wicked, wicked man who didn't give a damn who was watching."

"I don't give a damn who's watching," he murmured as he lowered his mouth toward hers.

"Neither do I," she answered, and then their lips met.

Silas had experienced many a passionate kiss in his lifetime. The most powerful ones came after a chase, a game where he wasn't entirely certain if he would obtain his heart's...or perhaps it was always only his body's...desire. But there had been no chase here tonight. The moment they'd begun talking, Silas had known they would end like this.

And yet it was one of the most passionate kisses he'd ever experienced. It was a kiss after being separated for a hundred years, a kiss after counting every graze of a hand and meet of a gaze across ballrooms and gardens. A first kiss, a last kiss and a lost kiss all rolled up into one.

Her lips parted beneath his the moment they touched and then she gripped his lapels with both hands, lifting into him with a muffled groan of relief and pleasure. One of his hands stole down her backside, cupping the shape of her, lifting her tighter against him as their tongues collided and clashed and yet somehow still welcomed and soothed. She tilted her head to change the angle and somehow everything got deeper, the exploration even more intimate as the world spun around them and they locked it out entirely.

He had no idea how long that lasted. When they surfaced at last, lips shining, panting breaths matched, eyes locked on each other in shock and wonder and desire unlike anything he'd felt in a very long time, the song the orchestra had been playing was just ending. Their dance was done. At least this one.

She looked as staggered as he felt for a brief moment and then she reached out and took his hand. He saw the knowing distance of an experienced courtesan slide back over that lovely face before she turned her back to him and began guiding him through the crowd toward the back rooms where members could take their pleasure together in slightly more private settings.

"Let's play," she said over her shoulder, and in his weak-kneed condition all he could was nod and know that this night would do everything he'd wanted when he came here. It was going to sear a new memory in him that would certainly erase something old and less pleasant.

~

Arabella had been trained in a great many things as a courtesan. She knew how to give pleasure and to pretend her own when it didn't come with the help of a lover. She knew how to compliment, how to make a man feel like what she wanted was actually *their* idea. She knew how to maximize her impact and gain the most from every arrangement. She knew how to comfort without losing herself in the process.

The skill she appreciated most though, as she guided *the* Silas Windham through the writhing halls of the Donville Masquerade, was that she could look unbothered when she was truly spinning inside.

She'd imagined kissing this man a great many times over the years. Sometimes it was the way she lulled herself to sleep, or brought herself to completion. But the reality of it was…different. Better because it was real and he tasted of a hint of whisky and smoky pleasure. Worse because in that moment he'd touched his lips to hers, she had forgotten every way she maintained distance from men who wanted to keep her.

She'd lost herself in that kiss, drowning in the pleasure, the sensation, the reality that *this* was the man who had starred in every single fantasy she'd concocted for herself over six years. And he was everything she'd ever hoped for.

But Arabella Comerford hadn't had her knees shake after a kiss in a very long time. The fact that she could barely stay upright as she reached the backrooms was…shocking. Still, she managed to nod to the servant keeping watch beside the dim hallway and drew Silas toward the room number the man indicated with his fingers. They entered the chamber together and she broke away from him, all but willing her heart to stop pounding. He would hear it when he came close enough and she didn't want to hand over the power by letting him know that she was shaken.

"Do you like to be watched, Windham?" she asked, then shook her head with a laugh. "A rather silly question considering our beginnings."

"I do like to be watched," he admitted. "And to watch in turn. But tonight…" He trailed off and then moved to the portrait mounted next to the fireplace warming the room. He slid the viewing area shut so that those standing behind it, the ones who liked to ogle, couldn't see.

She smiled. "Good. I think after waiting so long, it's best to let this be between you and me."

"I admit I hardly know what to do with you now that you're here before me."

She arched a brow. "You? After all the stories I've heard about you over the years, I can't believe that. But perhaps it been a long time. Do they not have willing women in America?"

"You *do* know a great deal," he mused softly. "And yes, they do have very obliging women in the former colony. But…it's been a while."

She cocked her head. That was a surprising admission. Every bit of research she'd obsessively done about this man said he was a love and leave kind of person. A charming rogue who gave pleasure and sought it with equal fervor and never connected anything deeper to either act.

"How long?" she asked.

He studied her a moment—reading her, she realized. The way people like them *had* to read people. Those who didn't belong, those who had something to lose if they chose wrong. How did she fare, she wondered, with this man who had been her fascination for so long.

"About a year," he admitted. "I got bored of the game."

"Perhaps you weren't playing it right," she whispered, and then reached to the front of her gown. Her seamstress made all of them so they were easy for her to remove and put on herself. She flicked a few buttons, unwrapped a little fabric, pulled a ribbon tie and the entire contraption fell around her feet in an artful pool of silk.

She was naked beneath, just as she always was. She couldn't even remember what it was like to wrap herself in layer upon layer of propriety as if a few scraps of fabric could protect her from the real demons out in the world.

She blinked away those thoughts, ones that were odd to find given the circumstances and smiled at the man who was staring at her, slightly slack jawed.

He was truly beautiful, even more than she had recalled. Of course her memories were shrouded in half-shadow and furtive glances. Now she could truly look at him. He was so tall and broad shouldered, with dark brown hair that was unruly around his forehead. He had green eyes, those eyes she knew so well, and they were focused and reflected all his desire. Up close he had an intensity and a wildness that seemed to come from every pore of his being. It called to her own. She wasn't going to refuse it.

"Are you going to stare all night?" she asked.

He laughed, a low, rough chuckle laced with more of that heady desire. "I think a man could make a study of you for a few days and be rejuvenated, but I'm not patient enough not to touch." He took a long step toward her and then stopped short. "Assuming you'd like me to do so."

He was asking for her consent, despite the circumstances. She blinked at him in wonder and then crooked her finger. "If you don't touch me, I'll combust and we'll burn the place down around us. Not very fair to the proprietor of this place and all he's built."

He laughed again at the mention of the man who owned the masquerade. "Well, considering Marcus Rivers is a good friend of mine, I couldn't have that."

He stepped to her, staring down at her in the dreamy firelight and candlelight of the chamber, and as he bent his head to take her lips again he whispered, "Oh, this is going to be worth the wait."

CHAPTER 4

Arabella knew all the colors in the rainbow of her pleasure. She knew how to coax them to the surface with very little effort and welcomed all the varieties. But tonight, as the man she'd fantasized about for years put his arms around her naked body and drew her against his chest, she found something new.

Or perhaps it was something she'd lost when her innocence had gone all those many years ago. It was the heated anticipation, the wild uncertainty that contained so much wonder and also a twinge of fear. And yet here it was as she lifted into this man and kissed him. Savored him, explored him. All the while her heart throbbed like she was some virginal miss.

He seemed to feel it too, for he drew back a fraction and stared down into her eyes once more. "You're trembling."

She swallowed and put all her effort into donning the costume of the experienced, playful courtesan once more. "Am I?" she said with a smile as she paced away from him. "Then don't make me wait any longer. I want to see you naked, Mr. Windham."

When she turned, putting her hands on her hips so she'd draw his attention there, he was still watching her face. Still reading her.

"Whatever the lady desires," he said with an incline of his head.

She kicked off her slippers, though she left her stockings tied as she watched him. Though he might not have been a courtesan, made his money from his body like she had, she still sensed something in him that was like her. He knew when to put on a show and he very obligingly did for her.

He shrugged from his jacket with almost a lazy indifference and let it fall to the floor behind him. The cravat was next, untied and unfurled without intentional speed. All the while, he held her gaze, playing with her.

She smiled. Most men expected her to play but didn't know how to play back. She was a toy to be put back on the shelf when a man was finished with her. But this was something different.

Silas tightened the fabric of the cravat between his hands, almost displaying it for her, then tossed it over his shoulder. He was faster with the buttons at the top of his shirt and then he tugged it off with one arm.

She froze and stared. There had been very many lovers, with varying bodies and she'd enjoyed them all. But this man was someone's masterpiece. His arms were something she could have written poetry about. Not just broad shoulders, not just spectacular biceps —no, even his forearms were something to behold.

"Your mouth is open," he said with a low chuckle.

She nodded and came across to him, uninterested in continuing the show if she couldn't touch the performer. "I think it wants to taste," she whispered.

She reached out a hand and drew just the edge of her nails down that truly wonderful, defined chest. He hissed in a breath as she did so and she reveled in the sound. A year since he'd had a lover. Well, she was going to be *such* a lover. Whether they did this again or not, she was going to burn a brand into him that would make it impossible for either of them to forget.

She stepped closer, watching him with every move. He could have caught her arms and done whatever he liked with her. She would have liked that too, truth be told. But he didn't take control.

He let her slide up to him, let her trace the naked lines of him without stepping back or taking over. And when she lifted her mouth not to his lips but to his throat, he dipped his head back with a shaky moan.

He tasted good. Of course he would. A man like this would always taste clean and somehow still masculine. Like a sweet treat someone had kindly crafted just for her.

She rested a hand on his stomach, letting her fingers tease at the waist of his trousers and he hissed in a harsh breath. "Arabella."

Oh, he was going to be her undoing. Just the way he said her name made her legs shake. So she kept herself from having to use them by dropping to her knees before him.

"I want that," she murmured, pointing to the cock that was so plainly outlined along the front of his fall front. "Please."

He cursed beneath his breath, though he unbuttoned the fall front obligingly. "It's the please that kills a man," he said.

"But just a little death."

She smiled up as she drew the fall front away and revealed him. It was a deep pleasure to her that this man was built the same in every part of him. If he was tall and broad and enthralling in the way he held himself, his cock was just as impressive.

It curved proudly toward that firm stomach, thick and hard as steel as she took him in hand and stroked him from head to base.

"Fuck," he grunted, and his hands came down into her hair, stroking against her scalp and making her body twitch with wanting him. And wanting to make him lose control.

She looked up him, holding his stare as she stroked him against her cheek, drew him across her lips but didn't open them. He surged toward her, moving through her hand and bumping those same lips gently. She smiled and then her tongue darted out to lick the head of him.

What happened next felt like a blur. After all these years of fantasy and memory, the heat of this moment finally being here exploded. She took him into her mouth and all the way to her throat, sucking and swirling her tongue around him as she did so. Whatever she couldn't take, she stroked with her hand and for a little while there was silence in the room aside from the occasional wet sound of her mouth on him and the soft groans he made in pleasure.

All of it aroused her beyond measure. Her sex was tingling, wet with wanting him and pleasing him. Achy with being so close to having her wildest dreams come true at last.

But just as his legs began to shake, just as his breath grew short and harsh and labored with the effort of waiting, he caught her under the arms and dragged her up to her feet.

"Maybe some time," he grunted as he pushed her back onto the bed and fell to cover her. "But not tonight."

There might have been some game to play where she protested and he bargained, where she toyed with him a little more, but he didn't allow it. His lips came over hers and his tongue drove into her mouth, exploring her, tasting her. Kissing had long ago lost its thrill for her, but this was like being reborn. Like being kissed for the very first time and feeling the explosion of want fill her.

She found herself lifting beneath him, trying to find some way to make their pelvises align when her legs were pinned shut and he was sprawled over her.

He lifted his head and chuckled. "In such a rush?"

She stared up at him, lost for words for a moment at the image of him like this, real not some foggy fantasy. "Aren't you?"

"No. Well, yes. Since the first moment you touched me every part of my body has been screaming at me to flip you onto this bed and rut with you like some wild animal."

"One of my favorite ways to fuck," she whispered, and glided her hands down his back, raking lightly with her nails.

He moaned a little at the touch and then cupped her cheek. It was such a small thing to do, so gentle and what could be construed as meaningless. But when he did it, everything in the room seemed to come to a stop. All there was was him.

"It's been six years since I first saw you. Six years since your face started invading the moments where I did this very thing with other women. So I intend to take my time. And you, Arabella, are going to let me."

He said nothing more and for what felt like a lifetime, she stared up at him. *He* had been the one to admit he'd thought of her face for so long, why did she suddenly feel dangerously vulnerable?

But she also felt even more deeply aroused. And the second outweighed the first. "I'm yours," she whispered. "To do with as you please for as long as you please, Silas. Close the place down while you fuck me if you want."

He dropped his mouth to her throat and began to suck gently, swirling his tongue against the skin and waking all the parts of her that were linked to her desire.

"Have you ever shut the Donville Masquerade down?" he asked as he dragged his lips lower, over her shoulder and then her collarbone. His tongue was so hot on her skin and she found herself squirming beneath him.

"No," she gasped out. "Do you think Rivers would kick us out?"

"If he did…do you have a carriage?" He was moving his hands now, down her sides, then in and across her ribcage. He slid up beneath her breasts and lifted them, massaging gently, flicking his thumbs over the nipples.

"Y-Yes," she gasped.

"Good. I came on my horse and doing this on his back doesn't seem very comfortable. So I'd fuck you in the carriage," he said. "And then on the stairs in the house I'm letting in Town."

She gasped as he lightly circled her left nipple with his tongue. "And then in the bed?"

"For a few hours in the bed," he promised. "And then we'd eat. And then I'd fuck you on the dining table. So don't you worry. If you're not sick of me in the next few hours, having the Donville Masquerade shut down won't be an issue."

She found herself laughing even though the images he created were entirely heated. Even the idea of sex on the back of his horse. It wasn't practical, of course, it seemed cruel to the animal, but the *idea* was lovely.

He smiled as he drew his mouth across the valley between her breasts and then focused his same attention on the right one. She dug her fingers into his hair, reveling in the electric pleasure that jolted from the place where he sucked her and the rest of her achy body. It was such a familiar path and almost comforting. Frustrating when he continued to lap back and forth, tugging, tasting, even gently nipping her until she was starting to rock beneath him with increasing urgency. God, who was the last man to make her so needy?

Finally, though, he drew his mouth lower, down the apex of her body, down over her stomach. She let her legs open wider and he took the space between her thighs, pressing them open with his shoulders. The lazy scruff on his cheeks abraded the tender skin there as he licked a trail upward. Finally he placed the flat of his hand to her, his fingers rippling over her. She turned her head into the pillow and let out a shaky sigh. Now to see how talented he truly was, for not every man could perform this act with any usefulness.

But the moment he spread her open slightly, sliding his thumb along her wet length, then dropped his head to her, he proved he was no average man with little thought or knowledge about the woman he bedded. The first stroke of his tongue along her entrance, then up to circle her clitoris, was heaven. The rest were something else. Something dark and deep that drew her right up to the edges of pleasure but didn't let her fall.

He held her steady with one hand against her hip, long fingers stroking there while the other massaged the outer lips of her in time to his tongue. She lifted to him, gasping for breath as wild sensations washed over her in waves, drawing her further out into the ocean where she would soon drown. But it was easy, somehow, and eventually she sank into the sensations, everything else forgotten as she dug her hands into his hair and rode with him as he teased her. He watched her as he did so, tracking her movements, changing with her sounds and shakes.

Just as he began to suck her clitoris, he slid two fingers into her to thrust in time. Her mind flitted back to the night at Vauxhall Gardens, to him watching Arabella as he sank into the pleasure. She rocked into him with a great gasping cry and then she came.

It was nothing like she'd ever experienced, that wild orgasm at the talented tongue of her fantasy. It was heavy and deep, the waves almost frightening as she gripped his fingers and rolled with the sensation. He never stopped pleasuring her as she did, drawing her through the crisis, lengthening it until she was almost screaming with the power. And only when she began to relax, when the waves became twitches, when her body relaxed with the warmth and glow of release, did he lift his head from between her thighs.

In the soft firelight, she watched him rise up, draw his mouth back up her body on the same trail he taken down, and then he found her mouth again.

"So lovely," he murmured against her lips.

She caught his cheeks in her palms and drew him closer, licking his slick lips so she could taste her release on him. She felt him shiver when she did so and the wicked power of that reaction made her body ache all over again.

"Very lovely," she agreed. "Now lie on your back, please."

He arched a brow as she scooted over and motioned to the bed. "So eager to be in charge?"

Even as he asked the question, he was following the order. "I think you'll enjoy it if you allow me to be," she said, and then slung her leg over his trim hips and mounted him. She didn't take him into her body immediately. She wanted to. She wanted to grip onto his shoulders, throw her head back and use that thick, lovely cock for her pleasure without thought of anything else.

But as he'd said, himself, this night had been a long time coming.

She wasn't going to rush through it just in case it wouldn't be repeated.

Instead she ground against him, letting him slip against the wet heat of her body, teasing and tormenting rather than satisfying. He watched her in the firelight glow, his angled face unreadable except for desire.

"Such a tease," he murmured.

She smiled and let her hair tremble around her shoulders and breasts. "I think a man like you likes to be teased." She arched her lips and almost let him slip inside. "I think you like to be a woman's plaything."

"Not always, but sometimes," he growled, and caught her hips in both hands. He slid her along his length and she was treated with her own game as the electric pleasure shot through her.

She reached between them, aligning their bodies and smoothing her wetness across his heat to ease the way. He groaned at the touch and groaned deeper when she shifted and he slipped inside first an inch then more and more until she took him fully.

The thick slide of him into her body was like heaven, stretching her in all the ways she liked best, making her want to cede control to him until he made her quake and curse and grip him. But he was hers. She had to keep remembering that. Tonight she was claiming *him* and whatever happened after that would be negotiated.

So she was slow as she began to ride that cock, gripping her fingers against his chest as she took him, rolled over him, clenching around him and all the while building her pleasure back to the soaring peaks she'd found against his tongue. He let her even though he certainly had the capability to steal her power. He watched her through it all, gaze hooded and heated and raw in its intensity.

But she knew her own pleasure far too well. Knew a man's pleasure just as intimately and the longer she rode, the closer she pushed herself to the edge. Her thighs began to shake, her breath grew short, the tingling sensations became sharper and just as she was about to lose herself, he sat up. His face was even with hers as he tucked her closer, cupping her backside to rock her in that same desperate rhythm as she came.

His mouth found hers and in the heated embrace of his strong arms she was utterly and completely lost. She squeezed her eyes shut and simply reveled in the flexing power of release, in the map of his touch all over her aching body, in the moans of appreciation that reverberated against her skin as he drew her pleasure out and out and out until she could hardly remember anything but being bound with this man.

At last she threw her head back with a last, broken cry and it seemed to shatter the dam in him. Whatever he'd been holding back so he could take every inch of her pleasure, he let it loose now. He shifted her onto her back, sprawled across the bed sideways as he rose up and started to take her hard and fast. The slap of their bodies joined with her gasps and his moans, a concert in the quiet around them.

She wrapped her legs around his hips and met him, grinding against him when he fully took her with each stroke and watching as the line of his control grew more and more taut and finally broke. He pulled from her with a gasping gulp of pleasure and came between them with shaky strokes against his hard cock. She reveled in the splash against her skin and smiled as she drew him down to cover her, taking his mouth as their panting breaths merged.

Whatever fantasy she had ever built in her mind, the reality had just lived up to it and gone even further. She had been his and she had claimed him as hers. It was more than just pleasure, there was something more wild and powerful and achingly beautiful to it than that.

It remained me be seen, however, if there would be anything more to it than this heated night and the uncommon passions they had shared.

CHAPTER 5

It had been a long time since an encounter had made Silas breathless. Oh, there was always release, he never missed it and he worked hard so his partners didn't leave without it either. But encounters were forgettable, meaningless most of the time. And every time in the last few years, especially. He didn't entangle himself very easily.

After all, he knew how much one could lose when one did so.

But here, with this remarkable woman lying in his arms, her dark hair down around his chest, her lush body tucked up close to him, it was hard not to feel like something very unique had just happened.

"Why were you watching me with Simone that night?" he asked.

She started a little, as if she hadn't expected him to question her about anything. There was a little triumph in that, for Arabella didn't seem like the kind of woman who would be easily surprised. Her armor was her knowing sensuality.

"It was the beginning of a road for me," she said after a moment's consideration.

He wrinkled his brow at the answer that didn't quite seem like one. "Ah, so you're saying it was early in your career?"

She shifted and those beautiful dark blue eyes moved away from his. "Yes," she said slowly.

He hesitated. There was part of him that felt the she was holding something back from him. But then again, women in the trade often had to do that. They didn't tell all because the secrets were both their greatest risk and their biggest currency. She didn't owe him the truth, so why did he want it so much?

She seemed to sense that and now she did look up at him again. "I-I didn't mean to spy on you with her."

"Did it embarrass you to see us?" he asked, arching a brow. "You don't seem the kind of woman who would be."

She shrugged. "I wasn't then. I'm not now. What you did that night, what we just did, it's as natural as breathing. To want is to be human. To fuck is to be alive." She sat up a little, her hands tracing his chest gently. "I know why that night stuck with me, why I couldn't stop thinking about you. But I was surprised when you told me you remembered me, too. Why?"

There was a flash of a moment when he considered telling her the truth. When he pondered blurting out that he didn't know why. That she had captivated him that night and tonight and he feared she might continue doing so. That he had thought of her both at his most aroused and also at his most broken.

But he didn't say any of that. He reverted to the rakish rogue that had served him well his entire life.

"Do you think," he began, dragging her a little closer and lifting up to kiss her neck gently, "that it's every day a man looks up on the edge of coming and sees a gorgeous stranger watching him from the shadows?" He kissed lower, nibbling along the lovely line of her to her collarbone. "Hands fisted at her sides, pupils dilated with desire she can't hide?"

She shivered as a response and he moved down her chest and latched onto her nipple. He licked her there, as she began to twitch against him most prettily. "It made the entire experience so much more intense."

He continued to lick lower, pushing her back. He reached what remained of the splash of his earlier release on her belly and began to slowly rub the evidence of his pleasure into her skin. She moaned. "Did you touch yourself after?"

She jerked under his fingers and whispered, "Yes." He brushed the roughness of his stubble against her thigh and then licked back to the sweet wetness of her pussy. She lifted into him and whispered, "And many times afterward thinking about it...and you."

He sucked her clitoris and she obliged him by starting to shake almost immediately. No wonder this woman was sought after, that men tracked her all through the hells like he'd seen them do tonight. He was certain they did the same in opera halls and ballrooms. She was a revelation, a sunburst of desire and pleasure and surrender that could wrap a man up and make him feel warm when he came in from the cold.

He sucked her harder and she came in long waves against him, her gasps and cries gorgeous in his ears. When she went weak, he looked up from between her legs and met her dark eyes.

"Do you want to do this for a while?"

She blinked. "Are you asking to be my protector?"

Protector. There was a loaded word for a man like him. Protectors in the sense she meant were rich and often titled and had a great deal to offer a lady who surrendered her favors. He didn't have nothing, but it still might not be enough in comparison to the dukes or marquesses or princes she could have claimed.

And protector in the other sense? He'd never been able to protect anyone he ever cared for. And he hadn't ever been protected by those who should. So what did he know of that sacred duty?

She sat up a little at his hesitation. "Or perhaps, Mr. Windham, you're just talking about being my lover."

He tried to read her, tried to determine if her little smile was real or false. He couldn't. She was too good at keeping the truth from her eyes.

"That might be better," he said softly. "I might not be here for long enough to take on any larger role than that."

She was quiet for a moment, as if she was letting that sentence sink in. Then she shifted out from under him and to her knees. She crawled toward him like some lovely, sleek tiger stalking her prey. "You know, Simone would caution me not to give away what I normally sell."

"She'd be very smart to do so," he admitted, and shivered as Arabella cupped his cheek and smoothed her fingers across his jawline.

"But…I think in this case I'll make an exception. For a while. For fun."

"Fun," he repeated as she reached between his legs and began to stroke the cock that was already half-hard again thanks to the taste of her pleasure on his tongue and the irresistible game of her. "I like fun."

She laughed. "I can tell that about you. And it's good, because we're about to have a great deal of it."

He laughed too as she pushed him back on the bed and then her dark head lowered so she could finish what he hadn't let her earlier. And as she took him in her mouth, he closed his eyes and let all the pleasure erase anything else he felt.

At least in that he could trust.

It was nearly six in the morning when Arabella's carriage pulled up to her townhouse in the heart of Mayfair. Silas hadn't been entirely wrong when he said they'd shut the Donville Masquerade down. By the time they came out of that lovely little room in the back, there were very few patrons left. They'd parted ways with a kiss and a promise to play again soon.

And now she was home and though she was deliciously exhausted from the demands of Silas Windham, she was also incredibly satisfied. It wasn't often one fulfilled a long-held fantasy and found it fully lived up to expectations.

Her driver helped her down and her butler opened the door for her as if he'd been expecting her. Barnaby was just entering his middle age, far younger than some of the senior servants she encountered. He was a handsome man, she'd picked that specifically when she made her household choices. Why not have something pretty to look at every day? His wife, her cook, was equally enamored and that was sweet.

But he was also efficient and strong enough to offer physical protection if she needed it. And as with all her servants, he didn't judge her.

"Welcome home, Miss Comerford," he said with the same tone as he would have had at six in the evening. "Would you like tea or straight to your rest?"

"Tea would be lovely and perhaps some of the scones left over from yesterday? I'm famished."

"Of course, miss. Right away." He inclined his head and left her.

She entered the parlor just off the foyer and smiled. Her home was not enormous, but it was very fine. Her third protector, the Duke of Kentwood, had gifted it to her to live in while they were lovers. He'd been a very good man to her after a very bad experience prior and she had spread her wings under his tutelage for over a year. Yes, he'd wanted to tame her wild, but he hadn't been cruel about it. When it was over, he'd given her the house outright, along with a small annuity to cover its upkeep and care for as long as she lived in it. It had been the height of generosity.

It had also given her enormous power and freedom in whom she picked as a lover and how she managed that person. And it had allowed her to offer a place to each of her sisters when they'd escaped the cruel machinations of their father. Even now, Julia stayed with her while she looked for her next protector. There was no fear of being put out into the street at the end of an arrangement, so therefore no rush to accept any man who might take her.

Arabella crossed to the window to look out on the street as the city began its day. Once again her mind slipped to Silas and his hands on her, his mouth on her. But also on his confession that he'd thought of her over the years just as she'd thought of him. It was funny that such a brief moment had silently bound them and brought them to this place.

"You are home very late."

Arabella started and pivoted to find Julia entering the parlor behind her. Her sister was still in her nightrail with a silky robe tied over it and she was barefoot.

"And you are up far too early," Arabella said.

"I couldn't sleep," Julia said, and came to stand with her at the window. "I waited up for you a while last night and then tossed and turned. So when I heard you, I thought I'd come down."

Arabella guided her to the settee and smiled up as Barnaby himself brought the tea service in. Likely because the other servants were busy doing other preparations for the day that didn't usually involve the interruption they were encountering now.

"Why couldn't you sleep?" she asked.

Julia let out a sigh. "Oh, you know. Just pondering my options. Unlike you, I don't have a line of gentlemen out the door to offer protection. It's always hard to make these decisions."

Arabella covered her sister's hand with hers and squeezed gently. Of the three of them, Julia was the least certain about her path. She had only been a courtesan for a few years, after Evelina and Arabella had swept in and rescued her before she could be married to a wretched man, their father's last attempt to use his daughters for his own gain.

Arabella had tried to protect Julia from the life for a while, but in these walls it was impossible for her younger sister not to understand what and how Arabella and Evelina made their way in the world. Ultimately, she had stepped into that world, herself.

"You judge yourself too harshly," Arabella said. "You have many gentlemen who are interested in you."

"But not like you," Julia insisted.

Arabella shrugged. "That's because my way is to dazzle them until they're so blinded by lust that they have to have me. But that isn't the way of everyone. Many men want someone soft and demure and gentle on their arm. They have an unpleasant relationship at home, perhaps, or they're of a shy bent and want their lover's company to soothe as much as inflame."

"I suppose."

"And there is the fact that you are..." Arabella hesitated. She had to go easy now, she didn't want to hurt or anger her sister. "That you are looking for a fairytale. You see Evelina with her arrangement with Harry and you want that same thing."

"A long-term lover who adores me and me alone?" Julia said with a laugh. "Oh yes, what a mad desire."

"It isn't mad," Arabella said, though to her it seemed mad. It seemed a recipe for heartbreak, though for a moment she thought of Silas again. No, that was fun. Just because he'd been her fantasy didn't mean he was her future. Her future was herself. "But it may not be realistic for women like us. What Evelina and Harry have is rare."

She didn't add that sometimes she wasn't even certain it was real. The duke made promises to her sister constantly about her being the love of his life and how he would keep her and protect her forever. For many women of their kind, that was the dream. And it did work for some.

But Arabella sometimes watched Southwater with her sister and wasn't certain.

She shook her head. Those were troubles for another day. If Evelina needed her, she'd be there and otherwise she wasn't about to intrude.

"You know, I could introduce you to a few gentlemen," Arabella said. "Help you pick if you'd like."

Julia got up and went to the sideboard where she poured them both tea and put two scones on a plate. When she returned she looked resigned. "Yes. That might be best. You've always been quicker to identify just the right gentleman to put in place. Perhaps I need that keen eye on my side."

"You always have it," Arabella said and then sighed with pleasure as she bit into her scone. "Oh, apricot. Mrs. Barnaby is a treasure."

Julia laughed. "She is that. Where did you go last night?"

Arabella sipped her tea. "Donville."

Both Julia's eyebrows lifted and Arabella understood why. She'd said many a time that she was taking her time choosing her next protector, letting the gentlemen sweat a little, gather some steam to fight for her, thus making her a bigger prize. Going to Donville was the very opposite of that measured plan.

"Does that mean you've chosen someone?" Julia asked.

"No." Arabella sighed. "I just wanted to have a little fun and forget the nastiness at Aunt Caroline's about Father's letter. Was Evelina very angry on the drive home?"

"You know Evelina," Julia said. "She blustered for a bit, but it wasn't about being angry. Father frightens her. I suppose he frightens all of us after everything he put us through. I distracted her talking about going to that new play at Covent Garden."

Arabella pursed her lips. "Well, hopefully she'll be past all that by the time I see her next. I wish Aunt Caroline hadn't pressed about it. There's nothing to be said or done."

Julia didn't look certain, but Arabella was pleased when she changed the subject. "So you just went to Donville to have fun. And you must have if you came creeping back into the house at dawn."

"I did," Arabella said.

Julia's brow wrinkled. "What aren't you telling me?"

Arabella hesitated and hated herself for it. The situation regarding their father aside, she tried to be honest with her sisters, but there was something about this thing with Silas that she didn't want to share. And that meant she had to do just that. It was dangerous to make an affair too precious.

"Do you recall when we saw Simone a few days ago?"

Julia nodded. "You two had your heads together for a long time."

"Yes. She told me…she told me Silas Windham was back in London."

Her sister's eyes widened. "*The* Silas Windham?"

Arabella felt rare heat rush to her cheeks. It was one thing to talk about the man, go on about her thoughts about him when he wasn't…real. But now he was here and very much real and it felt a little raw.

"Yes. At any rate, I went to the Donville Masquerade and he was there."

"Well, if I know you at all, which I do, I assume you sprung at him like some gorgeous, sleek cat and sprinkled all your magic until he couldn't resist you."

"Something like that," Arabella said with a chuckle. "You view me through very pretty glass, my love."

"I think I'm fairly accurate. You are a sparkling force of nature, Arabella."

Arabella ignored the compliment. "I *did* approach him, sleek cat or not, and we…there was an encounter."

"Ah!" Julia straightened up and set her teacup down. "And how was the man who has starred in every fantasy?"

"Spectacular," Arabella admitted on a sigh. "Oh, Lord, Julia, I haven't felt something like that in a long time. That spark, you know? When you want something so much and then you have it and it's so perfect."

Her sister's expression shifted slightly and she nodded. "I see. So is the man your protector now?"

Arabella got up and went back to the sideboard. She didn't actually need more tea, but she shuffled around like she did so she wouldn't have to look at her sister when she said, "Er…no. Just a lover."

"Oh, so just a night."

"No." Arabella still didn't turn. "I think I'll play with him a while longer."

"Arabella!"

She had to face Julia now and found her sister on her feet, hand clutched around a fistful of robe, dark blue eyes that were so like Arabella's own wide with surprise.

"*You* are the one who ground the rules of engagement into Evelina and me," Julia said. "Who told us both that it was a risk to play without protection. That it could reduce your value on the courtesan's market and set a poor precedent. And now you're considering taking a lover for more than just a night of fun? One who isn't in an arrangement with you?"

Hearing it said out loud in that tone with that shocked and slightly judgmental expression was like cold water on the heat of her night. Arabella folded her arms. "I have never been without a protector since the first few months after I started in the life. I have a sterling reputation that I've worked hard to cultivate amongst the courtesans and the gentlemen. Since I'm between gentlemen at present, why shouldn't I have a little something for me? A treat."

Julia rubbed a hand over her face. "I think you deserve all the treats in the world. All the fun and pleasure and anything else you want. And I know this man has captivated you for years. I just worry, Arabella. Our lives are on a knife's edge. One wrong step and the entire thing can come down around us. You've worked too hard and sacrificed too much to deserve that to happen to you. Even if he has the nicest cock in all of England."

Arabella choked out a laugh at her younger sister's rare foray into the vulgar. "It *is* a very nice cock." She shook her head. "I know what you're saying. I understand the worry. But I…I want him, Julia. And he says he won't be here long, so I think I need to do this. Just have something for me for a little while. What could it be? A few days, a few weeks? Before the Season is half-over I'll be back beckoning them to my side, deciding whose company will best provide for me. For us."

Julia was quiet a moment and then she nodded. "You always know best, Arabella. I know you'll be careful."

"I will. And now I'm going to bed because I'm exhausted." She stepped to her sister and enveloped her in a hard hug. "You are a darling love for reminding me of the rules. I know I need to follow them and I will again. I promise I know my path."

But as she parted from Julia and slipped away to go up to her chamber, Arabella ignored the nagging voice that told her her sister's fears were correct. That she might know the rules but that she was thwarting them. And that it could end in heartbreak and ruin for her if she wasn't very, very careful.

CHAPTER 6

Silas rolled over in his bed and opened one eye. Apparently he hadn't closed the curtains when he staggered home at dawn and the bright afternoon sunshine was flooding in. He lifted a hand to block it with a curse. He felt hungover even though he had hardly drunk a drop. No, it was something else that made him feel like he'd been addled last night.

It was her. *Arabella*.

He moved to his back and stared up at the ceiling as he propped a hand behind his head. God, but she had been magnificent. He could still feel the grip of her, hear the sweet, husky sound when she came. That had been magic and he didn't want to be let loose from the spell. Not yet.

There was a light knock at his door and he groaned as he thew the covers more fully over himself to hide the half-erection that had begun to bloom at thoughts of her.

"What is it?" he barked out.

The door opened to reveal the household butler, Poole. Silas hardly knew him, for he'd only just let the place upon his arrival back in London. The man always looked at him like he was something he barely tolerated and there was little different about him now as he sniffed at Silas's state and then said, "My apologies, sir, but you've received a missive from the Marquess of Pentaghast."

The servant arched a brow and Silas grunted. The message was clear. One of his betters had called for him and he had best get in line.

"My *brother*, you mean," he said sharply. "The marquess, my *brother*."

"Yes, sir," Poole said with a slight incline of his head. He continued to stand at the door with his little silver tray and his judgmental face.

Silas threw the covers back and strode, fully naked, to the man. Poole made a little sound of surprise and threw his gaze toward the ceiling. Good, at least he could shock the bastard.

He snatched the note and broke the seal to read the message.

Join me for supper. Eight tonight.

That was all there was to the note aside from his brother's mark. The mark of the title, not the man. Silas was put to mind of being summoned by his father years ago and only barely controlled a full-body shudder.

He tossed the heavy vellum back on the tray and said, "I grew up in that house. Of course you know. Below stairs always talks. You and Russell, my brother's butler? Used to be my father's. Probably you all talk between houses, eh?"

There was a moment when Poole's eyes went a little wider and then he schooled his expression, but Silas had seen it. "Fuck, you actually do? Christ, there's no way out of your tangled little webs, is there? That will be all."

He pivoted away and heard the servant exit and quietly shut the door behind him. Silas placed each hand on the edge of the table across the room from the bed and tried to calm his racing breath and heart. He'd always hated being the subject of gossip in his father's house. Hated when the servants watched him, when his siblings stopped talking the moment he entered a room. It put him on the outside so very firmly.

And there was no way back in from out in the cold.

Why that bothered him so much now, why it made him feel like a child again, was even more annoying. He pictured going to his brother, revisiting the same old arguments they'd had the night before and he couldn't stand it.

He pursed his lips and drew a few breaths to calm himself from his upset. He could never let them see what he truly felt, after all. He'd never give them that power.

He threw on a robe before he sat down and dug through the drawers in the small writing desk before the window. Once he had his materials, he stared at the blank sheet, trying to find the right words.

And at last he wrote.

Dear Arabella,

I'm riding in Hyde Park today at one. I hope you'll join me.

Windham

He folded the sheet and sealed it, then scribbled the direction she'd given him last night as they parted. Perhaps it was petty, but while he might show up for Charles's supper, he wasn't about to give his brother notice. Let him wait just as Silas had been made to wait so many times, standing in the shadows, not allowed to join in because he was bastard half-blood.

In the meantime, he intended to savor a day with Arabella if she would allow that. And anything else she'd give, too. At the very least, it gave him reason to cross to the bell and ring for his valet so he could dress. Until now his time in London had felt vague and shiftless and unpleasant.

But today it was going to be very different.

~

Two hours later, Silas rode through the main gate at Hyde Park and fell into a trot on the main promenade. He'd chosen the primary lane on purpose, because it was the place where people came to be seen. He *wanted* his family's friends and neighbors to observe him. To whisper about his brothers and sister as much as they had always done to him. Let them see he didn't give a damn about their rumors and innuendos regarding the kind of man he was thanks to his birth. No, he intended to embrace all that instead, lean into their worst assumptions if he had to.

He lifted up in his seat as he looked through the gathered crowd, right on time for the presentations before they all went off for their afternoon tea and gossip. He hadn't heard back from Arabella before he left for the park, but he still had hope she would join him. After all, a woman like her might enjoy making him wait. Wonder. It was all part of her game of cat and mouse.

Which role he would ultimately take was still uncertain, it seemed.

He began to feel disappointment as he let his gaze flit from group to group along the lane and gathered to the sides talking and exhibiting for the watchful eyes of their equals and betters. He certainly felt a great many of those on him and occasionally heard his name whispered on the breeze, along with his father's.

But just when he was ready to give up on her, he caught a glimpse of Arabella coming into the park from the opposite side. She was wearing a fine riding habit in a midnight blue that he was certain precisely matched her eyes. Her short jacket was of a similar shade and fit her perfectly. She even wore a small, jaunty top hat, once more in dark blue and it was tipped ever so slightly to the side.

She would have looked exactly proper but for the fact that her white chemisette was low cut and bordering on sheer, leaving anyone who looked a really lovely view of the tops of her two perfect breasts. And the gentlemen *did* look, even if they were standing with their wives and lovers. Those same ladies also observed her, their faces reflecting irritation, jealousy and occasionally just as much heated interest as the men.

If Arabella noticed any of it, she didn't make any indication. No, she rode through them all like some queen, without a care in the world for the paltry peasants at her feet.

She did see him at last and raised her hand when she did so. She urged her horse forward and rode a little faster in his direction, as he did in hers. It was remarkable how much his heart throbbed as they reached each other and she gifted him with a bright smile that seemed to challenge the sun.

"Mr. Windham," she said. "How kind of you to invite me to ride you today."

He choked on a laugh at the fact she had left out a key word in that sentence and he didn't think it was accidental. "Well, as you already know, I love nothing more than a good ride."

"Yes, I recall," she teased back, and then turned her horse so they could maneuver through the park side by side. They began a slow meandering through the neatly trimmed paths that cut through the trees. "I will say that I often require more warning than a mere hour and a half to meet with a man."

"It seems you are breaking all your rules for me."

He expected her to tease with him further, but something in her expression changed a little with that observation. A flicker of worry, even a hint of fear. He hated to see it, for he had no intention of hurting this woman who had somehow stormed into the swirl of his life and reminded him of a Silas Windham from before everything had changed.

"You look well for a man who must have gotten home and taken to his bed at least as late as I did," Arabella said.

"I sleep like a bear," he admitted. "Especially after such strenuous exercise. And I woke with more pep to my gate than I've had in years."

She glanced over at him. "What an admission. I should have you write my biography since you are capable of such poetry. *Arabella Comerford brought her lovers back to life.*"

"A fine opening for a wicked memoir. And I'm sure the sentiment is true and not just for me." He shifted a little in his seat. "You seem the kind of woman who would shock any man to life. Even the ones who would claim not to wish it."

She seemed to ponder those words at a deeper than surface level, though her expression betrayed nothing of her thoughts on the matter.

"I suppose I'm known for my wild," she said after a pause. She glanced at him apologetically. "My sisters and I used to call it that. My wild."

"Your wild," he repeated, letting the word roll on his tongue. It suited her. "I assume you mean your personality. That brightness to you."

She dropped her head with a soft chuckle. "And after one night he thinks he can spot it. And perhaps you can at that. I think it is also my tendency to laugh too loud and long, to do what I please without thinking of what is proper."

"To me, that only sounds like a woman who knows how to live well. I admire it."

"Thank you. I've always thought so too, but most men wouldn't agree. My father didn't, a very long time ago. And later, many of my lovers tended to want to squeeze every drop of it out of me. To tame it so that I would be more appropriate and palatable even though I was the woman they took to their beds."

They had slowed now and he moved his horse off the path and turned him to face her head on. "That's ridiculous. What fools. That...you called it your wild, yes?"

She nodded and was watching him through a hooded, speculative gaze that made him think he should choose his next words very carefully. He considered doing that, but in the end, he simply said what he meant.

"Your *wild* is obviously what draws people to you. That very spark you describe is a candlelight glow that brings people in. To think someone would have the honor of capturing that light even just for a moment and then only work to snuff if out is enraging, honestly."

He wasn't sure if he meant that purely on her behalf or if he was taking in some of that upset for his own, as well. After all, he contained a great measure of *wild*. It had been his defining characteristic for most of his life and he, too, had experienced many a person try to break it out of him. Occasionally violently.

"You certainly know the right words to say, Silas," she said softly. "And perhaps you mean them. I suppose it doesn't matter since we've determined that whatever we share will be fleeting, won't it?"

He hesitated. He *had* said that the night before, as they lay tangled after the first time they made love. He knew it was the correct offer, he felt no more equipped to be her long-term lover than he had in those heated, powerful moments. And yet when she repeated the sentiment back it felt bleak. Like he was losing an opportunity.

"Indeed," he said. "And perhaps that limited-time exploration is a perfect place to be wicked with the wild in both of us."

"Oh," she said her face lighting up. "That sounds like a challenge is about to be laid forward. What do you have in mind?"

He looked around. Those in the crowd were still watching, whispering, perhaps even more so now that Arabella had joined him. He supposed she brought her own kind of attention, after all. Together they might make the heads of some of the stuffiest gentry outright explode. What fun that would be.

"Are you an experienced horsewoman?"

She blinked. "I have no idea if you're asking me that as a euphemism or as a real question."

He laughed at her dry tone. "I know the answer in the first instance, don't I? No, I'm referring to real skill in riding an animal."

"Well, in that case, I'd say I am. I grew up around horses and rode them from the time I was very young."

"Excellent, then I propose a race, Miss Comerford," he said with a tip of his hat. "Back toward the Corner Gate."

"The *main* gate?" she said with a little shock to her tone. "Silas, the park is crowded with the gentry and they're already all watching. We'll shock the crowd if we race there. Plus, it's hardly safe."

"Oh, do you want *safe*, Arabella?" he asked with a wink. "What happened to all that wild?"

Her gaze narrowed. "What will I win when I best you?"

"A wager?" he gasped out. "I hadn't thought of it, though I have no idea how. It is the perfect place for one. Let me see…" He pondered the stakes for a moment and then laughed. "If you win, you'll come back to my home and I will do whatever you wish."

She arched a brow, but there was no denying the wicked interest that flashed through her gaze at that suggestion. "And if you win?"

"Then you come back to my home and I will do whatever you wish," he repeated with a wink for her.

She threw her head back and laughed so loud and hard that anyone near them who hadn't been watching certainly was now. He could help but stare at her, too. She was really something when she laughed like that. Untethered and glorious. "You have a wager, sir. It appears I cannot lose."

"We'll see about that," he called out as he turned his horse and urged him to jump forward into a gallop.

Behind him, he heard her squeal in playful frustration at his cheat and then they were off in earnest. He dodged the other horses on the path and she kept up with him, leaning forward on her mount, urging the filly with murmured words rather than a whip or crop.

They were neck and neck as they rounded the last curve toward the main gate of the park where dozens of people were gathered before they streamed in for the daily promenade. He heard men calling out to them to stop and the blurry faces of the crowd were certainly filled with irritation. It was perfect.

He pulled up to a stop just at the gate and she was but a few steps behind him, her jaunty top hat now at an even more off-kilter angle and her face lit up with laughter and exertion. He could hear the crowd around him murmuring and grumbling, clucking their tongues in disapproval. Of course Arabella seemed to give not even one care about any of that as she leaned in and cupped his cheek. The touch was electric, instant fire and passion that burned through him.

"Mr. Windham, I think *you* are a very bad influence," she said before she leaned over and kissed him right there in front of the Corner Gate with the crowd gaping at the very wicked display.

She only barely parted her lips, just traced his with her tongue, but he felt like she'd devoured him. The heat of her flowed through him, burning him to his core and leaving him panting and breathless when she pulled away. Her pupils were dilated, but otherwise she seemed unbothered by the entire interaction.

"I lost, *almost* fairly," she said with a wink. "And so it seems I must submit to your terms now. You may lead me back to your wicked lair, Mr. Windham. I cannot wait to see where such a villain lurks now that he's back in the city."

CHAPTER 7

It was Arabella's business to know about the lives and situations of the Upper Ten Thousand. She studied Debrett's with her sisters at least monthly, collected every paper and gossip rag that existed and used the courtesan network to find out everything she could. It was often tedious work, but when it paid off, it was very much worth the time and effort.

The side effect of that study was that when she and Silas rode up to his front door, she recognized the townhouse immediately. It was a beautiful place, with wrought-iron terracing and intricate white stonework along its carefully painted face.

"Wasn't this the Earl of Montague's place?" she asked.

Silas swung down from his horse and then offered her a hand down from her own. She was wearing gloves and so was he, but she still felt the heat of him when he took her hand. He released her as the front door opened and a very stern-looking butler stepped out to greet them.

"Mr. Windham," he intoned, all propriety, but Arabella heard the faintest hint of disgust behind it. She wrinkled her brow and glanced at Silas.

"Poole," he said. "Miss Comerford and I will require some refreshments."

The servant glanced at her. She could tell he recognized her name. That wasn't new. She'd built a reputation so nearly everyone would, down to those below stairs. What the butler felt about her presence here was less clear, but it didn't seem particularly positive. "I see. The west parlor is ready for guests, I'll arrange for tea."

As she and Silas walked into the house behind Poole, Arabella took the foyer in. It was very fine, with marble floors and stuffy art. Gilding was the fashion here, it seemed, for it seemed to dance along the edge of any surface that had been left still for more than a moment. A surprise since Silas seemed anything but a gilding man.

He led her into a parlor off the ridiculous front hall and she caught her breath. The gilding continued into this room, slashed across the edges of anything the designer could find. It was even on the ceiling, outlining the carved plaster in…well, she supposed the effect was meant to be elegance. Gaudy was the word she would use, herself.

"Will you be offended if I tell you this house doesn't seem to fit you?" she asked.

He stopped and looked around the room, almost as if he had never taken it in fully before. Then he glanced at her. "I'm letting it for the Season, so to be fair it isn't mine to fit. It is dandified, isn't it? Christ, the little figurines. They're atrocious."

He waved his hand toward a few of them on the mantelpiece. There had to be at least a dozen porcelain monstrosities perched there. Little people in different costumes, all meant to be the happy working class, she thought based on the tools each one held. One had a shovel, another a tray. They all had blank little faces and delicate paint jobs. She giggled. "Is that one meant to be a shepherd?"

He leaned in closer to the item in question and wrinkled his brow. "I *think* so. With silver, high-heeled slippers and a golden crook, no less. It's a patent misunderstanding of what those of lesser rank live like."

"Well, *they* all have that," she mused.

She walked past him and moved to the window. It had a nice view of the street and the park across from it. Not Hyde Park, from where they'd come, but a nice smaller park, Wildwood. It was still a fashionable address, but not as flashy.

"Why did you let a place?" she asked. "I think you had a home here in London before, didn't you?"

There was a slightest hint of a flinch that came across his handsome face. A pinching of his lips that told a tale before he even said a word.

"That house was given to me by my father. It was…complicated. When I left I gave it up. Sold it, actually, to help finance some of my adventures in America."

She swallowed. She wasn't in the dark about Silas's circumstances. After all, she'd made a study of his past for years. But it was different to look him in the face while he discussed that past rather than simply read things or hear whispers.

"You left right after your father's death," she said.

Again, there was the ripple of pain but it slipped away when Poole entered the room with the tea service. He set it on the sideboard and then turned back toward them. "Is there anything else, Mr. Windham?"

"No." Silas didn't look at him. "That will be all. Thank you, Poole."

The servant left and Silas shook his head as he moved to shut the door to the parlor behind him, then over to the sideboard. "That prick truly hates me." She blinked, uncertain if he was referring to his father or the butler. "I suppose I should be happy it was Montague's solicitor who made the arrangements for the rental, not his servants or else I never would have made the cut. Do you take milk or sugar?"

"Both," she said. "Generously."

He smiled over at her. "Of course you do."

As he applied both to the drink, she asked, "Why does Poole hate you?"

"Oh, you know how it is," he said with a grunt as he handed over her cup. "Their society doesn't like outsiders. He knows what I am and what I come from, just like everyone else. My father didn't try to shelter me from that and so all were allowed their opinions. In Poole's case, I assume he doesn't think my kind belongs in an earl's hallowed halls. Even if I have the coin to pay for them and his ever so proper lordship doesn't."

Arabella nodded. "Oh yes, Montague's fall from grace has been publicly marked. This place isn't tied to the entail, and he might actually lose the house. Someone ought to remind *Poole* that he wouldn't have a position at all if you weren't letting it."

Silas seemed surprised for a moment that she knew so much about Montague, but then he shrugged. "Yes, but the earl has the right blood in his veins so that can be overlooked."

They stared at each other a moment before she moved to the settee and took a place there. She sipped her tea and smiled up at him. "Well, this is perfect."

"Good."

She expected him to take the seat beside her, continue the seduction they'd started at the park. Instead, he sat one of the chairs that faced the settee. She felt his discomfort in that moment and what swelled up in her was a deep desire to offer him comfort. That desire startled her, for it was one she'd mostly tamped down over the years. If this man inspired it in her, that meant she had to be very careful. No, she couldn't get close to this one, not even a little. It was too dangerous.

She set her teacup down and got up. He staggered to his feet as she did so, still polite despite all the labeling of himself as a bastard who didn't belong. She smiled as she rested a hand on his chest and then slowly slid it up to wind it around the back of his neck. His breath caught, his pupils dilated, taking away some of that lovely green that was so interesting. When she lifted up on her tiptoes, he met her halfway for a kiss.

It was a kiss. That was the correct label, but just as before, when they'd kissed at the Donville Masquerade for the first time, it felt… different. There was something raw and hungry and desperate about the way their lips met. Like they lost who they were and found something else. His arms came around her, tugging her to his chest and the kiss deepened. She couldn't help but moan, there was nothing artful to it. The pleasure was just too sharp and deep and powerful not to react.

She dug her hands into his hair and held tight as the sensations washed her away for a moment or two. Then she fought back to the surface, gasping for breath when their lips parted. She stayed in his arms, staring up into that remarkable face and memorizing the lines of it up close.

"Show me the rest," she murmured.

He blinked like he was coming out of a fog. "Of…of the house?" he asked.

She arched against him a fraction. "Of whatever you'd like, Silas."

He caught her hand with a grunt and all but dragged her from the room. As they moved up the long hallway together, he pointed into empty rooms.

"Parlor," he said. "Another parlor. Too many parlors. If I don't name something, assume it's another bloody parlor."

She laughed.

"Library," he said. "Study." He pointed at the grand staircase they were rushing toward. "And the gateway to heaven."

"Very pretty," she said, even as she struggled to keep up with him when he tugged her up the stairs. At some point she staggered and he stopped, pivoting toward her.

"My apologies," he said before he caught her around the waist. He flipped her up over his shoulder and continued his way up the stairs.

"Silas!" she burst out, unable to control her laughter. Certainly, his disapproving servants would hear her, know what they were about to do. She had no idea if that would cause him trouble later, but for now he didn't seem to care. No, he was entirely driven to carry her up the hallway upstairs.

"I have no idea what any of these rooms are," he said as he passed by the doors, this time closed. "One must assume family chambers and…I don't know…let's say that one is a medieval torture chamber, just for fun."

He opened the door at the end of the hallway and carried her inside, through an antechamber and into the bedroom. He tossed her onto the bed and she was able to catch her breath from laughing and the excitement of being carried through a house like he was some barbarian bent on claiming her.

Being claimed seemed a very good idea, even better when he began stripping off his clothing and tossing it onto the floor without a care in the world for where it fell or how wrinkled it would be later. No, he was only focused on her.

When he was naked, he pressed his hands to the foot of his bed. She shivered at the sight of him, shoulders so broad, every muscle of him defined, his cock hard against his stomach and his green gaze locked on her. Oh, she'd chosen her fantasy man very well, indeed, for he was even better in person.

"Come up here," she said, crooking her finger for him.

He smiled. "You think you can direct me?"

She shrugged. "I think sometimes you'd let me. And sometimes you wouldn't. You'd take over and leave me breathless and pleading."

He began to crawl up the bed, his hands cupping her calves as he did so, then her knees, then her thighs. "And which do you think this afternoon will be?"

He covered her as she shivered. "Well, you seem determined to make it the second, but I have one little thing that makes me think I still have the upper hand."

"And what's that?" he asked, dipping his head to kiss along the side of her neck as he started to unfasten the spencer of her riding habit.

"You're exactly where I want you to be."

He lifted his head and flashed her a grin. "Little devil, I'm not even near where you want me to be yet. But I will be."

They didn't talk anymore then. He kissed her and she melted under him, giving over the control to him, at least for now. He took it adeptly, removing her spencer, finding all the hidden hooks and buttons of her specially designed dresses.

"This chemisette is absolutely lewd," he said as he pressed a hand to the nearly sheer fabric. "I adore it."

She smiled. "It does take some shifting and twisting to make sure I'm not flashing a nipple while I'm out riding." When he arched a brow she swatted him lightly. "A horse, you arse, a horse. Though I admit sometimes I have let the flesh slip a little. Given a few gentlemen and ladies a show when they've needed it."

He pushed what remained of her dress away and she shifted her hips so he could tug the fabric out from under her. He bent his head to her breast, still covered, albeit barely, in her chemisette. He cupped the naked flesh that peeked out around the sides and sucked her through the fabric. She shut her eyes and let herself be washed away by the stroke of his tongue, the feel of his hands squeezing just perfectly. He was unfastening her, pushing the last little bit of cloth away and then his mouth was on bare skin.

She pushed her hands into his thick hair, just as she had downstairs when they'd began. He made a little sound against her flesh, one of pleasure and surrender. Oh yes, he might be on top but she knew she was still in some level of control.

He slid his mouth lower, down her stomach, across her hip. Like he had the night before, he stroked his cheek against her thigh, only this time he was more freshly shaven and the skin was smooth. She wasn't sure which version she liked better.

And then it didn't matter because he spread her legs wider and covered her sex with his mouth. She bucked against him immediately, her hand fisting in the same hair she'd been threading through a moment before. He laughed against her and the vibration only made everything sharper.

Many of her lovers had been willing, if not eager, to have her like this, but not a one had ever been so damned good at it. Silas Windham was a virtuoso at the act, massaging her outer lips just perfectly, teasing her clitoris just to the edge of the limit and then easing back to keep her there. Without rushing, for over half an hour he ate her like a man starved, he worked her like it was his vocation, and when she was thrashing and begging and whimpering his name, he looked up from his feast and flicked his tongue just right and she fell.

The orgasm was enormous after such a long preamble and her back bowed off the bed as he slid two fingers inside her clenching sheath and worked her through the crisis. Her heels dug into the mattress and her vision blurred as she keened and cried out because she had no choice but to do so. He had drawn all the wild from her, celebrated it and released it into the world. When her body finally stopped convulsing, when she collapsed back into a boneless puddle on his pillows, she felt the strangest sense of peace.

He moved back up her body, his big hand cupping her hip as he kissed her again. He tasted of her, sweet and salty, earthy and powerful.

"Who was in control again?" he murmured against her lips.

She shivered. "I'll grant that it was most definitely you, Silas."

"Good. It will be your turn next time." He shifted her a little, pushing her still-trembling legs wider with his hips as he settled onto her fully. "But for now, I think I'll claim what's mine by right of conquest."

"Very much so," she whimpered, and lifted against him when he reached between them and stroked the head of his hard cock back and forth against her sodden entrance.

He took her in one long stroke, burying himself to the hilt in her. The little earthquakes that she couldn't control continued and he grunted her name against her neck as he started to rotate his hips. The taking was deceptively lazy and effortless, he moved just the barest amount.

But oh, what he did with those hips. She slid her hands down his back, letting her fingers dance along those gorgeous muscles, and cupped his backside. Together they worked on a rhythm, his pelvis hitting her swollen clitoris, her body massaging him with her pleasure. The quiet was filled with gasps and moans from both of them, with the slippery slide of their bodies together. The pleasure was building again, different than what she'd felt from his tongue, but just as good. This time when she came, he reared up and started to drive into her in earnest. She met him, her body shaking with release, with watching him as the control he wielded slowly cracked away and she was left with the wild animal beneath that seemed to match her so well.

He roared and pulled from her body, pumping over her skin with a few last strokes of his hand. Then he collapsed over her, his mouth finding hers, his hands holding her, their breath matching as the glow of what they'd shared fell over the quiet room.

How long they lay there, Arabella wasn't certain. She dozed in his arms, coming in and out of the dreamy afterglow of a good fuck. He seemed to do the same, his hands sometimes tracing her, sometimes still as he breathed a little deeper and heavier. At some point she woke to him stroking between her legs with those lovely fingers and she'd come around them and his cock once more.

At last, though, she became more fully aware of the room around them, cast in fading firelight for the sun had set long ago.

"This room is even worse," she said.

He was lying on his stomach, half-covering her with a muscular arm, and he lifted his head with a laugh. "Isn't it? That portrait above the mantel."

She looked over to the fire to find a portrait of the current Earl of Montague looking down his long nose at them. "Ugh," she gasped, and held up a hand as if to block the view of him. "Who puts up a huge portrait of themselves staring at the bed?"

"Rather dirty of him, I think. Wanting to watch himself rut with whoever he brought here," Silas said. "But honestly, I'm either going to remove it to an unused chamber or cover it with a sheet. Especially if you're going to be here. If we're going to have a third in this sparkling arrangement, it's certainly not going to be *Montague*."

"I agree," she said, and began to trace the line of his chest. "Have you ever had a third?"

"Of course," he said with a snort. "I'm not a monk."

She giggled at the idea that something so wicked could be considered commonplace. But his casualness about it was also arousing. "And was it a man or a woman?"

"Both in varying times," he said. "And before you ask, yes, I was involved with all parties. Pleasure is pleasure, my dear. I like all its forms."

"As do I," she said. "Good, we're finding so many things we're compatible about."

He placed a hand on her thigh and glided his fingers upward slightly. "So many things."

She gasped at the touch, surprised he seemed so capable of setting her aflame with such ease. She was experienced, after all. Occasionally she felt jaded when it took a great deal of fantasy and effort to truly become excited by a new man. Once she was there, it was fine, but this was… captivating. Instant. Volcanic.

She caught his wrist. "Before you start all over again, I must plead for some comfort. I'm famished. Is there anything in the larder of this gilded cage that we could share? Or perhaps we could take a little jaunt to my house where my very kind servants would whip us up a gorgeous meal to give us strength."

To her surprise, Silas sat up straight. "Fuck!"

"What is it?" she asked.

"Does that clock say eight?" he asked, leaning forward to look at the little clock on the mantel below the hideous portrait.

"Yes. Do you need spectacles? That would be adorable, I'd love to steam them up."

He gave her a playful glare but there was truly trouble in his countenance otherwise. "My brother, the marquess, demanded I join him for supper tonight at eight. I hadn't known for certain if I was going to attend, but I did mean to send him word if I refused. Now I haven't done either and I'm certain he'll be furious."

She sat up. "You could send word now and ready yourself quickly. I'm sure you could make it within the hour."

"I think being late might be worse in his estimation than not being there at all. No, I'm sure the damage is done and I'll hear about it from all sides eventually."

He ran a hand through his hair with a sigh. She wanted to press for more, but once again she silently cautioned herself on doing so. This was temporary. This man was not her protector, she didn't have a place to try to soothe his pains or worries. In fact, it was very much better if she didn't.

She leaned forward and placed her chin on his bare shoulder, looking up at him. "Well, if you intend to stay...I think I can make the trouble worth the while."

He glanced down at her and she watched the concerns bleed from his expression. She had done that, even if she told herself it wasn't her place.

"Could you now?" he asked with a chuckle. "I think you could."

"After food," she insisted, and batted her eyelashes. "Please, sir... just a bite."

"I like *sir*," he admitted, and leaned down to kiss her. "Come, let's get dressed and I'll see if I can have something palatable brought to us. But then I absolutely insist on you following through on this 'make the trouble worth it' plan of yours."

"Oh, I will," she said as she cupped his cheek and drew him in. "I promise."

CHAPTER 8

I t turned out Arabella kept her promises and in spades. After they'd eaten the night before, a reasonable spread despite the very obvious disapproval on his butler's face when he delivered it, she had pleasured him for hours. Until they were both weak with it. Until they couldn't stay awake from exhaustion and satisfaction.

And now she lay in his arms, still asleep despite it being late in the morning, and he felt…calm. That was the word for it, he thought. *Calm.* Like things were well for him somehow in a world that hadn't been balanced in years.

She shifted a little at his side and her hand, which had been resting against his stomach, slid up to his chest. His body reacted, despite the acrobatics of the night before. The wanting for this woman didn't seem to fade.

"How long have you been awake?" she murmured, turning her mouth against his shoulder and kissed it lightly.

He shivered in response and started to stroke along her spine lightly. "I don't know. Not long. A few minutes."

She inched closer and now her hand came down across his hip and her forearm brushed the half-hard cock that was already asking for more.

She lifted her head and smiled a little, that wicked flash of brilliance he was starting to crave. "Seems like something else has been awake a bit longer."

"*Something else* seems to be awake at all times with you." She leaned up to kiss him and he drew her over his body. "I think you might be a siren."

"No," she laughed as she began to gently stoke him. "They're half-bird and I can't sing, you truly don't want me to try. I think you mean a succubus."

He lifted his head, trying to focus when she was making his body tremble with pleasure already. "I definitely do not mean a succubus. Those are demons and they suck the life force from a man."

"I did that at least once last night," she said as she slid over him and settled herself over his cock.

He gripped her hips and started to rock her, easy and gentle in their sleepy states. She threw her head back, her breath short and he couldn't stop staring. This woman was gorgeous in all her forms, completely captivating. By design, he supposed, but also by nature. She would have been just as alluring as someone's country wife.

Though he was very happy in this moment that she hadn't chosen that path and was instead riding him, faster now, until she gasped out pleasure in the quiet and her pulsing sex milked his own release just to the edge.

He rolled her over, thrusting harder as he took her mouth and then spent between them with a long, shaky moan. Her arms had been pinned when he moved them and she wedged them free and wrapped her arms around his neck.

"What do you think about getting dressed and coming back to my home? I have the most amazing bath there, big enough for two. We can take a soak and have food prepared by people who don't sneer while they do it and then do all this again for the rest of the day."

He smiled at the idea. She was talking about the most lovely, wicked fantasy and that certainly sounded better than trudging over to his brother's home and getting scolded for missing supper. He could put that off another day, couldn't he?

He opened his mouth to answer when there was a knock on the chamber door. Not the outer one, but from the antechamber. He pursed his lips and twisted to look at it.

"Ugh, what it is?" he called out.

It was Poole's voice that responded, as always, thick with censure even through the barrier. "You have a guest, sir."

"Christ," Silas muttered, and kissed her once, then got up. "I must have summoned him."

"Who?" Arabella asked, sitting up a little, but making no attempt to cover herself as he threw on a robe and started for the door.

He hesitated. "The marquess. That must be who has come because I missed our supper. Climbed out of his sick bed, even." A flash of guilt rushed through him at that thought, but he shook it off. "I'm opening the door if you wish to cover up."

She responded by throwing the sheet over herself, though she didn't move from her sprawled position. If the servant looked, and Silas had a good reason to believe he would do that, he was going to see her and know exactly what they'd been doing all night.

Not that everyone in the house hadn't already guessed *that*.

Silas opened the door. "A guest?" he repeated. "And who is that?"

"Lord Reginald," Poole said.

Silas froze. "My middle brother?"

Poole inclined his head. "I did tell him I wasn't certain you were in residence and he told me to tell you to *sober up, climb off your whores and come down, I'm not leaving.*" There was a twitch of pleasure to his lips as he spoke. "His words, of course, not mine."

"Tell him I'll be down in half an hour. I need to dress and ready myself."

"Very good, sir."

"And offer him breakfast," Silas added as the butler turned away.

At the outer door, Poole stopped. "I would do so, sir, but it is nearly noon. I will offer other refreshment, though."

With that, he was gone and Silas turned back into the bedroom. He shook his head, trying to absorb this. He glanced at Arabella, still wrapped in his bed. "I'm sorry about what he said. The whore comment."

"It's strictly true." She shrugged. "I've been called worse, I assure you. This is your second brother, yes?"

"Yes," he said. "Charles and I got along so much as we could. Reggie...well, he's something different. He hated me as a child and I'm certain he hates me now."

"Why?"

He indicated to himself with one hand without responding.

She surprised him by getting out of bed and crossing to the window, throwing open the curtain so that the room filled with light. "Because you're so much younger and more handsome than he is?" she asked lightly.

He snorted, though his brother being here gave him no pleasure. "I'm certain that doesn't help."

"It sounds as though you're being given no choice but to join him."

"Yes." He sighed. "If he says he won't leave, he won't. He's singular that way. And now I must call my valet and get ready like some dandy fop and take my medicine."

She tilted her head. "I can't help with the second, but I'd be happy to help you ready yourself so you could forgo the valet."

He arched a brow. "You?"

She arched hers right back at him. "If you don't think that a courtesan knows how to put a gentleman back together, you haven't been with the right lovers."

Put a gentleman back together. He knew she meant that as a throwaway sentence, something playful and teasing in the midst of this upset. But it hit him harder than that. A woman like this...no, not like this. *This* woman. She could put him back together. What a concept.

"Silas?" she said, concern coming over her face.

He shook off the wild thought and motioned to the dressing room door. "If you want to dress me up like some doll and make me acceptable to my brother, I won't stop you. Though I admit, I think I'll be distracted by you being naked while you do it."

She laughed and grabbed for her clothing that was still scattered around the floor. "I'll dress while I look at your wardrobe and find your armor for the encounter. I won't be but a moment."

She slipped off then and he sank down on the settee with a sigh. He hadn't meant for things to become complicated when he came back to London, when he started this affair with Arabella. But both of those things were becoming quickly and increasingly just that.

And he had no idea what that would mean in the end.

Silas Windham really did cut a fine figure when he was dressed and groomed. His broad shoulders filled out his finely made jacket perfectly, the greens in his waistcoat brought out the beauty of his eyes and when he was freshly shaven and hair in place, she couldn't help but shiver.

He looked like a gentleman, as refined as any duke Arabella had ever taken to her bed. He could have fit into their world, she could see. Only people like that never let someone like him, no matter if his father had brought him into his home. Silas's bastard blood, his courtesan mother…that would never allow him to be anything but an outsider. Just like her. It made her wonder why the last marquess had done such a thing. It was not a kindness.

She squeezed his hand. "You are ready, Mr. Windham. And you look very handsome, indeed, so that ought to frustrate that brother of yours all the more."

"What fun," he said, but the tone was flatter than the teasing words implied. He shook his head as he looked at himself in the mirror. "If you ever retire from the game, you should take on the role of a valet. In half an hour you shaved, dressed and fixed me up."

"Yes, but one minute more and you'll be late to meet with him. So you ought to go."

He hesitated a moment and then turned on his heel to face her. "Come with me."

She stepped back. "You wish me to come downstairs and join your meeting with your brother? He knows who I am, you know. He's seen me at Cyprian balls and at the Donville Masquerade and even at the opera."

Silas's expression twisted. "You two have never…"

"Oh, God no!" she said with a shudder. "I draw a hard line at going between siblings."

"But you didn't know you'd have me and he has power."

She shifted slightly. "Well, I never wanted to close the door on you just in case you reappeared in London. Now *why* do you want me to join you?"

He shrugged, like it was meaningless. "It would tweak him, wouldn't it?"

She forced her expression not to change. She'd been used as a weapon before. Sometimes that was the entirety of her role. Step out with one person, hurt someone else. But the fact that Silas wanted to use her that way…well, she wasn't especially fond of it. But perhaps that was good. It helped remind her that even if he behaved otherwise sometimes, she was still just a whore to him. Just as she was to his brother. She couldn't forget that was a line between them.

"If that's what you want, I'll go." She briefly touched the hair she had fixed. She knew it was fine. She had trained herself to become quickly presentable under any circumstances. Part of her own armor.

Silas brightened up and held out an arm. "Good. Thank you."

She took it and they stepped through the antechamber and out into the hallway together. He didn't release her until they'd gone downstairs and stood outside the parlor. He was almost vibrating with anticipation, shifting his weight a little back and forth.

She squeezed his arm briefly and he looked down at her. For a breath's time, their eyes locked and then he nodded, released her and opened the door.

～

The last time Silas had seen his middle sibling had not been pleasant. It was the morning after their father's death. There had been thrown blows and angry words, so when he stepped into the parlor, Arabella on his heels, his heart was pounding.

Reggie was standing at the window, looking out onto the street he'd come in on. When he turned, Silas caught his breath. He didn't know why he felt so surprised that his brothers had aged. It had been six years, after all, and all his siblings were at least ten years his senior. But still, seeing Reggie with the gray in his temples, the heavier lines on his face, was startling. So much had changed.

Then his brother pursed his lips and Silas realized nothing had changed at all, actually. It seemed Reggie's annoyance picked up just where he'd left off.

"Silas," Reggie said softly, and stepped toward him, hand outstretched.

Silas met him halfway and they shook briefly. "Reginald."

His brother's gaze flitted past him toward Arabella, still in the doorway, giving this reunion space. Silas turned toward her slightly. "May I present Miss—"

"I know who Arabella Comerford is," Reggie interrupted.

Arabella stepped up then, casting Silas an *I-told-you-so* look and then she extended a hand to his brother. "Good afternoon, Lord Reginald. What a pleasure to meet you."

"Miss Comerford," Reggie managed to grind out past what were obviously clenched teeth as he briefly shook her hand. His gaze didn't linger on her but narrowed on Silas again. "Is this what you do instead of having supper with your *dying* brother?"

Silas flinched at the plainly stated question and the deep disappointment that laced it. He'd been hearing that tone from his father's side of the family for years and years. Somehow his first reaction of guilt and shame was never muted.

He could feel Arabella staring at him even though he didn't look in her direction. He did hear her though when she whispered, "Dying?"

Silas pushed aside all the weaker emotions that crowded in his chest and shook his head. "He's not dying. And I never said I was coming to supper."

"No, you never said anything at all, did you?" Reggie threw up his hands. "You didn't bother to answer the invitation, like some petulant child who—"

Silas stepped up to him. "I'm not a child, though, am I, Reg? And what you're really angry about is that you can't make me dance to some drum anymore. I don't give a damn about your opinions about me."

That wasn't entirely true, no matter how he wished it were.

Reggie shook his head. "Then why come back?"

"Why ask me back?" he shot back.

"*I* didn't!" They stared at each other for a long moment and then his brother shoved a hand through his hair. "Fuck, you are impossible." He let out his breath slowly and then smoothed himself. The high emotion fled and there was nothing but coldness and formality to him when he said, "Whatever you're going to do, Silas, just figure it out. I have children of my own, I don't need to spend time chasing around one that's thirty. Good day."

He pivoted on his heel and stalked from the room. In the distance he heard the murmurs of Poole speaking and then the slam of the door as his brother left.

It was in that charged moment that Arabella touched his arm. He felt every warm finger fold over him, even through the layers of propriety they'd put on him earlier. He drew a shaky breath and forced himself to look at her, somehow expecting her to be captivated by this encounter. After all, that was the currency she collected for her own protection.

And yet there was no prurient interest in his family dramas or his pain. There was nothing but gentle understanding in her stare and he was surprised that a sense of peace moved over him as he lost himself, albeit briefly, in the endless blue of her eyes.

"Silas," she said softly after that moment passed. "Is your brother truly dying?"

～

Arabella could see the unspoken and always had. It was something she'd nurtured in the years since she'd entered the game as a courtesan. After all, to be able to tell a man's mood was one way to avoid being harmed, either physically or emotionally. And it also helped her preemptively provide for her lovers, which was part of her charm, she supposed.

Right now she felt Silas's pain radiating off of him in long, sharp waves. Oh, he showed none of it on his handsome face, in fact he looked angry in that moment, not at her but at the world. But the pain was there, pulsing below the surface. And she wanted to ease it, not as part of a seduction, not because it was expected of her...but because she truly wished to help.

He let out a long sigh. "He's not...dying," he said, repeating the words he'd said to his brother a few moments before. But now he didn't sound as certain in that statement. "Well, it's not entirely clear, actually."

"How so?"

"He's been ill for a while now. It has gotten worse in the last six months, he was on the brink a few times."

She nodded slowly. "That's why you came home."

"Home," he repeated, and she wasn't certain he knew he'd done that. He shook his head slightly. "Y-yes. My sister Phoebe asked me to return. I'm closer to her than to either Reg or Charlie."

"I see."

He scrubbed a hand through his hair, deconstructing the formality she'd helped him put on less than half an hour before. "My mother was a courtesan," he said.

She nodded. "Yes. I…know."

He glanced at her. "Oh yes, your research. I'd forgotten you delved into every facet of my life. So you know what everyone knows at the very least, that I was a product of her ill-conceived arrangement with the previous marquess."

"Yes, and then he took you into his home. A very odd arrangement."

He pursed his lips. "Most men would have sent me off to some other family. But he wanted to claim me for some reason. To control me when he couldn't control her. Whatever his reasons for such a strange decision, I was raised in the same house as my siblings, from the time I was five, but they were older than I am. There was distance. Walls." He turned away a fraction. "Never mind, it's a boring, sad story."

She wasn't so sure of the boring part, but this wasn't the moment to push. It wasn't her place, either. After all, she wasn't keeping him.

He shifted and she saw him put a mask on, cover up the vulnerability she had found there with this topic. "What about you, Arabella? Do you have siblings?"

She laughed at the loaded question he didn't even know he'd asked. "Yes. You've been gone a long time, but we're actually quite infamous."

"Infamous," he repeated with a small smile. "How so?"

"We're called the Comerford Courtesans. I'm the eldest, Evelina is the middle and Julia is the youngest."

"And all three of you are courtesans?" She heard his surprise, but not his judgment.

She nodded. "They followed me into the life."

Now it was her turn to put on the mask. To cover the discomfort she somehow felt at this topic. It was such an odd thing, for a great many in Society knew of her and her sisters. The answers to his queries weren't ones she often had to give. And yet this man appeared and when he pressed his finger to this particular nerve, she found it to be raw. What a surprise.

He held her gaze a moment and she felt him reading her. "You don't have to tell me, Arabella."

She shrugged. "Well, it's a boring, sad story."

He smiled slightly at the fact she'd used the same words he had. There was no denying the effect, though. They'd both shut the door on a deeper connection in that moment. A connection that had been right there, begging to be taken since the first moment they'd seen each other all those years ago. Certainly since she'd discovered him at Donville just a few days prior.

It was better that the wall had been erected, though. She knew it. Attachment, closeness, those weren't things she gave easily, nor truly, very often. And she couldn't get close to this one. There was an inherent danger to that possibility that felt sharper than any she'd sensed in a long time.

She forced a smile of her own, one that felt false, and stepped up to press a brief kiss to his lips. "I think I may have overstayed my welcome. I'm sure you have much to think about and do."

He held her gaze a beat. "Ah, I see."

"But perhaps we can see each other later?" she said, hoping that softened this. She didn't want to stop playing with him, after all, she just wanted to make sure what was happening between them didn't end up crossing a line.

"To try out that big tub you promised me," he suggested.

Her smile became less false at that idea. "I'd love it. Until later."

She slipped away then and he didn't follow. When her carriage was brought around, she got in, but the moment it began to move, her legs got shaky. She gripped her hands against them, drawing a few deep breaths.

Every part of her that had ever protected her was now screaming that this affair was perhaps a bad idea. That it couldn't only lead to heartache.

And yet she didn't want to end it. Not yet.

CHAPTER 9

Despite the fact that he hadn't truly belonged in the world where his father had raised him, Silas *had* developed friendships there. There were gentlemen, even those with title, who were wild and fun and didn't count his parentage as his only value. And a day after his encounter with Reggie, a day after Arabella had all but dismissed him, he was seated with one at Fitzhugh's, a club he found far superior to the stuffier White's.

The Earl of Ramsbury had once had a wild reputation that nearly rivaled Silas's own. But upon his return to London, he'd discovered his old friend was now married and, he shuddered, *settled*. Still, they'd fallen into good conversation and better whisky like no time had passed.

"It's good to have you home," Ramsbury said with a little smile when there was a lull in conversation.

Silas smirked. "Well, I'd say it's good to be home but..." He trailed off and yet his mind rushed to Arabella. The time they'd spent together had made his return much better, after all. She was the bright spot in this dimness.

"You came to handle things with your family, yes?" Ramsbury said, and speared Silas with a long glance.

He shifted beneath it and stared into what remained of the amber liquid in his glass. "I don't know. Yes."

There was a silence long enough that Silas looked up from his drink and found Ramsbury watching him far too closely. "And you're avoiding them," the earl said.

Silas arched a brow. "How do you know that?"

"I know everything," Ramsbury said.

"God, you're insufferable now that you're married," Silas grumbled.

Ramsbury laughed. "Don't disparage Marianne with your grumpiness. She isn't the reason I can see right through you."

"No, I suppose not. Though how you managed to land yourself Delacourt's sister after he so strenuously warned you off her all those years is beyond me. But as far as *my* family goes, I suppose they would tell you I'm best at avoiding everything, yes?"

"They wouldn't be wrong, considering this conversation." Ramsbury sipped his drink.

Silas threw up his hands. "Fine. Yes. I'm avoiding them."

"Perhaps you shouldn't," Ramsbury suggested, leaning forward on the edge of his chair. "Perhaps you have a chance here and now to form some real bonds with your brothers and sister. The ones that circumstances prevented when you were all children."

"God, I thought you were supposed to be the fun one, Ramsbury."

He smiled a little. "All my fun comes from home, I fear. From her."

Silas wrinkled his brow. He'd known this man most of his life, and even though what Ramsbury was describing was something that would have once made his skin crawl, today there was a peace to him. A quiet joy to the way he declared he'd surrendered his old life and now made a new one.

And as inexplicable as that was to Silas, he also felt envious of it. Of the certainty that seemed to erase all pain and fear and doubt.

He found himself thinking of Arabella again and shoved those thoughts aside with violence. She was a lark and while he certainly was having fun with her, she had no place in these reflections. She'd made that clear when she slipped from his parlor the previous afternoon.

"I know you're right," he said slowly.

"That must have taken a great deal to admit that," Ramsbury said with a long laugh.

"You've no idea," Silas said, and laughed with him. "God, those words are actually bitter in my mouth. Let's change the subject."

"I hear you've been spending some time with Arabella Comerford," Ramsbury said.

Silas rolled his eyes. "The rumor mill is in full swing, I see."

"Your race through Hyde Park was well-documented in several gossip rags."

"Yes." Silas had seen those reports. The scandal sheets that were delivered to the eager hands of those in high Society often didn't fully reveal the identities of those they wrote about. But there were always enough clues to determine the names. What was the fun if one couldn't?

Ramsbury shrugged and continued, "And even if it weren't, there's a great deal of interest amongst certain parties when it comes to her and whoever will be her next protector. You can't help but hear about it."

"I suppose not."

"She's quite a person."

Silas nodded. "She is. It's like catching lightning in your hands."

"Hmmm. Interesting."

Ramsbury's gaze had gone speculative. He nudged his friend's boot with his none too gently. "Oh, fuck off."

"Excuse me, my lord, Mr. Windham." The men glanced up at the servant who had stepped into their space, a tray balanced in his hand. "You have a message, Mr. Windham."

Silas shot Ramsbury a glance of confusion but took the message and thanked the servant. When the man had stepped away, he gave his friend a look of confusion. "It's not a secret I'm here, but I've no idea who would send a message to me."

He thought briefly of one of his brothers and flinched. Neither of them held a membership at Fitzhugh's, but it seemed to fit the form of their strained bonds.

He turned the missive over and found that the wax seal was a flourished *C*. He looked again at his name on the front of the envelope. It was written in a feminine hand.

Arabella.

He opened it and read:

Silas,

I find myself wanting a partner at Flynn's tonight for some gaming. Are you available?

Arabella

He found himself reading the message again. Well, it wasn't an invitation for a big bath and an intimate supper. He shouldn't have been disappointed, but found himself exactly that.

"From that look on your face I'd say it's not an unpleasant message," Ramsbury said with a chuckle. "Perhaps that very *interesting* lady is calling for you, and you are off to dance to her tune, it seems."

"As long as she'll play it," Silas said and laughed along with him. "You couldn't deny a woman like that even if you wished to do so. I hope we can see each other soon, Ramsbury."

"Perhaps you can join Marianne and me for supper one night." Ramsbury rose and shook his hand. "It is good to have you back."

Silas slapped his friend's arm and then hustled from the club. He had a good deal to do to prepare for his next night with Arabella. And a good deal to conceal about just how excited he was to do just that.

~

Arabella was putting the final touches to her hair, winding a few bright red flowers into the wonderful work her maid had done for her. She'd grown up with maids, of course, and was accustomed to having a great deal done for her, and yet there was an independent part of her that didn't want to depend too much on anyone. Or give anyone too much power, even just over her toilette.

There was a light knock on her door and she called out, "Come in."

Julia stepped into the room and Arabella faced her briefly. Her sister was in a plain gown, nothing meant for the hunt, and her hair was done simply. She looked young and fresh, just as she always had.

"Oh, look at you," Julia said, and rushed over to stand beside her at the dressing table. "I love those flowers. Would you like me to put a few in the back?"

"Thank you, yes," Arabella said, and turned toward her mirror as she handed over some of the pins. Julia leaned in to take a flower and Arabella watched her in the reflection. "You're not going out tonight?"

Julia glanced up at her, their eyes locking in the glass. "I wasn't planning to. I'm knee deep in the most remarkable romance and I cannot wait to see what fantastically gothic thing will happen to the heroine next."

She fussed with Arabella's hair a minute longer before Arabella said, "You know, you don't have to follow the path Evelina and I have taken. You can just stop. I have the means to continue to protect you and you could decide to do something else."

"Like what?" Julia asked with a laugh that sounded like it was filled with little humor. "I've been a courtesan for over two years now, and thanks to the success of my sisters, I'm not an anonymous one. I couldn't just go back to being a lady."

Arabella shifted. "Did I...do the wrong thing by taking you away from Father's house? By rushing in to break up the wedding he arranged?"

Certainly her father thought so. His wretched letters, including the one she'd received that very morning, always followed the same pattern where he accused her of ruining him, ruining Evelina and Julia. Ruining *everything*. Arabella tried not to be affected by those heated, cruel, even violent screeds, but occasionally they hit a nerve.

Julia's hands faltered. "God, no. He was trying to marry me off to a man in his seventies, a man who used to…to paw me and smelled of sick half the time. It was awful. You and Evelina arriving at my window and sweeping me away was the best thing you could have done. I'm afraid I sounded ungrateful and I'm sorry."

Arabella turned to face her head on. "You have never been ungrateful in your entire sweet life. But *I* chose this life with my full heart. And Evelina ran away of her own volition. That you wanted to escape from Father's grasp doesn't follow that you wanted to be a courtesan like your sisters. If your heart isn't in it…"

Julia shook her head. "It is. It's in it. I just want to find my Harry, like Evelina has. A man who is dedicated and wants to keep me. Someone who cares."

Arabella bit her tongue. Julia was only twenty and she idealized Evelina's arrangement with her duke almost as much as Evelina did, herself. But Arabella sometimes wondered if it was the best option. And if her sister, perhaps both her sisters, would end up heartbroken by expecting these kinds of things to last.

That made her think of Silas and she frowned as she turned back to the mirror to allow Julia to finish pinning the flowers in her hair. She had to keep reminding herself to not get too close to the man who had been her fantasy for years. She couldn't fall into the same trap she worried about for her sisters.

"Do you mind if I ask you something?"

Arabella blinked and refocused on Julia. "Anything in the world. We three don't keep secrets, do we?"

"Where exactly have you been spending your time lately, Arabella?" Julia asked. She stepped back from her work. "There, I think that's perfect. Not too many but enough to draw the eye."

"That's the preferred effect," Arabella said, and stood up. "And what do you mean where have I been spending my time?"

Julia laughed. "You think me innocent despite all this." She waved her hand around the room. "But I'm not foolish. You spent several nights away from home and I heard about you racing with that man, the one you mooned over all that time. It was in all the papers."

"Silas Windham. Are you pretending not to know his name?" Arabella asked.

"I don't remember any of their names until they become important," Julia said with a shrug. "Is that who you've been out with?"

"Yes." It was odd that the admission gave away nothing and yet it felt vulnerable regardless. "You know I'm having an affair with him."

"Still not an arrangement?" There was a disapproving quality in her sister's soft question.

"No, as I said before it's just a bit of fun on my own terms."

Julia's brow wrinkled but she murmured, "I see."

Arabella grasped her sister's hands. "Why don't you come with me to Flynn's tonight? I'll give you a little blunt to gamble with."

"And I assume you'll also push me toward any man you think might be a good fit?"

"I haven't since you parted ways with that last one...the baronet."

"Lloyd," Julia said softly. "No, I suppose you haven't."

"I just want you to come out, not lock yourself up and read all night. Have *fun* with me."

"And meet your fantasy man?"

Arabella froze. That would be, she supposed, the side effect of the invitation. And while plenty of men had met her sisters over the years, they were somewhat of a package collection, after all, the idea that Silas would come in contact with Julia felt...different. Charged in some way.

"Yes. But you must behave yourself and not ask him a thousand questions and tell him awful stories about how I mooned over him." Arabella laughed. "He already knows that anyway."

Julia seemed to consider the suggestion a moment and then she threw up her hands. "Fine. I'll come along. How long to I have to ready myself?"

"As long as you need," Arabella said. "I rule the roost at Flynn's. I can be as late as I wish."

Julia rolled her eyes at that declaration and grabbed Arabella's hand. "Well, come with me then and help me find something to wear."

Arabella went with her, giggling as they had as girls, at least in the times that their father hadn't been looming over, threatening and controlling. They would have fun tonight. And then she would have a very different kind of fun with Silas once she reached the hell.

CHAPTER 10

When Arabella and Julia entered Flynn's gaming hell together an hour later, the eyes of the room turned toward her immediately. She smiled like she was a queen ruling over the regard of so many. Yes, some leered and only saw her as a prize to be won, but that was what men did and it only made them easier to control.

The rest saw her as powerful, desirable. She had the respect of a great many of them for the way she had handled herself in this life. They were willing to negotiate with her in a way no other woman was ever allowed to do, at least directly.

She also saw friends. Other courtesans, a female boxer she'd met a few years before, the owner of a dress shop whose real money was made creating toys for lovers. *These* were her people. *This* was where she belonged.

Julia gripped her arm a little tighter. "Oh, I see Bianca Reynolds over there. She just parted ways with her protector and we've been meaning to chat. I'll come find you to game later?"

Arabella nodded and watched her sister skip off to her friend. Eyes followed her as she did. Julia might be hesitant to pick her next conquest, but she wouldn't be hurting for options. Arabella could ensure she had even more when the time came.

She pivoted and looked into the crowd again and that was when she spotted Silas. He was coming toward her from the back of the hell. He was slightly slack-jawed as he looked her up and down and suddenly she was very happy she'd made herself up to be her most alluring. It was all for him, wasn't it? She could pretend otherwise, but that was the truth of it.

And she felt just as stunned as he appeared. He was so entirely beautiful, after all. Like a god plucked from Mount Olympus. That broad-shouldered, lean-hipped line of him was as perfect in clothing as it was sprawled naked across a bed.

He thwarted Societal expectation by the fact that he clearly hadn't shaved. His day-old scrub of stubble across his jaw only made her long to feel it brush her thighs. When he reached her, his green eyes were bright with desire but also delight, as if seeing her was some singular pleasure.

And she was warmed by him. Such an odd thing to feel.

"Good evening," she managed to choke out without revealing too much in her tone.

He took her hand and lifted it to his lips, his warm breath leaving tingles in its wake. Then he stepped back to see the full effect of her. "My God, look at you," he murmured.

She laughed and spun around in a circle to let him see it all. She'd chosen her favorite dress for hunting, deep red, scandalously low cut, highlighted with pink silkiness. The flowers in her loosely done hair were also blood red. The gown was purposely created to make her, as she had always said, *all shoulder and décolletage*. Other courtesans always laughed when she said that, but they all knew the truth: what she was doing was making herself a mouthwatering treat right here on display in public.

And this was the man she most definitely wanted to unwrap her and try it all.

"I'm glad you came," she said.

He nodded. "I'm *very* glad I came now that I'm seeing you here like this." Many men would have continued with seduction, but he seemed in no hurry. Instead, he looked around. "I don't think this hell existed before I left London."

Arabella pondered that. "I suppose it didn't. I think Flynn's opened just three years ago, but it's all the rage. As you can see by how well attended and fine it is."

They looked out into the hall together. Many tables were laid out in a neat pattern and every one of them was full or nearly full of patrons playing various card games.

"Are you good at cards, Silas?" Arabella asked.

He winked at her. "A cad like me? Very good. And that isn't just me being a self-congratulating shit. I doubled my fortune playing cards, you know."

She lifted her brows in surprise. Though the specific number wasn't known when it came to Silas's inheritance, whispers said it was no tiny sum. If he had truly doubled it through his skill at card play, that was impressive.

"In America?" she asked.

He stiffened a fraction, almost as if thinking of that time was difficult. "Yes. They even have these riverboats where they game. That was becoming quite popular when I left."

"What fun," she said. "I love the idea of sailing around, being debauched."

"Who was the woman you arrived with?" he asked.

She smiled. "My youngest sister, Julia. She went to speak to a friend, but I'm sure you'll meet her tonight. For now, why don't we join a game? You can teach me a few things, it sounds like."

He snorted as he placed a hand on her lower back and guided her through the crowd toward a table with two open seats. "Me? I doubt that. I think you, Miss Comerford, are probably very good at everything you've ever tried. I have pegged you for a talented bluffer and I can't wait to see you strip every man at that table of his coin… and probably his dignity."

She laughed even though the weight of his fingers against her spine was shockingly distracting. "Even you?"

"Probably me first," he said, and they took their places and began.

❧

Arabella didn't strip him of his dignity, as Silas had teased her, but it was impossible not to be impressed by her skills at cards as he played against her. She knew how to bet, which was often more important than what to play. She wasn't reckless, but she had few tells, so when she did bluff, she was almost always successful. She was also charismatic beyond belief. Every person at the table hung on her every word, and not just because she looked like a goddess. She was simply that good at handling people. It was no wonder she was so sought after as a lover.

And yet she was giving her time to him without expectation or demand. There was something about that which gave him a sense of...pride. She was the sun and somehow she'd chosen him briefly as her moon, and that was worth a great deal in the midst of the upheaval he was experiencing at present.

But now the night was growing long. She glanced toward the door and gave him a little smile that brought heat to his blood. He pushed back from the table and said, "I think we may have to take our leave, gentlemen."

Lord Archibald, the second son of some earl or another, who had been playing and losing to Silas for the last hour, glared at them. "You can't go now, Windham. You must give me the chance to win my blunt back."

"You didn't win it back over the last fifteen hands, there's no chance you're winning it back in the next fifteen and I'm finished here." Silas barely sent the man a glance as he took Arabella's hand and pressed it between his own. Her smile widened. It was clear they were already playing a very different game. Together they rose, but Lord Archibald got up too, banging into the table with his thighs as he did so and rocking it slightly.

"Bollocks, Windham. You're a cheat."

That did snap Silas's attention to the man. There were many things he would proudly admit to being, but a cheat was not one of them. He arched a brow. "Do you want to repeat that? Or take it outside?"

Arabella's hand tightened slightly in his, like she was trying to draw his attention back to her. But it was quickly becoming too late for that.

"Why not settle it here?" Lord Archibald staggered around the table and shoved Silas. He released Arabella and shoved back. The eyes of the entire hell were now on them as official employees of the club started toward them.

But they weren't needed. Without fear of two slightly tipsy men who were much larger than she was, Arabella wedged herself between them. Her hand flattened against Silas's chest and she lightly pushed him back even as she met Lord Archibald's eyes.

"Now, now Archie, you don't want to make a scene, do you? That won't do at all."

Some of the starch went out of the other man's expression though he glared at Arabella. "My money—" he began.

"Look over there at the table two rows over," she said and motioned one elegant hand. "That's the Duke of Beckingham and he is so deep in his cups that he's barely upright. Everyone knows he's far too loose with his wagers even when he's not. So why don't you take what you have left and go sit there? I would imagine you'll end up tripling your money before two hours have passed."

Lord Archibald stared off at the table which contained the duke and then back to her. As Silas watched in wonder, she stepped up to the angry gentleman and patted his cheek lightly. "Off with you now."

Without further argument, Lord Archibald gathered up his sad little pile of money and headed off to do just as she had suggested.

Once he was gone, she gathered up the blunt she'd won from the other men at the table and smiled to the group at large. "Best of luck to the rest of you. Good night."

Then she grabbed Silas's hand again and together they moved away. He glanced over to her. "You handled that with great aplomb. I'm impressed."

She shrugged. "There are times for a brawl at a hell and times where such a thing must be diffused. I'm adept at diffusing angry men."

He frowned at the idea that she'd had to be over her life. Men who had been meant to protect her, he was certain. Perhaps other men before that. In the life she'd led before she was a courtesan, long before he'd seen her in the garden.

He stepped to the right to dodge another gentleman and when he moved rapidly, he found the room spinning just slightly. She laughed and clung to his hand a little tighter. "I'm just as good at tending to men who are in their cups. You're good at cards even when you've had two too many."

"Was it two exactly?" he asked with a smile.

She returned it easily. "*Exactly*. You were perfectly in control and then the waver started just after two drinks ago. Not drunk, but tipsy enough to start to make mistakes."

"And that's why you decided to end the game? To protect me."

There was a moment when a flicker of something came over her face. A trouble that shadowed her usually bright expression, but then it was gone. "That's what I do." She looked past him. "And here comes one of the subjects of my unwanted protection now. Good evening, Julia."

He turned and watched as Arabella's sister approached. She was a lovely young woman, with a heart-shaped face and eyes very much like her sister's. But though their familial connection was clear, especially closer up, Julia lacked something Arabella had. It was the bright spark, the bubbling joy, the intense explosion that was in Arabella's every move and word.

"May I present Mr. Silas Windham," Arabella said. "Silas, this is Julia Comerford, my youngest sister."

"Miss Comerford," he said with a slight bow toward her.

"Mr. Windham," she replied, her gaze flitting up and down him briefly. "So this is you."

"Julia," Arabella said softly.

Silas laughed. "Good Lord, is it really true all she said about talking about me for all these years? I thought that was a way to make me feel better about myself."

"Arabella is singular," Julia said. "Once she has something to think about, she really does gnaw it to pieces."

He winked at Arabella, who was going a shocking pink in her cheeks. "Sounds like fun."

"Stop it both of you, or I shall storm out very dramatically." Arabella's words had no heat and he could see she was smothering a laugh.

Julia shook her head with a giggle and then said, "I've heard you've recently been in the former colonies, Mr. Windham."

"Silas, please," he said. "And yes. I was in Virginia for a while and then a territory that just became a state before I departed for London: Louisiana. Both beautiful places."

"Is it as wild as everyone says?" Julia asked, her blue eyes shining.

He smiled. "As wild as you'd like it to be."

She shook her head. "To travel sounds like a treat. I've really only been here in London and out in Granger before that. Granger was boring as dry toast and London is...*London*."

Arabella continued to smile, but Silas caught the flicker of concern at the edges. She was worried about her sister, it seemed.

"Well, perhaps the next gentleman you make an arrangement with will take you traveling," Arabella said.

Julia dipped her head. "Perhaps." When she lifted her head again, any worries were gone. "Well, I've been chatting all night with dearest Bianca. Her parting was *not* on mutual terms, Arabella, I have all the details for later. But I told her I'd come spend a night with her and have breakfast tomorrow, so I'll travel home in her carriage."

At that, Arabella's hand tightened a little on Silas's inner elbow. He glanced at her. "So I have you all to myself."

"It seems you do. I wonder what you shall ever do with me."

"I don't," he said.

Julia rolled her eyes playfully. "And that is my cue to leave. Goodnight, dearest." She leaned forward and kissed Arabella's cheek and then extended her hand to Silas. "And goodnight, Silas. It's not every day you meet a man of such legend. You did live up to the talk."

"Go away," Arabella said, her tone still filled with teasing.

Julia slipped into the crowd with a light laugh and Silas pivoted toward Arabella. Even a little tipsy, he just couldn't get enough of her face. He reached up to trace the line of her jaw with a fingertip and watched the shiver move through her in response.

"Should we have another drink?" he asked.

"No, I think we should go get in my carriage and go back to your home," she said with a falsely innocent smile. "Right now, if you please."

"You don't have to ask me twice," he said, and drew her toward the door and whatever the rest of the night would bring.

The moment they got into her carriage and the vehicle began to move, Silas came across the gap between them and pinned her to the wall behind her. His mouth was harsh and hot against hers, all semblance of control wiped away by the handful of drinks he'd partaken in during their night of cards.

She rather liked this untethered version of him. How hungry he was for her. She was certainly equally filled with heat and desire for him.

His hands roved, fingers gripping and massaging and flicking as she rose beneath him, sucking his tongue, nipping his lower lip.

He rumbled with pleasure as she did so and began to drag her skirt up her legs. His palm skimmed her stocking, thumb stroking the spot where her bare skin began.

"I wanted to do this all night," he murmured against her throat. "Watching you drove me mad."

She gasped as he cupped her sex, thick fingers opening her and stroking her right to the edge of madness with such speed that she felt like she was the one who was a little tipsy, not him.

She caught his lapels and deepened the kiss, tasting the liquor and desire on him in equal measure. When she pulled away, she held his stare and flicked her head toward the seat next to her.

"Sit," she ordered.

He arched a brow at her and she waited for his response. Would he deny her and engage in a battle? That could be fun. Or would he acquiesce and let her do what they both wanted?

He did the latter and eased onto the carriage seat next to her. She moved to straddle his leg and just before she kissed him again, she whispered, "Good boy."

He chuckled against her tongue, but then the humor was gone. Their mouths warred, desperate and heated. He got his hands back under her dress and cupped her bare backside to grind her against him. And somehow she managed to wedge a hand between them to unfasten his fall front.

He was hard already. She'd known that from the first moment he pressed against her and she could feel him there, this luscious treat just waiting for her to claim.

So she did. She claimed him in one heavy, slick slide that took him inside to the hilt. They both shuddered. He rested his head on her shoulder, his breath harsh as she began to ride him.

She watched him as she rode. In his slightly inebriated state, his expression was a little softer, even in his pleasure. Like some fraction of his mask had slipped. All his need, all his longing, all his pleasure was reflected on every line of him. He moaned louder, he gripped her tighter, she saw him lose himself in the way her body rolled over him and when he rapped his head back against the carriage seat and grunted out, "Arabella," the power of it was almost too much.

She arched, her orgasm rolling through her in long, heavy waves. He watched her from below, eyes wide as she threw her head back and took every drop of the pleasure.

Normally she would have continued that way, taking him until he felt close to the brink and then trusting him to shift her away so he could spend. But tonight was different because of his state. She could see he was beginning to feel the effect of the last drink he'd had before they left. He might not be able to stop himself when his own orgasm hit.

So she removed herself from over him.

"Oh, not that," he grunted.

She laughed. "No. This."

She lowered herself to her knees before him and took him in her mouth. Her taste was all over him, pleasure and release, and it mixed with his clean flavor. She took him as deep as she could, stroking him with her hand and her tongue as his fingers came into her hair and he lifted to her. His legs were shaking, his breath was hard and without warning, he came.

She took every drop of him, reveling in him like he was fine wine. When she was done, he caught her arms and pulled her back onto the seat beside him. He kissed her deeply, rumbling at the taste of himself on her lips. Then he tucked her in beside him and just held her in silence for the remainder of the ride.

As they reached his home, she smiled up at him. "Are you going to put that lovely thing away or shock Poole entirely?"

Silas glanced down at his fall front, which was still unfastened. He shook his head. "Poole deserves a shock. He delights in his little acts of disrespect. As if I don't know who I am and where I certainly don't belong."

She wrinkled her brow at the pain that laced those words. A man like Silas always appeared as if he didn't give a damn about what others thought, but it was clear the servant's disrespect rankled on some deep level.

He managed to tuck himself back into place before the carriage door opened. He stepped out first. Well, staggered was more like it. He barely managed to avoid depositing himself on the drive and braced himself on the carriage door with both hands as he leaned back in. "Are you coming?"

She realized she ought to say no. When she felt so much draw, she should always say no. But instead, she came down from the vehicle. "Gregson, wait here, will you? I think I must help poor Mr. Windham inside."

"No, I—" he began, and then his knees wobbled a little.

She stepped up and slung his arm around her shoulders. "Lean on me. I'll deliver you safely to your bed."

"Mmmm, as long as you're in it," he grunted. They reached the door where Poole now stood. The butler looked down his nose at them even as he let them into the foyer. "Poole, how nice of you to greet us."

"Quite," Poole sniffed. "Are you well, sir?"

"He's fine. Just a bit in his cups."

Poole turned away and Arabella was certain he muttered something beneath his breath. She glared at him, but then drew Silas forward. There was no reason for him to have to spend even another moment in this vulnerable state with someone who was so cruel.

They somehow managed to get up the stairs and to his room. She got him inside the bedchamber and started to unfasten his jacket. He smiled down at her, the expression cock-eyed. "I like when you undress me."

"I'm sure you do. You're a man, after all," she said, swatting his hands away when he tried to help or distract her. She pushed the jacket away and unwound his cravat so he wouldn't choke himself on it. She unfastened his shirt and somehow he managed to get it off and only caught his head in it once.

"Lie on the bed," she ordered, and couldn't help but smile again as he staggered to it and flopped across it, his booted feet hanging off. "Look at you, still trying not to dirty the sheets even in this state. So polite."

"I just want to dirty the sheets in more pleasurable ways," he hiccupped, and then stared at her a moment as she struggled to get his boots off. "I mean with you."

"Yes, I got that." She smiled at him. "I like this Silas. He's a very silly man."

She expected him to smile or reach for her again. Instead, his expression grew darker. Sadder. "Silas isn't silly. He's rotten." He sighed, a broken sound that made her turn her head. Then he did reach for her. "Tell Poole to send your carriage away and just stay here and fuck me."

"Men are such singular creatures," she said.

"You don't have to fuck me, then. Just stay with me," he corrected himself. "Warm everything up with your sun."

"My sun?" she repeated. "I don't think anyone has called my quim that."

His expression grew softer. "Not that. *You.* You are the sun, Arabella."

She stared at him, this now far past half-drunk man who was telling her she was the sun. Many men had given her compliments over the years, none of them left much of an impression, but this one felt powerful. Like the brightness everyone else tried to dim was so lovely to him.

She turned away, trying to regain some purchase over herself when her heart was throbbing traitorously and her hands were shaking.

"You—you are very sweet when you're drunk, Silas," she said. "But I would wager what you really need is a good sleep. So I should go."

She waited for him to argue. To repeat the request. If he did, she wasn't certain she was strong enough to refuse him. After all, what he asked for was what she wanted, herself. She wanted very much to climb into his bed and into his arms. She wanted to have him again, that longing didn't cease, but then she just wanted to stay. To wake up with him as she had a few days before, and watch the shafts of light around the curtain illuminate his handsome face.

She blinked at the intimacy her mind created. Then she turned back toward him. To her surprise, he was not waiting to argue with her, but he was asleep. It seemed like that last drink had finally fully entered his bloodstream and taken over whatever control the man had over himself.

She moved toward him, feeling like a thief as she brushed a hand over his cheek, tracing the feel of his stubbly jawline. "Years ago, I might have jumped at the chance to be your sun," she murmured. "But…but now I know better. I know these things can only create pain for everyone involved."

She leaned in to kiss him and then slipped from his room. She came through the hall and down the stairs, only to find Poole standing there, arms folded and pointed, hard expression on his face.

"What a pleasure you are," Arabella said with a humorless laugh. "You'll be happy to know I'm leaving, so no need to stand guard all night. But I do think that it would be a kindness to have the kitchen staff be ready with a curative in the morning for Mr. Windham. I think he'll need it. If you don't know a recipe, I can write one down."

"I don't take orders from someone such as yourself," the butler said. "And I don't need your opinions or recipes."

She stared at him a moment. There it was. The judgment of a man who had no idea of her life. Not that it mattered. Servant or no, he was elevated above her. And oh, how men like this liked to lord it.

"I suppose you don't," she said softly. "Though I assume it bothers you mightily that you must take orders from *him*."

"Just for another month and then the period of his lease will be up," Poole hissed. "And he can go back to wherever men like him belong."

Arabella flinched. He'd talked about longer, but he must have been hedging his bets. Ready to run if things didn't go well. But a month? That felt like so little time. He'd be back on a ship then, back to being unreachable. Probably better for her, at that, because when she was with him she felt longings she had erased years ago. Dangerous desires that went beyond sex.

The same dangerous desires that made her want to defend him against this utterly nasty man. And that, at least, she could do. With great pleasure.

"Do you think the people you dismiss don't know things?" she asked. "The reason your master, the Earl of Montague, is so close to losing this place, that he has to let it, and *you*, out to someone you have so little respect for…isn't for any of the reasons that go around in public."

Poole's nostrils flared a little, but he said nothing and so she continued, "He wants people to believe it's gambling, poor investments. The usual things the Upper Ten Thousand can dismiss with a little bit of pity. He'll still get invited even if they cluck their tongues. But what would they say if they knew about his payouts? His victims?"

"You don't know what you're talking about."

"Interesting that you've gone so pale then," she said. "I wonder if that's because you helped him. That seems like something such a loyal servant might do. And when he loses this house, you'll also be out of a job, I think. At least you might be if someone were to find out what was really going on around here and your role in it."

There was a long pause as they stared at each other. Then Poole let out a shaky breath. "What do you want?"

"A little respect for the man who is currently living in these halls," she said with a small smile. "The man who is fifty times the one who owns them. Now, do you know the recipe for a curative?"

"The cook used to make them for the earl when he drank too much," Poole said, softer now, not meeting her eyes with such cheek anymore. "I'll make sure one is included on Mr. Windham's breakfast tray."

"Good man. I'm sure I'll see you again soon. Good night."

Arabella turned on her heel and exited the estate back to her still waiting carriage. She took her place and folded her arms. There was triumph in using what she knew to put someone horrid in their place, but she felt little pleasure in it.

Her life had been spent protecting others. She did it easily for those she loved. She never did it for her lovers, though. They were powerful and had money and they didn't need her to swoop to their rescue. She tried not to even know their troubles, not at any deep level, and her comfort was always surface.

But tonight she had threatened a man in order to give Silas just a little more wellbeing. She wanted to give him that relief, and she knew what a foolish notion that was. No, not foolish, precarious. It meant she cared, no matter how many times she kept telling herself she wasn't going to get close to this one.

It seemed it was impossible to stay away. And she had no idea what to do about it.

CHAPTER 11

Despite all his desire to avoid it, Silas found himself sitting in his brother's parlor two afternoons after he'd woken up alone, no Arabella. He'd heard from her since, of course. She'd checked in on his state the morning after. He'd written her about racing again in the park. There was something romantic about sending letters back and forth that he didn't want to explore.

Certainly he wasn't going to do that now. Not in this moment as he sat on the settee, his sister Phoebe at his side and his two brothers across from him in chairs. Charlie looked better this time. Unlike the first night Silas had encountered him, he was dressed. His cheeks were less pale and pasty. In truth he looked so much like a marquess…so much like their father…that Silas had to keep blinking to make sure he wasn't imagining it.

Reggie's expression was pinched, but thus far he hadn't said or done anything to antagonize or accuse. And Phoebe was, as always, kind. Silas smiled at her and she returned the expression as they continued awkward small talk with their tea.

How Silas wished it were whisky.

He shifted, his discomfort blooming in his chest and making him watch the door restlessly. At last he set his cup down. "I appreciate this moment of familial bonding, but I think we all know you didn't call me here, call me back to London, so we could discuss the state of the weather or the roads."

"Always so direct, Silas," Phoebe said softly at his side.

He smiled toward her, masking his nervousness. "My position forced it, I think. I'm sorry if it makes you uncomfortable."

"I suppose in this case, it is a good thing," Charlie said, and glanced at Reggie briefly. "You've been home for almost two weeks and we've avoided this subject long enough. I've tried to tell myself that I've done so due to my illness or the fact that you were still getting accustomed to being in London, but the truth of it is that I didn't quite know how to say it."

Silas stared at his oldest brother, trying not to think of Reggie's statement that Charlie was dying. Perhaps all this was about that fact and he didn't know what to think or feel about that possibility.

Charlie smoothed his hands over his thighs and then said, "After Father died, we were all...emotional. There were things said, actions taken, that I think didn't reflect anyone's true feelings."

"You mean that fact that Reggie punched me in the face for declaring the marquess wasn't much of a father to me and so I couldn't mourn him?"

It was poorly done to point out the specifics, and he knew it even before all three of his siblings flinched. And Charlie was correct that what he'd said that day wasn't true. He'd spent years afterward doing exactly that: mourning a man whose inconsistent affection had left a hole in him that no amount of whisky or cards or lovers could fill. Well, most lovers. The edges of that hole felt a little less sharp when he was with Arabella.

"Yes," Charlie said softly. "Just that. When you left, I always regretted it."

Charlie glanced at Reggie and he pursed his lips. "As did I."

Silas couldn't help but laugh. "That sounds very sincere, Reg, thank you."

"Just because I think you're a colossal prick doesn't mean that I wanted to do something that wretched," Reggie said, then shook his head. "Christ, you make everything so difficult."

"As you keep saying," Silas snapped.

Phoebe reached out and touched his hand. "Silas, this is something the three of us have *truly* spoken of many times over the years. Our remorse over a great many things, not just the words and actions after Father's death. We all know that your treatment as a child under this roof wasn't always...kind. We might have contributed to that unkindness, certainly none of us questioned it as we might have done."

Silas stared at her, uncertain what to say when these entirely unexpected words were coming from her mouth.

"My illness gave my thoughts more urgency," Charlie said. "There were moments when I lay there on the brink, cataloguing my regrets, and chief amongst them was the way you'd been cut away from the family. Pushed out, or at least I think you'd see it that way. I asked Phoebe to bring you back, to ask you back, because we want to...to..."

"Have you back in the fold," Reggie finished with a shrug. "*All of us.*"

Silas stared at them, uncertain how to respond to this utterly unexpected declaration. His whole childhood he'd longed to be fully accepted by this family, had tried to mold himself and make himself more palatable to them all, including his father.

Eventually when he realized nothing he did would make them love him, he decided that they would bloody well not ignore him. And thus, Silas the rake and rogue had been born. That version of himself had felt more real than any other he'd created to make *them* happy.

But now they were talking about being a family. About acceptance. The flutter of anxiety and joy that blossomed in his chest made him see that the lonely boy he'd been hadn't been entirely smothered. He still wanted the family he'd been denied.

"I...I don't know what to say," he began softly. "I realize my existence was difficult for you all. As an adult I understand why far more. But what do you mean by back in the fold?"

Reggie leaned back in his chair. "Everyone knows you're our half-brother."

"Brother," Charlie said softly.

"Yes, of course. Our brother. It's never been a secret. I suppose what we mean is more inclusion in family events, requests of your opinion in decisions made for the good of our father's legacy."

"You have as much right to steer that, after all, as anyone else," Phoebe said, and touched his hand briefly. "We would more publicly and full-throatedly accept you."

Silas shifted. He'd stopped wanting to be some Society fop years and years ago. And yet this was still a sparkling decoration being dangled before him.

"I see." He looked from one sibling to the next. "And yet I sense there is a caveat, something bitter to follow this seemingly sweet offer."

Charlie let out a long sigh. "Well, we would, of course, need to discuss your activities. Your behavior."

Chest tightening, Silas forced out his next words. "My activities. Which ones, specifically?"

"Racing like a lunatic through Hyde Park?" Reggie said. "Getting drunk at Flynn's and losing how much at cards?"

"I actually won a hundred pounds, but do go on," Silas said, waving his hand with flourish as if this was all some presentation.

"And what about the fisticuffs with Lord Archibald that same night?" Charlie said softly.

Silas shook his head. "That didn't happen, no matter what was written in the scandal sheets. There was a little pushing, yes, but no punches thrown. And it was Archibald who started it."

Reggie made a sound of frustration, but said nothing as Charlie lifted a hand to stop him. He met Silas's gaze evenly. "And then there's Arabella Comerford."

Silas froze at that. "And what is wrong with Arabella?"

"She's a courtesan," Reggie burst out, getting to his feet and pacing the room.

"Indeed, she is." Silas leaned back and putting on a show of casual nonchalance even though he felt none of it. "Are you certain you wish to discuss her then with Phoebe sitting here? Our innocent sister."

Phoebe let out a snort. "I'm forty years old and have been married and widowed *twice*. Not to mention born five children. I haven't been an innocent for years. Even if I were, I think *everyone* knows about Arabella Comerford." She glanced at Silas. "She's uncommonly pretty."

"She is, isn't she?" Silas agreed with a wink for her.

"And *infamous*," Reggie snapped, slamming his hands down on the back of the chair he had abandoned a moment before.

"Why do you care?" Silas asked. "Christ, I'm certain both of you have had mistresses in your time. And Reg is married. So why does my connection with a courtesan make a fucking...apologies, Phoebe...bit of difference to whether I'll be accepted by you lot or not? It sounds like it's just some excuse so that you can offer me this but not truly mean it. Some little game."

"It's not a game," Charlie insisted, and reached up to rub his eyes. He looked a little pale now, tired. "Christ. Yes, gentlemen have mistresses...apologies, Phoebe."

"Good Lord, please stop apologizing to me, all of you," she interrupted with a wave of her hand.

Charlie continued, "But it's one thing to have a discreet arrangement with some level of propriety and composure. It's quite another to rush around with a woman who is sought after, yes, but also known as entirely wild."

"Imprudent, *foolish*," Reg added.

"She brings out the worst in you."

Silas flinched. The worst in him. What his brother meant, of course, was the most natural in him. When he was with Arabella, he felt…free. More like himself than he had been since his father's death and his self-exile from the life and family he'd known.

They wanted to tame his wild, he realized, using the same term Arabella had said to him when they first met each other again at the Donville Masquerade. They wanted to take that center of him that wasn't just like them. Take away his spirit. Take away the one thing that gave him real pleasure, and not just the physical kind.

He shook his head. "Arabella Comerford is neither imprudent nor foolish. Spend two minutes with her and you'll know she's one of the most intelligent people in this or any country. She *is* wild, but that is because she is only entirely herself and does not let people like *you* dictate how she views herself and the world. You cannot control her, which is what you don't like."

"Oh, Silas, really," Charlie said on a long sigh.

"And the fact is that you cannot control me, which you also don't like. Have never liked. So as for your offer to let me into the fold, as long as I dance to your tune, I think I shall have to decline."

"After all these years, I don't think anyone in this family would be so foolish as to believe anyone could control you. Christ, you can't even control yourself," Reg said, taking a step toward him.

Phoebe got up, holding up a hand like she feared the two men would come to blows. "Don't do this. Please."

Silas glanced toward her. "I don't intend to do anything, Phoebe, I promise you. For all I've been accused of being out of control, it's our dear brother who you need be concerned about when it comes to throwing blows. I don't care enough to do so."

Both his brothers flinched at that and Phoebe sucked in a sharp breath. He wished for a brief moment that he could take that last sentence back. He didn't mean it, after all. But he had to start, it seemed. He drew in a shaky breath.

"Years ago, I might have jumped at the offer to be a real part of his family," he continued. "I would have loved it. But I gave up on that decades ago. I am here. I've come at your beckoning, my lord. But the loving family ship sailed long before the one that took me to America. And I will be sailing back to my life there in a few weeks. Then none of you will have to be concerned about what I do or who I fuck."

He pivoted on his heel and exited the room, ignoring Phoebe calling his name as he did so. He had held his head high as he stormed down the dark path to the stable for his horse instead of waiting for it to be brought to him.

But as he thundered from the drive, the emotions he wished he didn't feel rose up in him. Regret, anger…loss. Pain. He hated those weaknesses. Hated that he had felt a swell of hope at the idea of being a real family before he was brought back to reality.

He wanted it to stop. And he knew one way to make sure it would.

~

Arabella loved going out, playing her games, wearing her costumes, but the nights she planned to stay in were always a relief. There was something so comfortable about wearing her flannel dressing gown and wrapping her hair in rags so it would have a curl the next day. Then she'd sit before her fire and talk to her sisters if they were there, or read a book and sip madeira if they weren't.

Tonight she was alone, for Julia was the only one living at Arabella's home at present and she was out with a friend for the night. Arabella tucked her bare feet up next to her on the settee and pressed her chin into her hand as she turned the page of her book, reveling in the story she was in the middle of at present, an adventure tale of a man traveling around the world. One who made her think of Silas from time to time.

When there was a light knock on the parlor door, she lifted her gaze in surprise. "Yes?"

Barnaby opened it and inclined his head. "I'm so sorry to intrude, Miss Comerford. I did try to tell the gentleman that you were not in residence, but he asked me to check again and seemed quite wild about it."

She blinked. "Who?"

But she knew the answer. She felt it in her bones.

"Mr. Windham, miss."

"Of course it is," she said, and bent her head. "Well, let him come."

"Do you want a moment to prepare?" Barnaby asked.

She swallowed. She must have her emotions on her face if he was asking her that. She nodded and he left her. She got to her feet and paced the room, shaking out her hands to get the tingles that now worked through them to stop.

It had been two days since she left Silas. Since she threatened his temporary butler so he would get better treatment. She hadn't stopped thinking about him since. Hadn't stopped running over and over in her mind how her protective instincts had come out and how wrong that was. How it violated every rule she had about the men she took into her life and her body and her bed.

And now he was here and somehow she had to stop her heart from throbbing and her body from trembling like she was some little innocent about to meet with a man for whom she had a *tendre*.

"Stop," she ordered herself.

It didn't work and her door opened again. She faced it and saw Barnaby's brow wrinkle before he announced, "Mr. Windham."

He stepped away and Silas entered the room. He had a fiery expression to his face, one that faded as he looked at her. When Barnaby had closed the door behind him, Silas stepped forward.

"That's a new look for you, Arabella."

She gasped as she realized what she was wearing and what was in her hair. She reached up and touched the little rags rolled through her locks to curl them.

"Oh damn, that was why he asked me if I needed a moment," she gasped, and began to unknot the little pieces of fabric.

Silas laughed and moved forward. "I actually think you look adorable."

"Well, adorable isn't the effect I'm *ever* going for," she huffed, still tugging the fabric away.

"A pity," he said, and reached out to slide one of the strips of fabric out of her hair gently. "But I suppose we all wear masks, don't we?"

She wrinkled her brow because his playfulness had gone now and the intensity she had felt from him when he entered the room had returned.

"I suppose we must," she said carefully. "Are you well?"

"Perfectly well," he said, but that was clearly not true as he began to pace the room. He looked rather like a caged predator then. Restless and sleek and dangerous beyond the bars. But also lost. Longing to be free.

Something had happened. She ought to make herself not care about that, but she couldn't. She did care. It was too late.

"Do you want to tell me what happened?" Arabella asked, hating how her breath shook as she retook her place on the settee and continued to tug the curling fabric from her hair.

Silas continued to pace back and forth in front of her window, his hands clenched at his sides. "You told me before that your sisters followed you into this life."

That felt like a change of subject from her question and one she didn't understand. "Y-yes."

"They never judged you for who you are, what you are? Your bond wasn't shaken by it?"

She hesitated. What he was asking her for felt very vulnerable. Oh, she was often asked about her relationship to Evelina and Julia. Men who tried to seduce her into their protection were endlessly titillated by the idea of three sisters who were all in the life. The ones who wanted to include her sisters in their sexual fantasies were always roundly rejected.

But none of them ever delved into the emotional element of their bond. What Silas was inquiring about now was *real*. It was truly about family.

When she didn't answer, he turned toward her. His gaze wasn't just intense, it was pained. And that pain called to her own, drew it from the corner where she always placed it so it would remain hidden from everyone.

Including herself.

She swallowed hard and answered carefully, "I'm sure they must have judged me at first. This wasn't how we began, after all. We were all raised to be gentlewomen. Raised to marry as well as possible and live genteel lives. When I left, when I changed everything and dared to use my own name to do it, I'm sure Evelina and Julia must have resented me on some level."

He appeared surprised. "So Comerford *is* your birth name. Do you mind if I ask why you didn't take on a new one like so many courtesans do?"

She gave a half-smile. "To make my father angry. To ruin him a little. I would perhaps do it differently now."

She frowned as she thought of her father's letters. The angry, violent, desperate letters that just kept coming no matter how many years she and her sisters had been out of his control. Would that situation be better if she hadn't dragged him into her mud? If when papers wrote breathless recountings of her adventures, it wasn't his name that echoed through the scandals?

Silas let out a short breath. "Well, I certainly understand *that*," he said. "I was reminded tonight how much I've lived my life as a direct *bollocks off* to the man who sired me and the family I was raised beside. Not in, though. Never *in* the family. Just slightly next to it."

There was such bitterness in his tone that she got up and moved toward him. She took his hand between her own and held it there. "What happened, Silas?"

He shivered. "Am I so obvious?"

She nodded wordlessly and threaded her fingers through his. He let her and for a moment they both simply stared at the intertwined digits. His breath became ragged and when he looked up into her eyes that pain she'd already seen seemed even sharper. Her heart ached a little at the sight of it, even if she knew she shouldn't allow it to do so.

"I've *never* belonged with them, Arabella. They made sure of it. My *father* made sure of it. I was in their house, but not their family, not truly."

"You were a child when you joined them, yes?" She hesitated. "It seems an…odd arrangement."

"To bring a bastard child into the family so publicly? Yes, entirely odd. He could have sent me to live with some family in the country. Someplace I'd have a chance to belong, but no. He wanted his revenge and his control because my mother had the gall to deny him."

She let out her breath slowly. "I see. He was her protector, I know."

"He was obsessed with her, at least so I've heard and read in his journals from before they broke. I used to steal into his study when he was out and read them, try to imagine some fairytale life where he loved her and we were the family I so wanted. But now, as a man, I know it wasn't love. Not ever. It was obsession and control."

"Yes, that happens sometimes," Arabella said softly. "A danger of the profession. Was he her lover all the years before he took you in?"

"Off and on," Silas explained. "He'd go months away and then show up. Give me a gift, shuttle me off so they could be alone and she would hope again. He would crush her within a few weeks and disappear back into his real life. She would crash into despair and I would try to pick up the pieces."

"Oh, Silas, you were so young," she whispered.

He shrugged. "You don't get to be young when you're raised like us."

She flinched, for truer words had never been spoken. Children had to become adults when they were raised by adults who acted like children. Who never considered their families before themselves.

"What happened at the end?" she asked, pushing herself back to his story so she wouldn't linger long on her own.

"One day she refused him. He had sent word he was coming and she made sure she wasn't at home. She left me there with a letter ending it. He was livid. I thought he would destroy the house around me he was breaking things and swearing and cursing her for her audacity. And then he just stopped and stared at me. Just stared at me until I could hardly breathe. Without a word he left. She grew more broken after that. Weeks of slow collapse. I found out later he was sabotaging her. Writing her these awful letters, forcing her to be cut off at shops and with other courtesans. And once she was at her weakest, he used it as an excuse to steal me. And he did it publicly so she would hear about me, know about me. See me being raised as his son out of her reach."

She shivered. "That was why he stared at you. He realized you were the way to hurt her the most."

He didn't answer for a moment. He seemed incapable of doing so. Like the words would shatter something. She knew there was more to tell, more hidden beneath all the boldness his masks. But if she pushed for it, she feared the consequences, not just for him but for her. For *them*. The them that couldn't be, not truly.

"That must have been difficult," she said.

"Impossible, at least until I trained myself not to care." He shook his head and some of the heartbreak softened a fraction. "But tonight, tonight *they* tried to change all that. They offered me a place there with them. To be a part of their family in a more genuine way."

She tilted her head. "But?"

"But only if I become everything I'm not. Give up everything that matters."

She sucked in a breath at that broken admission. At the true emotions behind it. And at the pure, powerful anger that bubbled up in her when she heard it.

She didn't know much about the Marquess of Pentaghast and his legitimate siblings, but at this moment she could have scratched all their eyes out. Torn them into pieces without a thought because they'd made the light in Silas's eyes dim.

And in that moment the danger of her reaction didn't matter to her even a whit.

"If they couldn't see your value," she said, "If they cannot see it now, then they are *all* fools and they don't deserve you. I hope you told all three of them to go straight to hell."

His gaze became distant. "I did just that, actually. I lashed out. The likelihood that I destroyed my relationship with all three of them, including my sister, who I've been closest to, is almost one hundred percent."

She cupped his cheek. "Oh, Silas. I know better than most how much it hurts to walk away. Even when you must. But you shouldn't compromise who you are for whatever scraps of affection someone dangles on a string for you. I think you know that from experience as much as I do."

He smiled, though there was little pleasure in the expression. "Do you know why I came here tonight?"

She returned the smile. "I imagine you wanted to fuck the pain out, make it go away. Pour it into me as passion until there was nothing left but pleasure streaking through you?"

His eyes widened. "That's exactly it."

"Then I'd suggest you put me on a settee or a chair or the floor and bury yourself in me until that happens."

She grasped his lapels and pulled him in. This, at least, she could do without risking any part of herself. That was better for both of them. She couldn't forget it.

S ilas dug his hands into Arabella's hair and then his mouth was on her, hard and heated. She took the heavy need of him without argument and arched against his chest. What she had suggested, what he had intended by coming here, was already working, for pleasure burrowed through his veins like molten lava. It muted some of the pain.

Of course, talking to her had done that too, releasing some of the pressure that had been building in the wound for decades. Her empathy and understanding had been a long-needed balm.

But no. He pushed that thought away and focused on this now. On backing her across the room toward the fire. She'd mentioned settees and chairs, but when she'd said the floor, that had sounded rough and animal and perfect for his mood. There was a rug in front of the fire and he tugged her down onto it, covering her as her arms came around him.

He reveled in the silkiness of her locks, tangled now but no longer bound up in the twists of rags she had in them when he entered the room. He kissed her, deeper, harder and she opened to him without hesitation. Opened her mouth, opened her legs so he could wedge between them with his hips as he pressed into her.

She arched against him, sucking his tongue, rubbing her pelvis against his. She knew exactly what she was doing, what her role was in erasing his emotions and memories. She played it to perfection.

Her hands clenched against his back, gripping at his shoulders, sliding down his spine so she could cup his backside and grind him harder against her. He moaned against her lips because he could already feel the heat of her even through his trousers.

He wanted to feel it even more.

He rose up onto his knees and shrugged out of his jacket, ripped his cravat in his haste to remove the propriety his family had earlier required. It felt too stifling now. She caught his hands as he moved them to his shirt buttons and shook her head.

"Easy," she murmured, and unbuttoned for him.

Easy. Yes, she made this easy. He let out a shaky breath as he pulled his shirt over his head. She stared up at him, swallowed hard and then gripped the edge of her flannel dressing gown and simple nightshift, tugging them up around her stomach to bare herself from the waist down.

He shuddered at the sight of her, sprawled on the carpet, legs open, half naked. It all felt so out of control and animal.

"Stop thinking," she ordered, reaching out to flick the buttons of his fall front open, freeing his cock. She dragged her fingers along the length. "Stop thinking and just take what you need."

"And what about what you need?" he choked out, shocked he could be so coherent when she was touching him.

She wrinkled her brow as if she didn't fully understand that question. "Silly boy, I need *you*. Don't you think I've been aching for you for two days, since that last time you were inside of me in the carriage?"

His heart was pounding at that declaration. He tracked her hand as she took it away from his cock and instead slid it down the apex of her body, between her legs. She spread herself open a fraction and circled herself lightly. "Arabella—"

"Don't you think I've been touching myself to thoughts of you ever since, longing for you? Put yourself inside of me and see how slick I am. Feel me rise beneath you and pulse around you because there is no way that I won't come the moment you grind against my clitoris." She arched against her own fingers and her breath became shaky. "Do it, Silas. Use me. And know I'm using you just as much."

"Shit," he grunted, and took himself in hand so he could align to her entrance. He thrust hard and found she was correct, she was wet and hot and ready for him. With that permission gained in every way, he lifted her hips slightly, cupping her against his lap, and then he took.

Thrust after thrust, he took. He was hard and fast and angry. He took her with *anger* even though it wasn't directed toward her. She matched him with every stroke, her pupils dilated, her body twisting with pleasure. He reached between them to stroke her clitoris and her fingers joined his. Together they worked her as he took and he felt her legs shaking around his hips, saw the tension enter her face as he brought her closer and closer to the brink.

When she fell, her body gripped him in long waves, squeezing in time to his thrusts as she cried out and shook. He rode her as long as he could, lengthening her pleasure alongside his own until he could no longer stand it. Then he withdrew and spent against his hand, against her thighs.

"Fucking hell, Arabella," he moaned, and collapsed over her on the rug, his mind empty for the moment, just as he'd wanted it to be.

She smoothed her hands along his bare back, tracing little patterns there. Their panting breaths slowed together and at last he rolled away onto his back to stare at her ceiling.

He'd been with a great many women in his life. He'd experienced a great deal of pleasure. But somehow it was nothing like this, nothing like her. And it would be easy to dismiss that as merely a byproduct of her experience as a lover. Or her knowledge as a courtesan, able to make a man dance on her string.

But to think that was to diminish what had just occurred between them. And somehow he didn't want to do that, even though perhaps he should. Perhaps he should pretend it away and make it something casual and without true meaning.

"They want me to stop running around London with you," he said.

She gave no response for a moment. When he glanced at her face in the firelight, there was no indication of what she felt about that fact. She didn't move, she didn't change anything about her body or expression. In fact, she was entirely blank, like the statement made no difference one way or another.

"Well, you and I have made no agreements," she said at last. "And if you decide to bow to their requirements, I could do nothing but understand. After all, I'll need to make my own arrangements soon enough. You'll be leaving to return to America in a few weeks anyway."

He lifted his head. "You know my schedule? Is that how far your research goes?"

"I was told it, I didn't seek it. But whatever the timeline, this is temporary, isn't it? We knew that from the start."

Temporary. His entire life felt temporary sometimes. And yet the fact of it stung this time. He pushed to his feet and fastened his trousers, then slung on his shirt and gathered the rest of his clothing. "You're right, of course. But I'm not ready for it to end just yet."

She sat up on her elbows, watching him, so utterly gorgeous when she was disheveled from sex. Then she nodded. "Well, I'm here as long as you'd like me to be, Silas. As long as you need me."

He held out a hand, which she took and allowed him to help her to her feet. He pulled her in for a kiss, which she also allowed without hesitation. But she also made no move to keep him against her when he pulled away.

"Thank you for this, Arabella. It did help," he said.

"I'm glad." She smiled at him, but he noted it didn't entirely reach her eyes. "Goodnight, Silas."

"Goodnight," he repeated, and then he left her parlor to go back into the night, feeling both better and somehow worse after the encounter.

And feeling forever confused about what exactly this woman was and how she could spin him around so easily.

Arabella watched from her window as Silas swung up onto his mount. He was all sleek and easy strength, a physical specimen unlike any other lover she'd ever had. He urged the animal forward and rode away from her home.

She ducked her head. In her heart, she knew it wasn't his physical prowess that made him different, not truly. No, the difference with him was something much more powerful and so much worse.

She didn't *want* to be shaken to her core by a man. That wasn't something one did and remained successful as a courtesan, she'd seen that firsthand with friends and rivals. And yet Silas Windham did shake her. Not just body with his wicked, wild touch, but he touched her heart and mind, too. She thought of him too much, wanted to protect him too much, wanted to ask him for protection too, and not the kind that usually went along with arrangements between her and lovers.

Those were all barriers she couldn't allow him to pass, just as she didn't allow *any* man to pass them. She would stop now. Any meeting between them would be light and meaningless and fun, just as they'd promised from the beginning.

And since he would be gone soon, perhaps it was also time to put her focus back on her own future. The one that would not, could not, ever include Silas Windham.

CHAPTER 13

In the three days after the encounter in her parlor, Arabella had somehow stuck to her promise to herself. She and Silas had met every day. They never discussed the painful subjects that had been brought up that powerful night. Instead, they attended a public fete in Hyde Park and danced to the music there under the stars. They went to yet another hell and played cards until dawn. They rode together and laughed together and after it was all done, they made love in carriages and against walls and at his home.

It was light and airy and the exchanges were completely without meaning. Or at least that was what she told herself. It was evident he was trying just as hard as she was to maintain the connection, at least in some way, but she felt their bond pulling apart.

Perhaps he had decided to eventually follow his family's edict that he separate from her. That this was the last hurrah. She could understand why. She wasn't appropriate, even as courtesans went. That was part of her charm, but also part of her poison.

She couldn't be upset about it either way. Or at least that's what she reminded herself over and over when she felt empty after they parted. This man wasn't her future, he was a lark. A purging of desire that had clung to her for years. He would leave, she would file him away with all her other former lovers. When she thought of him, she would smile and that would be enough.

It had to be.

She drew a breath and refocused for what felt like the tenth time on the room around her. She'd accepted an invitation to a gathering hosted by a courtesan, Gretchen Loveland, and her current protector, the Earl of Shrewton, and this was a hunting ground. Not a place to spiral off into weak and pointless emotion.

She sipped her drink and smiled across the room at one of the unattached gentlemen who was watching her. There were no small number to choose from. All of them were potentials for the next man who would hang her on his arm, take her to his bed, and ultimately, if she bargained correctly, fill her coffers a little further. Make her life easier.

She focused on that and batted her eyelashes a little to draw one of the interested parties near. Her come-hither expression was excellent bait for she didn't only bring him, but two other gentlemen to her side. With all her might she tried to focus on them, not stare into her drink, pondering Silas.

No, she *wouldn't* think of Silas.

"Good evening, gentlemen," she said with a small nod of her head as the three men reached her almost in unison. They gave each other little glares, like stags competing for a mate who weren't quite ready to come to actual blows yet. It likely wouldn't come to that. Though there had been courtesans who had experienced it. Men really were so endlessly predictable.

Almost all of them.

"Good evening, Miss Comerford," the Marquess of Saltersberry began, for he was the man of the highest rank. Arabella searched the collection of information in her mind to find any facts she could recall about him. He was older than her by at least a decade and a half, but that didn't mean much. She'd had far older lovers and they'd been fine.

But now that she stared at him she recalled he'd been linked briefly to a friend of hers, Lavinia, and she'd said he sometimes had a harsh temper when drunk. That certainly knocked him down a fraction in Arabella's mind. Abusive situations were intensely difficult and dangerous to escape for women of her ilk. She tried to avoid getting even remotely near them.

Viscount Saxton was the next to greet her. He was the man who had been staring. He was handsome enough to look at. He had an interesting smile and a Roman nose. He also had ten thousand a year and his last mistress had been settled reasonably well. Arabella though she remembered Betty complaining about his lack of skills in the bedroom, but one could bring their own orgasms when one needed them. Still, months or even years of fruitless fumbling? Ugh.

The final gentleman was Mr. Patrick Murray. He was a grandson of the Earl of Jacksnewton, untitled himself, but certainly not without means. She thought he'd gotten himself involved in some kind of mining investments and made himself a fairly tidy fortune far beyond the small inheritance spread about by his grandfather. He seemed intelligent as he spoke to her and he wasn't startlingly attractive like Silas, but he wasn't hard to look at. His dark brown eyes seemed kind.

She talked to all three for a little while, using the mask of her personality and the draw of her wild to dangle them on her string. To play them off each other. Of course, it worked. She knew it would, it always did. By the time the three gentlemen excused themselves, two had asked to call on her later and one was talking about his wealth in the kind of terms that were part of the negotiation of these types of arrangements.

It was successful and it drew the attention of even more men in the room, which was the purpose, after all. But God, it was boring. Arabella had never found the hunt boring before, but tonight she was pleased when she was left alone for a moment and could gather herself.

"Here, have a drink."

Arabella started at the sound of her sister Evelina's voice. She hadn't realized she was even in attendance tonight, which was evidence enough of her distraction. She turned to find Evelina approaching, a glass of punch outstretched toward her.

"Thank you," Arabella said and took it. "Where is Harry?"

She looked around the room for Evelina's duke and found him with a small group of gentlemen gathered by the punch table. He was frowning and talking.

"Negotiating something to do with parliament with those men," Evelina sighed. "He scooted me off, told me I wouldn't understand."

Arabella pursed her lips. Evelina was the cleverest person she knew. The fact that the duke would think she wouldn't understand some debate about farms or roads or taxes was ridiculous. Her sister could likely talk circles around those fops about it all.

"Why do you look so sour?" Evelina asked as she slid an arm through Arabella's and squeezed gently.

Arabella glanced at her. "Do I look sour?"

Her sister nodded. "Yes. Not for more than a flash of a moment after the latest group of popinjays walked away from you, but I saw it. Were they so terrible? I noted Saltersberry was amongst them."

There was a waver to Evelina's tone. Concern for Arabella, so she quickly nipped the reason in the bud. "Yes, and before you say anything, I recall the talk about his temper. I've already crossed him off the list, though he was certainly charming enough for the little while I spent with him."

"They always are," Evelina said softly.

They both flinched. Her sister had been through a great deal with her second protector. The topic of violent tempers and what they could lead to was always a tender one.

"I would never consider him, Evie," Arabella promised, and squeezed her sister gently.

"Good. But what about the others?"

"The viscount seems interesting enough to get over his lack of prowess in bed. And Mr. Murray is rich *and* fascinating. Double points for him, even though he isn't titled. I don't think I've ever been with a protector who wasn't titled."

"Except Silas Windham," Evelina said.

Arabella looked at her. There was a certain tone to her sister's voice that was meant to elicit a reaction and she fought to keep it from doing so.

"Silas isn't my protector," she said and stared off into the crowd as if that didn't matter. "We're both very clear on that."

"And is whatever it is between you over? I thought I heard you were out last night, but here you are on the hunt."

"It *will* be over. Probably sooner rather than later since he'll be leaving London in a very short amount of time." She swallowed, wishing her eyes didn't burn with that reminder. She wasn't about to shed tears about a man. That was ridiculous.

"I see." Evelina was quiet a moment. "You've always liked the hunt. It's always been magical to watch you stalk your prey and make them think it was them who drew you not the other way around. And don't misunderstand me, you *are* doing that right now. But I know you. I *know* you, Arabella. I can see that you're only going through the motions. Do you want to talk about why?"

Arabella turned her head. Her sister saw far too much. Under normal circumstances she *would* talk to her about it. They'd often compared notes about lovers and discussed tactics—she adored Evelina and trusted her opinions.

But right now the answer to the question of why Arabella didn't have her head in this most important game wasn't one she wanted to consider for herself, let alone bring her intelligent sister into. She feared Evelina would see even further than she did now.

So instead, she laughed and shook her head. "Oh, you're seeing things. Go away and dance with Harry. He seems to be finished with his cronies and I'm sure you'd rather do that."

Evelina arched a brow. "I see you, whether you like it or not."

"I'm the oldest, you know," Arabella muttered as she bodily

pushed her sister toward her protector. "I'm supposed to be the one who uses that judgmental look, not the other way around."

Evelina laughed as she finally walked away, but Arabella felt no pleasure as she immediately turned from her sister and toward the terrace doors that led from the ballroom. The orchestra had begun playing for the couples and nearly everyone in the room was pairing up to dance. That meant the terrace would be emptier than usual and perhaps she could have a moment to herself to regather.

She apparently needed it.

She slipped through the doors and quietly closed them behind her. To her great delight the terrace was, indeed, empty and she drew in a deep breath of cool night air. Peace was a rare commodity at such gatherings. When one found it, it was like a pocket of gold.

She paced to the terrace wall overlooking the garden and began to plan. She could stay out here for two songs, perhaps, without being missed. And then she would go back in, she would school any sourness from her expression and she would hunt, damn it. She wouldn't let something temporary affect her long-term plans. Not even something *lovely* and temporary.

She had only just declared that to herself when she heard someone exit the ballroom. She prayed it was a couple, that they'd go to the other side of the terrace and she could slip to the shadowy privacy closer to the house wall.

But as she glanced over her shoulder, her heart skipped a beat. It was Silas who stood there, decked out in full finery, all that wildness smoothed a little for the consumption of others. He watched her with intensity for a long moment before he stepped forward.

"You look very pretty," he said without any other preamble or greeting. As if they could just pick up so easily without formality.

Now why did her heart pound at that rather innocent compliment? Why was she so flummoxed by it?

"I—so do you," she said, and before she could correct herself and tell him she meant he was handsome, he motioned up and down his body with one hand.

"Oh, this old thing?"

She laughed at his teasing and he joined with her as he reached out to take her hand. She realized in this moment that what she felt when she was with him was something so *easy*. She never ran equations with her knowledge when she was with him, never searched for topics that would please him or avoid ones that wouldn't. She didn't play her game. Or at least, not her usual one. Life was a game, after all.

No, when she was with him, she was just...*there*. In the moment. Genuine.

She swallowed. "Are you following me, Mr. Windham?"

He stepped even closer, lifting the hand he held to rest against his chest. She felt the faint comfort of his steady heartbeat even through the layers of his clothing.

"I missed you," he said, "and went to call on you at your home without even sending word ahead."

"How flagrantly you ignore societal rules, Silas."

He shrugged. "I do. I really do. Much to the great consternation of everyone in my orbit, it seems. But it came back to bite me tonight because you, of course, weren't home. But I did manage to overhear where you were going as I left. So I suppose, yes, I *did* follow you here."

"Considering I used the courtesan network to research every little fact I could about you over the years, I suppose you following me to a party makes us even."

"Does it?" he laughed. "Very well, then we're even." He was quiet a moment, just watching her in the light coming from the windows that looked into the still-spinning ball behind him. "You are glorious in your element, you know. Drawing the men in, making them dance to your tune even though every one of them would leave thinking they were in control of those interactions. Turning your head just so and making them all track you. Remarkable."

Her eyes widened. "How long were you watching me?"

"For a little while," he admitted.

She swallowed, for she suddenly felt exposed by that admission. It was one thing for her beloved sister to see all her moves from a height that let her track the machinations, but quite another for this man.

She shifted. "Does it…bother you to see it?"

His brow wrinkled. "Bother me?"

"I've had lovers in the past who didn't want me to even look at another man. Who hated that I went on the hunt even when our arrangements were over."

"Hmm, sounds familiar," he said, and the words brought her to mind of his confessions about his father's obsession with his mother. But he didn't delve into those intimate topics. Instead, he shrugged. "But it's not me. I find it arousing to watch men want you. To watch them trail after you like some kind of erotic Pied Piper. You are a master, Arabella, I can only respect your skills." Now he traced the line of her jaw with his fingertip, his green gaze holding hers and forcing her to spiral into the beauty of it. "I suppose it also helps to know that it was *me* dripping down your thighs just last night. That I have what they want, even temporarily."

She shivered at the erotic words, spoken so softly because they were so close in the cool dimness that felt intimate even with a party going on ten feet away.

"Silas," she whispered.

He shook his head and to her surprise the playful sensuality left his expression, replaced by something else. Something regretful and pained. "I wonder if I'm being selfish toward you, though." He hesitated. "Well, I suppose I'm always selfish, some would say. It's one of my traits. But in this case, too selfish."

"What do you mean?" she asked. "How are you being selfish toward me?"

She truly couldn't find the answer. In the time they'd spent together, he'd been nothing but generous. With his passion, with his time, with his humor and *his* wild. He'd given, she'd never felt taken from.

And yet he looked genuinely concerned.

"I'm taking what they would pay for," he said. "I'm keeping you from the next step, perhaps. From the next man who will tend to your comfort and your stability, just because I can't stop..." His breath came out in a shaky sigh as he smoothed his thumb across her lower lip. "...touching you. So doesn't that make me selfish, Arabella? Because it certainly doesn't feel selfless."

CHAPTER 14

Silas found himself holding his breath as Arabella stared up at him, her gorgeous face soft in half-light and half-shadow. He couldn't read her expression, she had schooled it a moment ago, but before she had he'd seen surprise and a little pain in it.

What that meant for her answer to his question, he didn't know.

"What are you saying, Silas?" she asked at last, tone even. "That you don't want to keep doing this?"

The words pierced him like a sword passing easily through cheap armor. "I want to," he said immediately. "But I fear it's unfair."

Now there *was* a flicker of emotion. She released his hand and walked back to the terrace wall where he'd first found her after he stepped out. She looked toward the garden a moment and then she faced him again. Rare vulnerability lined her features.

"My life isn't about making choices," she said, barely loud enough for the words to carry. "I pick a man, yes. I negotiate for terms of an arrangement that will be best for me. I suppose that seems like choice to many. But the fact is that once I'm his, I must do what will keep him happy. To *be* what will make *him* happy. I don't choose what opera we go to or what we eat. I put my clothing on, yes, but I don't really pick the color, I pick what he'll be most attracted to. I laugh at his jokes, even if they're not funny. I believe in whatever politics he holds true, even if I hate every part of them. I become his doll and I put a great deal of myself away in the process."

Silas winced at that description. "That sounds deeply frustrating."

"It is sometimes," she admitted. Then she drew a shaky breath. "But I want to make something clear. Since you reappeared in London, since we connected, I haven't had to do that. I *chose* you, Silas. And I didn't try to water myself down or fluff myself up for your pleasure. I was just…me. Christ, you even saw me with my hair rolled."

"I'm not sure *that* was your choice," he said with a chuckle. But the humor of that moment didn't reduce the weight of the rest. The absolute power of her saying she had chosen him.

"You were what I wanted all those years ago at Vauxhall Garden," she continued. "And it turns out you're what I still want. So please don't take that from me out of some misguided attempt to protect me. *That* would be selfish."

It felt like someone had given him wings and now he could soar to dizzying heights. Or like Arabella had reached into his chest and placed a gentle hand around his throbbing heart. He could see that the honesty, the vulnerability shook her. She was trembling as she looked up at him.

He knew how to ease her, of course. And how to celebrate this unexpected admission that rocked him to his very core.

"So you're using me then," he said, and made sure the teasing was very obvious in his tone.

Her gaze lit up and she smiled. "I suppose I am. There's a shift. Usually it's you lot that use me."

He shifted as he thought of the night he'd come to her, pained from his encounter with his siblings and he *had* used her. Pinned her to her carpet and poured all this desire and pain into her quaking body until it was all dulled. That had mattered, even if they'd pretended it away since. He wanted to do something that mattered as much to her.

"Would you like to do that tonight, Arabella?" he asked.

There was a fraction of a moment where her breath caught and her pupils dilated in the lamplight. He felt the longing coming off of her in waves. Desire, yes, of course there was desire there. But there was also something deeper. Something more powerful that called to a matching sensation he tried to ignore and pretend away and close off so that it couldn't hurt him. But it was there, hovering between them like some beautiful mirage that he feared would vanish if he tried to move toward it.

She began to back into the darkened corner of the terrace, away from the doors and the windows that allowed those in the ballroom to see outside. He followed without hesitation and when they reached the darkness he crowded into her space, caged her in with a hand on either side of her head against the outer wall of the house and leaned down to kiss her.

The touch of lips was explosive, just as it always was. It could be a day or an hour without her and he would crave her like he'd been starved. He wasn't even surprised by the intensity of feeling anymore, it was almost like an old friend.

She wound her arms around his neck and lifted into him, making the ache in him even sharper and more powerful.

"You said you have to do things for them, be things for them," he murmured against her mouth. "Play for their amusement."

She drew back a little, her gaze barely glittering in the impossible dimness of the night. "Yes."

"Then why don't I play for yours?" he whispered, and lowered to his knees before her, dragging his mouth on the path he had to take to do so.

She gripped her hands into his hair with a gasp and he watched her look around as he began to inch her skirts up bit by bit.

"Silas," she whispered, then whimpered as he brushed his lips against her stocking-clad knee. God, even through silk, she was impossibly sweet.

"Yes?" he whispered, even as he dragged his tongue up the inside of her thigh and pushed her gown higher. He could almost scent her desire now, feel the tremble of her.

"Anyone could come around the corner," she gasped. "Anyone could see."

He smiled up at her as he handed her the bunched skirt of her dress to get it out of his way. "Let them. Let them watch you shatter around my tongue. Or better yet, listen to them dance and drone on about whatever foolishness pleases them while you scratch at the walls as you come."

"Fuck," she breathed, that one word so sweet a surrender.

He smiled as she widened her stance, granting him further access to her body. He took it, stoking her soft flesh with his palms and fingers, then brushing her bare sex with his thumbs. He peeled her open and she jolted, one hand coming back to his hair. He paused, wondering if she'd push him away or pull him in. She hesitated, perhaps debating that decision herself, then she tugged him closer.

Permission fully granted, he licked her length once, then twice. The taste of her was maddening, sweet and earthy and rich with desire. He swept his tongue over the tender flesh, just playing for a moment. Not too long, though. Game or not, he doubted she'd like being tormented for too long out in the open. Later he could do more. Later he could torment and torture and play until she was screeching and twisting.

For now, he wanted to make her come in a shocking, heated, instant burst. So he focused his attention upon her clitoris. He smoothed the sheath aside, exposing the slickness of it beneath. When he just darted his tongue across her, she bucked against him. A demand for more. For now, he obeyed that command. This was for her, after all.

He swirled his tongue over her again and again, increasing the pressure and setting the rhythm as she began to ride his mouth in earnest. He matched her, stroking and stroking as her wetness increased, as her moans grew louder and joined the sound of the party around the corner of the terrace.

People came outside as he licked her. He heard the door open and voices become clearer. They were talking about the roads, something so benign, and she removed her hand from his hair and covered her mouth so they wouldn't hear her.

He began to suck, strong and steady, and the muffled sound of her drove him on, pulling him toward the inevitable moment when she would fall and he would revel in the clench of her, the burst of her, the waves of her.

She gasped out his name on a harsh whisper and did just that. He pinned her hips against the wall with both hands and sucked harder, drawing out her orgasm, forcing her to ride every single gorgeous ripple of it as she wriggled against him, breath sharp and body trembling.

Only when she went weak, leaning against him for support, did he lift his head from between her legs. She widened her stance a little more, giving him a place to push into, to take her. It was a temptation, the idea that he could have her in the fading glow of her pleasure, still feel the shutter of her release massage his cock until he spent between them.

Instead he rose up, smoothing her skirt back down and straightening her carefully before he leaned in and let her taste herself on his lips.

"This was for you, Arabella," he whispered. "Just for you."

She stared up at him and then cleared her throat. "Well, what if I want that for me?" she asked, cupping him through his trousers and sending shockwaves of pleasure up his cock from her touch.

"You can have it later," he said. "If you're very good. Now why don't we go back in and enjoy the rest of the party?"

He offered his arm with all the politeness and propriety his father had tried to scream into him over the years and she took it.

The intruders on the terrace had gone back inside while she writhed in pleasure, so they weren't seen as they stepped back into the fuller light.

She looked up at him and snorted out a laugh. "Oh dear, I've mussed you," she said, and then reached up to smooth his hair back into place. "Not perfect, but I doubt anyone will notice."

"You'll notice," he said. "And you'll know why." He stepped forward and opened the terrace door. "After you, Miss Comerford."

She shook her head as she re-entered the ballroom. He moved her directly onto the dance floor and as the orchestra began to play a waltz, he drew her to his chest and spun her into the crowd of dancers.

She smiled up at him, her face bright with remnants of her pleasure and also just true enjoyment. She was achingly beautiful in that moment, genuinely perfect in every way. And he realized that he was truly coming to care for her. Perhaps more than just care, even though that made no sense and could have no good end. He would leave. She had made it clear she only wanted an affair.

To long for more was folly.

"They're all watching us, you know," she said softly.

He looked around and shrugged even as he turned her. "I'm sure. You are in great demand, after all. I'm sure it irritates them to no end that a bastard no one is the man with you in his arms."

"They're watching us because they want to know how I tamed such a wild thing," she said. "How I made you dance with me like a very proper gentleman."

"That's because they don't know what I was doing on the terrace a moment ago," he said. "They wouldn't think I was a gentleman then."

She tilted her head. "Perhaps, despite your best efforts, you are both, Silas. A dashing rogue, yes. But also a little bit of a reluctant gentleman."

He stared at her as the music ended and the other couples took their bows. She'd said something so seemingly benign and it felt like it cracked him open a fraction. Let some light into places that had always been as dark as the corner where he pleasured her.

He had no idea how to respond to her observation, but was relieved of any obligation to do so when they were approached by a couple. She smiled at them and Silas realized this was the sister he hadn't yet met, Evelina. Like the youngest, Julia, this woman looked a great deal like Arabella. Her eyes weren't the same—Evelina's were brown—but otherwise they had a similarly shaped face, the same dark hair.

"Evelina, Harry!" Arabella said, and drew their group off the dancefloor so they wouldn't block the next set of dancers. "What excellent timing. I don't think you've met my..." She trailed off and looked at Silas. "My friend, Silas Windham. Silas, this is the Duke of Southwater and my sister, Evelina Comerford."

"Your Grace," Silas said with a slight incline of his head. He actually knew Southwater, though he doubted the man recalled him. They'd been acquainted with each other as boys in school. Southwater had been a few years older. Silas had watched him bully some of the younger children and had ended up with a black eye for the trouble of defending them.

"Mr. Windham," Southwater said, all disinterested politeness. "I'd heard you were back in Town for a few weeks. Pleasure to see you. How is your brother?"

Silas glanced toward Evelina, who hadn't yet had a chance to greet him thanks to the intrusion of her protector. "He's doing better, thank you for the inquiry. And Miss Comerford, I've heard so much about you."

Evelina extended a hand at last and he shook it. "And I think you know I've heard so much about you," Evelina said with a glance toward her sister.

"Evie," Arabella said, and actually blushed. "She is terrible, she'll tell you awful tales. All lies."

"Hmmm," Silas said with a wink toward her. "That only makes me want to ask questions."

"Dearest, would you like some punch?" Southwater asked.

Evelina glanced up at him with a soft smile. "Oh, that would be lovely, thank you."

The duke inclined his head and then left the three of them to weave his way through the crowd. Silas watched him with a frown. To fetch punch for his lover seemed kind on the surface, but Silas wondered if it was more out of disinterest in talking to Arabella and him rather than truly looking out for Evelina's care.

Not that it was any of his business.

"You know I met your younger sister, Julia, at an event not so long ago," Silas said, refocusing on the two women.

"Yes," Evelina said with another wink for Arabella. "She told me all about it. And so you've met all three Comerford Courtesans. Do you have an opinion on the lot of us?"

He felt Arabella tense beside him. Just a little bracing for whatever he'd say, which made him wonder what other men had talked about when they discussed the sisters. Actually, he could well-imagine the disgusting things some men would come up with when faced with three sisters in the life.

"I think I'm most stuck by your strong bond," he said, and meant it. "I'm afraid I'm not particularly close with my siblings, so to see how easy you are together is a true pleasure."

Something on Evelina's expression softened and she reached out to briefly squeeze Arabella's hand. "Well, you ought to see all three of us together, then."

"A tornado is what that is," Arabella teased.

He smiled. "I've seen a tornado, in America. Terrifying things, but intensely beautiful."

Evelina laughed. "Then it sounds like the perfect description for us. Terrifying but beautiful."

"I find all three of you lovely," he agreed. "But only *slightly* terrifying."

Evelina watched him a moment, her humor still on her expression, but her gaze focused. She was reading him, just as Arabella did sometimes. "How did you find the former colonies?" she asked. "You were there a long time, yes?"

"Over five years," he said. "I traveled a great deal, saw cities and the countryside. There is great beauty there. And their wilderness is very different from ours. Here, you walk for a little while in one direction, you'll find a town or house of some kind. There...well, if you wander too far you'll never be found. Lost to the woods and the brush forever."

"That sounds fascinating," Evelina said with a sigh.

"I-I made some sketches during my time there," Silas admitted, almost not realizing he was going to be so honest.

"You did?" Arabella asked, her eyes wide as she turned to face him more straight on. "I had no idea you were an artist."

"I wouldn't say an artist, but it's impossible not to be in such a place and not capture it in some way, and I've never been much of a writer."

"If you've brought the pieces, I'd love to see them," Evelina said. "And it sounds like Arabella would feel the same."

"I'm happy to share, as long as you do not judge my attempt at art too cruelly," he said.

Evelina glanced over her shoulder. "Where in the world is Harry? He's always been interested in America. Thinks we should take it all back by force, I think, for the resources there." She slightly rolled her eyes, just barely perceptible.

"I think I see him there with..." Arabella pursed her lips. "I'm not sure which earl that is, it's hard to tell when they're not facing me."

"He must have gotten sidetracked," Evelina said. "I'll go fetch him, as we intended to go home early before we spotted you two dancing. It was a great pleasure to meet you at last, Mr. Windham."

"Silas," he said. "Mr. Windham is far too formal."

"Silas," she repeated. Then she leaned forward and kissed Arabella's cheek. He thought he saw her whisper something, but couldn't hear it. "Good night, dearest. We'll work out when I can have the grand exhibit of his work."

"Good night," Arabella said, and together they watched her make her way toward Southwater. The duke glanced down at her when she reached him, put his arm around her as he continued to speak to his companion.

When Silas looked at her, Arabella was frowning slightly. He caught her hand and lifted it to his lips. "Another dance, my lady?"

She nodded. "I'd love to."

They went back to the dancefloor and spun back out together. This dance was a little more lively than the waltz had been earlier, but it wasn't a country group dance, at least, so he could keep her in his arms even as they hopped and skipped their way around the floor together.

"You worry about her," he said.

"Evelina?" she asked.

He nodded. "Do you not approve of her duke?"

"She's been with Harry for two years now. That's a lifetime in the world of courtesans. She tells me she's happy, she even seems happy most of the time. But I suppose old habits die hard and I always look to how I can protect her."

Silas tilted his head to look at her a little more closely. There was more to it than that, but he doubted Arabella would say more. On some level, he understood it. If there was trouble between Evelina and Southwater, that was their business, not anyone else's.

"Well, both your sisters are amazing women," he said.

That slight change of subject caused Arabella's face to light up. "Thank you, I agree. I do adore them both. We were close as girls and to still be so close now is a true pleasure."

"I can picture you all easily as girls, giggling together and causing trouble. What about your mother since I know you weren't close to your father based on our earlier conversation."

The pleasure that had come over her face when she spoke of her sisters faded now. Replaced by pain and then by the mask she put up around subjects that had real impact on her. Her expression became calm and blank and her gaze darted to the side slightly.

"My mother was long dead," she said.

Silas wrinkled his brow because she made no effort to tell that story, nor more of the one she'd already mentioned about her father. She was shutting the door on him. Shuffling him into the same category where she put her protectors. He had opened up to her, but she wouldn't do the same with him.

And he understood it all. He knew exactly why she kept her emotions, her pains, separate from everyone around her. Yet he wished he could find a way over that wall she had erected around herself. Wished he could delve deeper and find the depths of her that hadn't seen the light in years.

And that was most definitely unfair of him. For both their sakes.

He turned her on the dancefloor as the song faded and when she changed the subject, he didn't pursue it. He let her be light and fun and nothing more. And even as he reveled in all that she was, he also felt bereft with the knowledge that he could only see a tiny fraction of her.

And that she'd likely never allow him more.

CHAPTER 15

Simone Stanhope's London townhouse had been the first place Arabella had felt safe when she left her family and began on her path to becoming a courtesan. Simone had allowed her a room and full use of her library of naughty books. Her education had been first theoretical thanks to the books and then practical as Simone took her out into the world and let her see and experience the expectations Arabella would encounter as a courtesan.

Memories of long talks and spied upon moments flooded her as her carriage entered Simone's drive on an early afternoon two days after the Cyprian ball. As she exited the vehicle, servants rushed to help her and she smiled at them. They were the same people who had served Simone all those years ago.

Get good servants and keep them happy. She could practically hear that edict in Simone's voice. It was one she followed religiously. She took care of those in her employ and she trusted them to take care of her...and her secrets.

"Miss Comerford," Simone's butler said as he stepped from the house to greet her. "We weren't expecting you today."

"Good afternoon, Buttons," Arabella said with a warm smile for the man.

She had no idea if Buttons was his true last name or if he'd been a pirate at some point and that was his nickname. Honestly, she might believe the second. He had a scar on his cheek, after all, and a rather rakish air for a butler.

"I assume you've come to join your aunt and Miss Simone?" he asked as he took her hat and gloves.

Arabella blinked at that unexpected question. "My—my aunt? Er, yes. Of course."

He led the way to the parlor. Arabella was surprised to find the door shut. He knocked lightly and waited until he heard Simone's voice, "Yes?"

"Miss Arabella Comerford," he announced as he cracked the door.

"Oh. Yes. Well, have her come in," Simone's voice came from behind the door.

He stepped back and Arabella entered the room. She found her aunt first. Caroline stood at the window, her hands clasped almost nervously in front of her. Simone was also on her feet before the settee. She must have been entertaining her protector before Caroline's arrival, because Arabella recognized her gown. Normally it was one she wore at the beginning of a new arrangement. It was low cut and accentuated Simone's lush curves. Something to make them want, she always said.

"Simone," Arabella said, and crossed so they could kiss each other's cheeks. Then she turned on her aunt. "And Aunt Caroline. I...I admire I'm shocked to find you here. I didn't realize you and Simone shared tea."

Her aunt blinked and reached up to smooth her dark hair before she cast a quick look toward Simone. "I—we don't. Or we didn't. Not often at any rate. I just wanted to talk to her about—"

"Gracious, Caroline, don't give yourself an apoplexy," Simone said smoothly. "Your aunt and I share something in common, our affection for you and your sisters. We bumped into each other at

Mr. Mattigan's bookshop and decided to have tea. I'm not sure one should say they are *shocked* to see us together."

Arabella wrinkled her brow. That did make sense, of course. It was only that her aunt was always so missish when the topic of Simone ever came up. She'd had such a sheltered life and the idea of the courtesan seemed to make her nervous.

"Well, I'm happy for you two to be friends," she said carefully. "To have you two both looking out for us is a very powerful idea."

"Yes," her aunt said, and seemed to find the ability to move from the window at last. "But it seems you have something to discuss with Simone...with Miss Stanhope, and I think it's best I not be involved in the details of your arrangements. I'll excuse myself." She glanced toward Simone. "Thank you for—for today."

"It was my pleasure," Simone said with a smile. "May I escort you to the door?"

"No, I'm fine. I can find my way. Good afternoon."

Her aunt scurried off and shut the door behind her. Though muted through the thick wood, Arabella could still hear her voice as she asked for her carriage. She glanced at Simone.

"What did you do to my aunt?" she teased.

Simone shifted. "Nothing at all, I assure you. You know we've had a few interactions over the years."

"You have? I thought it was only the one time."

Simone shrugged. "You don't know all her business, you know. Or mine."

"We delight in teasing her at how red she blushes when your name is said."

"Does she now?" Simone said with a husky laugh.

"Well, she was raised in a very sheltered way," Arabella explained. "That she didn't cut herself off from me, and later from Evelina and Julia, speaks to her loving heart. Still, the facts of our lives are still shocking to her, I'm sure. Was she concerned about something specific?"

"Don't you worry. I took care of it," Simone said. Then she motioned to the tea that had been laid at the sideboard. "Would you like a drink? I have this, but also a great many somethings which are stronger."

Arabella took a seat on the settee. "The tea is fine."

She watched as her friend prepared her a cup just to her liking. That was another skill Arabella had learned at Simone's knee: that a courtesan must always pay attention to the small details. Being able to prepare a cup of tea just perfectly to a partner's liking was almost as important as knowing what kind of sex he liked.

How did Silas like his tea? They'd shared tea once, back at the beginning of this seduction, but he'd prepared it for her, not the other way around. Did he recall how she liked it? She had a sneaking suspicion he did, down to the exact amount of milk.

"What are you doing?" Simone asked as she set the cup before Arabella and took a place in one of the chairs across from her.

Arabella blinked. "Doing?"

"I've heard the whispers, you know. Actually it's all louder than whispers now, though not quite shouts. You and Silas."

Arabella's first instinct was to play it all off. To act like it meant nothing. But she'd come here to talk to Simone about just this. She couldn't be a coward now. Even if she tried, she had a sneaking suspicion that her friend would see right through her.

"Well, it's all supposed to be breezy," she said carefully. "It's just meant to be a bit of fun."

Simone sipped her tea. "But?"

Arabella shifted in her seat and stared at her hands. The words she was about to say came very hard suddenly. Like they were stuck in her throat. She cleared it and forced them loose. "Have you ever… cared about a man?"

"No," Simone said, but her gaze went faraway. "I've cared about a lover, though. You are saying you care about him."

Tears stung Arabella's eyes and she blinked them away. "I do. I think I'm falling in love with him."

There. It was out. The fact that terrified her more than anything was free into the world where it could fly and sting and maybe poison her in the end. And yet saying it didn't feel painful, it felt glorious, at least for a moment before it became utterly terrifying.

Simone set her cup down and leaned forward in her chair. "Arabella, you've been falling in love with him since you first saw him at Vauxhall Gardens. This is not news."

Arabella let out a shaky sigh and scrubbed a hand over her eyes. "Possibly that's true. *Probably* that's true. He's just…he's special. He's so intense and passionate."

"You've been with passionate men before," Simone said gently.

"But he's also bright and he's…he's caring."

"And he's leaving."

That was said firmly and Arabella shut her eyes against the weight of it. "I know. I *know*. And even if he wasn't, what do I know about sharing myself? About loving someone?"

"You think he wants your love?"

"I know he wants more of me, even if it's not the love he craves. He presses me, tries to crack me open. I've always run from anyone who did that and I feel that same desire to run with him. But I also feel this need, this want to—to tell him everything. To give him everything he ever wanted. Even though I know if he sees me, truly sees me…how will I ever protect myself?"

She waited for Simone to lecture. She deserved a scolding, after all, didn't she? This idea that she could care for Silas, even love Silas, went against every creed she had agreed to when she became a courtesan. She broke every rule by even thinking about it.

Instead, Simone let out a shaky breath. "Oh, Arabella, I wish I knew the answer to that question. I never taught lessons on love aside from avoiding it because I didn't know it then. And right now, looking at you, my gut tells me not to support this. To tell you to hide yourself away, to break with him as cruelly as possible so that he won't pursue what could hurt you."

"But?"

Arabella was breathless as she awaited the answer. Simone was just as breathless as she gave it. "But I know him and I know you. You two together, truly together…it makes some kind of sense."

Two sensations rushed through Arabella at that answer. First was joy, pure and unadulterated joy. But the second was a terror unlike anything she'd ever felt before. A full knowledge that she could be torn to shreds by this if she allowed it. That she could surrender all she'd built around herself and never fully recover. That she could force Silas to lose his family and the future he pretended he didn't want. But she wouldn't share that fact with Simone. It was too private and intimate to whisper his secrets and pains to anyone else.

"I came here so you could talk me out of this," she gasped as she leapt to her feet and paced to the same window where her aunt had stood a few moments before. "Christ, Simone, don't tell me it makes sense, none of this makes sense!"

Simone was quiet for a moment, long enough that Arabella faced her at last. She found her friend watching her, expression unreadable. "But what do you want to do?"

"Want to do? When did *want* ever come into it? Need was first, wasn't it? That was what you taught me. Access what I need, determine how to get it. Want would only get me in trouble."

"You quote me back to myself so easily," Simone said, and now she got to her feet, too.

"Because I memorized every line. You are successful because you don't fall, you don't even waver. You give exactly the amount that is needed but never an ounce more. You mentored me to make the same choices and I have. I have and I've been…happy."

She faltered in that last word because it felt heavy on her tongue. Like it was a lie.

"Happy," Simone repeated. "I'm not sure I ever taught you to be that. Just to survive. Happy might take a little more risk than I've ever been willing to take."

"If you haven't been willing, then how can I?"

"Because you are young, Arabella. And Silas isn't like anyone else. He isn't some duke who pretends to care while he is just getting what he wants." Arabella winced because she feared Simone was using Evelina as the example of what not to do. Worse, she feared Simone was right. "Silas is...singular. So what do you *want* to do with this emotion in your chest?"

She kept coming back to want and Arabella pushed at it with all her might. She had to focus on need, no matter what Simone said. And need was very clear.

"Perhaps what I must do is...end it."

Saying that felt like slitting her own throat. She almost couldn't breathe.

"Oh, Arabella."

"I should end it, and get a new arrangement and be finished. He'll go back to America or...or do something else that will be better for him. Make him happy. What was between us will become nothing more than a pleasing memory I'll recall when I'm trying to orgasm with some fumbling gentleman."

She expected Simone to laugh at that. She didn't. Instead she crossed to Arabella and took her hand. "Are you certain?"

"No. Yes. No. But that doesn't mean I shouldn't do it."

"I'm sorry."

Arabella let out a shaky sigh and let her friend hug her. "So am I. So am I."

CHAPTER 16

Silas was faced with two feelings as he fingered the note in his pocket. It was from his sister, asking if she could come call this afternoon. The first feeling was anxiety. He had no idea what she would say. Their last encounter, when she'd sat beside him as his brothers demanded he change to earn their love, had been unpleasant.

But the other feeling was relief. He truly cared for Phoebe. He didn't want to be estranged from her.

As if conjured, Poole suddenly appeared at the door to the parlor and said, "Mrs. Broughton to see you, Mr. Windham."

The butler stepped aside to allow his sister into the room and Silas smiled at her. "Phoebe, I'm so glad you've come."

She crossed to him and took his hand to squeeze it gently. "I'm so glad to be here."

"Will there be anything else aside from the tea, sir?" Poole asked.

Silas shook his head. "No, that will be all." The servant stepped away and Silas let out his breath. "I've no idea what suddenly made the man all politeness, but I cannot argue the change."

"The butler was not polite to you before?" his sister asked, and nodded as he motioned to the tea set.

He moved to pour her a cup and snorted out a laugh. "Well, he came with the house, of course, and I suppose he knew of my status as bastard prodigal son. But suddenly last week his attitude changed and now he at least tones down the nastiness."

"Well, I'm glad of it." Phoebe sighed as he handed over her cup and the two of them took a place together on the settee. "You certainly don't deserve to be mistreated by anyone due to your birth. Not the servants, not…not your family."

He set his tea aside untouched. "Come, Phoebe, you've always been kind to me. How old were you when I was brought to the family?"

"Well, you were about five, so I must have been fourteen or fifteen," she said. "Which would have made Reggie seventeen and Charlie twenty."

"It was a big change for all of you. And I'm sure it wasn't comfortable to have your father's by-blow running around, causing talk."

She pursed her lips. "No, it wasn't. And we all know that Father didn't make it easier. He encouraged the gulf between us, I think. But after I got over the shock, all I could see was a sweet little boy when I looked at you." She sighed. "Why do you think he wanted separation between you and us?"

Silas blinked. He hadn't intended to have this conversation with his sister today, perhaps ever. He tended to play off these sorts of topics, try to steer away from any kind of vulnerability. But he'd opened something in himself when he'd told part of his past to Arabella. It had eased the hurt a fraction to allow the pain out. And now he thought of her, she just popped into his head like an angel trying to get purchase on his shoulder. She whispered to him that to discuss this with Phoebe might make it hurt even less.

And he drew a shaky breath and said, "He never really wanted me, I don't think, he just wanted to take me from my mother. Oh, he'd tell you it was because she wasn't…stable…and that was true, though I think his treatment of her made all that worse. But he also despised her for ending the affair before he could. He wanted to hurt her. He wanted to do it so she would always know. So she could always be fully aware where I was and what I was doing because it was all so public."

"He was vindictive, yes," Phoebe whispered. "I could see him doing that. Trying to make her hurt by stealing you, claiming you not just dragging you away."

"And once he had, he had little use for me. When my mother died, he…he told me so matter-of-factly. So coldly."

She winced again. "Yes, I recall that. I only knew she died because of servant whispers. And when I asked him if I could offer you comfort, he was furious. He told me that your mother didn't… didn't…"

"Didn't matter, yes. He told me the same." He turned his face and drew a few breaths. "I thought he might send me away then, but I think I was a bit like a project for him. Could he turn the bastard son of a courtesan into a suitable gentleman? Mold what he saw as the worst of me out of me. So he kept me under his roof, under his watch, tried to shape me, but I'm not sure he ever truly saw me as a son. So why would he want his real children to be close to me? Why would he want to foster the full acceptance he never gave?"

She seemed to ponder that a moment and he saw the pain in her. Pain for the past, pain for him, but also pain for herself. Slowly, she nodded. "You are probably right. Like many men of his stature and disposition, he saw his children as tools. Charlie was his legacy, all he cared about was making him marquess, and he didn't care if he broke him in the process. Reggie was just a spare. He hardly even gave a damn about him unless it was to punish. And I was his way of linking our family to an equally important one, whether I liked his choice or not."

Once again, Silas thought of Arabella. She had run from her father, dragged her sisters behind her. She wouldn't tell him much, but perhaps it was a similar tale.

And he also thought about the childhoods of his siblings. They'd all been so much older, he hadn't given much time to what they'd all gone through because he was so focused on surviving, himself.

"Charlie is ten times the marquess our father ever was," he said.

Phoebe smiled. "I agree. You should tell him that sometime—I think the idea that he is as awful as our father weighs on him."

"And Reggie may be an arse, but he's certainly done well for himself." She laughed softly. He continued, "And you...you may have been forced into a first marriage that made you unhappy, but the second was better, wasn't it?"

"The second was my choice," she said with a slight nod. "And I did love Gregory, as he loved me, God rest him. Plus, I could not regret my children, or my life as it has unfolded. So we all survived. Thrived in some way."

"Well, except for the bastard," he said, turning his face. "I know all I've done is create trouble. Otherwise, you all wouldn't want me to be different."

Phoebe took his hands and it forced him to look back at her. "I very much regret that last encounter. I think Charlie and Reg do, as well. It came across wrong, as a judgment."

"You don't think it was a judgment in truth?" he asked with an arched brow, challenging her to deny it.

She struggled a moment and then sighed. "It was. But do you know why Charlie asked me to call you back to London?"

"Guilt? Obligation?" Silas shrugged. "Bile?"

"Because he truly wants to fix things," she said. "That last day you were here, the day after Father's death, there have been so many conversations about that awful day. About how badly we all handled it. About how sorry each of us was that you felt chased out, accused. Six years is too long, Silas."

He got up and paced away. "But the cost of what they're requesting is awfully high, Phoebe. You all want me to just throw away all I am, all I've built myself to be, just because it isn't what you approve of. You want to make me a puppet to dance on your string in order to earn the affection of my family. Do you know what that sounds like?"

"Father," she said with no hesitation.

They stared at each other a long moment, that one word and all that surrounded it hanging in the air between them.

"It wasn't a fair request," Phoebe said softly. "I told them that after you left. They were both chastened when I said it because at their hearts they're good men who don't want to be like the one who raised us all. But Silas, if you run away back to America, then it will never be fixed, will it?"

"I don't know," he muttered. "I suppose not. I just don't know if I want to stick around and wait for them to decide I'm worthy of consideration as I am. If they would allow me to be who I am and be with who I chose and not withdraw their affection as a punishment for it."

He turned and went to the window. He intended it to be just to gain a little distance, but as he looked down he saw a carriage on his drive. It wasn't his sister's, though. It was Arabella's. His heart caught. Was she here? She hadn't sent word, but then again, that was her way. She didn't ask for permission, she didn't mince or pretend.

She was exactly who she was at all times.

"A moment, Phoebe," he said, and rushed to the door. He opened the door to the parlor and the moment he did so he heard loud voices in the foyer.

"I'm telling you, you have no place here, Miss Comerford," Poole was saying. "Mr. Windham is not in residence."

"You will not even ask him if he'll see me?" Arabella was saying, her voice laced with rare pleading.

Silas strode down the hall and into the foyer without hesitation. "I say, Poole, what is this about? You're telling Arabella that I am not in residence without even inquiring about my availability? What right do you have to make those decisions?"

The butler pivoted toward him and Silas could see the hatred sparkling in his eyes, the disgust. "Sir, you could not possibly wish that your sister, the widow of both a viscount and a decorated colonel in His Majesty's army, be exposed to this...this blackmailing hoyden."

To Silas's surprise, Arabella flinched a little at that statement. As if this man's judgment of her actually stung. She stepped back. "I'm sorry, Silas, I didn't realize your sister was here. Obviously, I wouldn't wish to intrude or—"

"Wait," he said, holding up a hand. "I didn't ask you to go. Please don't back away." He swung his attention back to Poole. "Miss Comerford is my friend, Poole. She will not be spoken to in that manner. Not in my house, certainly never by *you*. You who are not fit to shine her shoes. Do I make myself perfectly clear?"

The butler shifted and his nostrils flared. "Yes, sir." He accentuated both words. "I only thought you would want to be gentlemanly enough to keep the proper part of your life away from...from *this* part."

"Excuse me."

All three of them froze because it was Phoebe's voice that interrupted. She had come into the entrance to the foyer from the hall and stood staring not at Silas, not at Poole, but at Arabella. To Silas's surprise, Arabella's cheeks turned bright red and she stared at the floor.

"Poole, my brother is absolutely correct that you have no right to keep a friend from him. You should know better." She moved forward and extended a hand. "Miss Comerford, I'm Phoebe Broughton, Silas's elder sister. I've heard a great deal about you and have always wished to meet you. You're even more beautiful close up. Won't you come join my brother and me for tea?"

Arabella lifted her chin. "I would not wish to intrude."

"It's no intrusion if you are invited, is it?"

Arabella glanced at Silas, then shook Phoebe's still outstretched hand. "I suppose not. You're very kind."

"Good." Phoebe pivoted back toward the parlor. "That's settled. Come along you two."

Silas began toward the parlor, but Arabella caught his hand. He looked down into her face, trying not to catch his breath at her beauty and the raw emotion she normally hid which was now plain in her eyes.

"I can leave," she whispered. "I shouldn't have barged in."

"I want you here," he said. "And apparently so does she."

She sighed, but let him take her arm and guide her to the parlor. Phoebe was already preparing Arabella a cup of tea and glanced up from the sideboard as they entered together. "Do you take sugar and milk, my dear?"

"Er, yes," Arabella said. "Both."

"Generously," Silas added, and smiled at her as he recalled the first time they'd had tea together. In this very room, in fact. A very early moment in their affiliation that made him smile.

"A woman after my own heart," Phoebe said, and handed over the cup. "Hopefully this is enough."

Arabella sipped the brew and nodded. "Oh yes, thank you."

They sat together, though this time Phoebe took the chair across from the settee and Silas made his place next to Arabella on the couch. He could feel the tension in her, coiled in every muscle, vibrating even through her hair. She glanced at the door from time to time, as if she might bolt.

"Tell me about yourself, Miss Comerford," Phoebe said.

Arabella blinked. "I...I don't know what to say. I think what I'd normally share isn't fit for your ears."

To his surprise, Phoebe laughed and leaned forward. "That sounds fascinating. But I can see you're very uncomfortable and that won't do. You are clearly important to my brother and thus you must be important to me. I'm not trying to embarrass you or make you question yourself."

Arabella shifted. "You're a lady, though."

"But not an entirely innocent one. My first husband was Viscount Musgrave."

Silas wrinkled his brow that his sister would bring up her first marriage as a way to put Arabella at ease. But he watched as Arabella's expression shifted, her lips parted and her eyes widened a fraction.

"Oh," she said softly. "I-I see. Yes, I knew of him. Not *knew* him, though, Mrs. Broughton. I want to make that very clear."

Silas's eyes went wide as he realized the reason his sister had brought up her husband. She had known he would be recognized by a courtesan. And though Phoebe's chin was lifted, the pain in her eyes was clear. He hadn't realized she had suffered so much. Of course, he'd been very young during her first marriage. But it was a reminder that she was a person with a full life of her own. Pains and fears and regrets of her own. It was easy to forget that when he thought of his siblings.

"That's kind of you," Phoebe said. "I didn't think you did *know* him. I think you were not old enough to be in the life when he died, but I assumed his name must still be bandied about in the circles you are associated with. His proclivities and cruelties weren't something people forget and I'm certain he expressed them on his lovers as much or even more than he did with me."

"Phoebe," Silas whispered, and reached for her hand. She let him take it and for a moment their gazes held. "I-I wish I'd known."

"You were a little boy when I married him, just barely a man when he passed. I love the suggestion that you would have ridden to my aid, but you could have done nothing, just as Charlie and Reggie could do nothing. It was what it was." She looked at Arabella again. "But I bring this up not to inspire further discomfort in you or grief in my brother, but because I may not be as innocent as you assume. So I will ask again, will you tell me a little about yourself? I truly wish to know."

Arabella nodded. "I was born in Granger."

"Oh, that's a lovely area."

"It was beautiful in places, yes," Arabella's lips thinned slightly. "And not as much in others. My father is Albert Comerford. He was not particularly well known. The second son of a second son and made his way as a solicitor in the country there."

Phoebe nodded. "And what of your mother?"

"She died when I was very young," Arabella said with a quick glance toward Silas since it was a question he'd asked himself not long ago. "I have two sisters, which I'm assuming you know."

"I do. I once saw who I think is your middle sister...is her name Eve?"

"Evelina," Arabella corrected.

"Evelina, a very pretty name. Well, I saw her at the opera last year, with the Duke of Southwater. She's truly lovely. I think more people were watching her than paying attention to the presentation."

"That's likely true," Arabella said. "She's impossible not to watch when one is the room with her. Not only because of her beauty, but she's kind and very witty."

"I'm certain she must be. Have you met Miss Comerford's sisters, Silas?"

Silas had been so caught up in this conversation between these two women who were so important to him that he had almost forgotten he might be included in it. He blinked. "Er, yes. Julia, the youngest, a few weeks ago and Evelina just two nights ago."

Phoebe nodded slowly and then turned her attention back to Arabella. She was clearly about to ask more questions, but Arabella spoke instead. "What about you, Mrs. Broughton? I know you have two other brothers. And you have children, as well."

"Yes," she said. "Three from my first marriage and one from my second. A daughter and three sons. All of whom think their pirate of an uncle is fascinating." She turned toward Silas. "You have only seen them twice since your return, though. Once when you first arrived and in passing at the bookshop. Certainly you must come over soon and see them again."

He smiled at the thought of his niece and nephews, who he liked a great deal but also tended to avoid so that he wouldn't bring them harm or confusion. "I think I might be a bad influence."

Phoebe laughed. "I'm certain you are, but all children need a little bad influence in their lives. Besides, I think you are not quite so wicked as you play at."

Arabella snorted and he pivoted to look at her. "Et tu, Arabella? You participate in this slander?"

"Your sister has the right of it, I fear. You may at your heart be the best of men, play acting at being a scoundrel."

He arched a brow and she blushed ever so slightly. Good, he hoped she was thinking of the very many ways he'd been the perfect scoundrel with her lately.

Phoebe seemed to miss the intensity of that connection, though, and was laughing full out now. "Good, I'm glad to see I have an ally in this thought."

"If you two spread this nonsense around, I will be forced to take legal action." He leaned back, folded his arms and gave them both a playfully stern look. "Don't think I won't."

"I'm certain you will," Phoebe said. The clock on the mantel chimed and she sighed. "And now I fear I must leave you two. My daughter has a fitting this afternoon that I want to attend."

They all rose together and Phoebe extended her hand to Arabella without hesitation, just as she had in the foyer. "I'm very pleased you stopped in so I could meet you, Miss Comerford. A friend to my brother is very much a friend to me. I hope that if I see you out and about in the world, you won't mind if I greet you."

Arabella's lips parted, for if a lady such as Phoebe greeted her in public that would be a shocking event. But she inclined her head. "I -I would be very pleased to meet with you. Perhaps we'll bump into each other in Mattigan's bookshop."

"I hope so, it's one of my favorite places in the city. Good day. Silas, will you see me out?"

He nodded and gave Arabella a quick glance before he led his sister from the room and into the foyer. He could read her expression—she had something to say.

And he just hoped that her kindness and warmth to Arabella wasn't just some act and that whatever she would say about the woman who had come to mean so much to him wouldn't put a further wedge between him and his family.

CHAPTER 17

As they entered the foyer, Poole came into the space, still looking sour. Silas nodded to him. "My sister's carriage, please."

The butler left to make the arrangement and that left Silas alone with Phoebe. "You must have something to say," he said, feeling nervous and breathless as he waited.

She nodded. "My God, what a beauty she is. But I think that's not what draws you, or not entirely. The woman is impossible not to like. Not to mention, there's something between you that practically crackles."

He tilted his head. "But?"

She blinked up at him. "What makes you think there's a 'but' that goes along with all those observations?"

"Because you know what she is. And even though I'm not of your world, she isn't either. I know what you and our brothers asked of me and it most definitely includes many less charitable thoughts about her than what you've expressed."

"I have no uncharitable thoughts about Miss Comerford," Phoebe said. "Our brothers have been able to choose their wives… or lack thereof…and futures. That is a privilege and one they may not fully grasp. But having not had that option, at least not for my first marriage, I have a very different view about love and happiness. I don't know your intentions with this woman or hers with you, but if you were to make her a more permanent fixture in your life, I wouldn't say a word against it. In fact, I'd very much support it, especially if it kept you in London."

Silas glanced back over his shoulder, in the direction of the parlor. He'd never sought acceptance for anything he did in his life, but right now Phoebe offered it. And somehow it mattered. Just like Arabella mattered, more than just a lover, more than just a friend. In the time they'd connected, she'd grown to matter a great deal more.

"I always appreciate your support."

"And I offer it. But not just in private. I should have said something at our gathering last week. I should have spoken up in your defense to Charlie and Reg. I'll do that now. I'm going to tell them again that I disagree with their edict that you must change yourself in order to fit into our family."

He wrinkled his brow in confusion and shock and, yes, happiness. "You'd be my defender?"

"If you need one? Always," Phoebe said, then lifted up to kiss his cheek. "Better go back to her. I'm sure she's waiting to talk to you about this and be reassured I wasn't offended by her very existence. Which, of course, I'm not. I hope we'll see each other soon."

The carriage pulled up then and Silas watched as his sister was helped up into the rig. She waved from the open window as she pulled away and he was left alone with his thoughts.

And alone with the woman he wanted to be with more than anyone else in the world. He just hoped that the reason she'd descended upon his home today was a good one.

❥

Arabella's hands shook as she paced the parlor waiting for Silas to return after his farewells to his sister. She had come here to end things with him after her talk with Simone and the fact that his sister had been with him had thrown off her entire plan.

Truth be told, his *presence* threw her off. The moment she'd looked up to find him entering the foyer, defending her against the butler, her heart had started pounding and all her certainty about what she must do had faded.

She didn't want to walk away. The very thought of it made her chest ache and her eyes sting.

Silas returned to the parlor and shut the door behind him. Without a word, he crossed to her and gathered her up in his arms. His mouth came down on hers, firm and warm. The kiss was gentle at first, then deepened until her breath seemed to fall away from her lungs and all there was in the world was him.

At last he parted from her and smiled down into her face. "I've wanted to do that since the moment I realized you were here," he admitted.

She smiled. "I cannot imagine your sister would have been quite so polite to me had you started out that way."

He set her aside gently and shrugged. "I'm not so certain. She told me before she left that she likes you. And given that she told you something about her marriage that I didn't even know, I think all her connection to you was very real."

She frowned. "I am sorry about that, Silas. About her first marriage and that you didn't know what kind of man he was."

His expression looked so pained in that moment, so filled with real love for his sister. It put her to mind of her own feelings for Julia and Evelina. And the heartbreak when she couldn't protect them from harm.

"I wish I'd known. I'd have done anything to keep her from that pain."

"That I *do* understand," she said. "But sometimes you can't save someone you love. And it seems like she ended up happy enough in her second marriage."

"Yes. It's been two years since he died and she still mourns him and wears his ring. She truly loved him and he her. I'm glad she got to experience that in her life, even though she lost it."

They stared at each other a moment. Suddenly the air felt thicker, like those words hung there as an accusation between them.

He cleared his throat at last. "Do you mind if I ask you why you came today? I don't think I was expecting you."

"You weren't," she said. "I was just at—at Simone's before this."

"Oh," he said with a smile. "And you two were talking about me, comparing notes on my prowess and you had to rush right over?"

She froze. He was teasing her and she should have laughed, but she couldn't. He was too close to the truth.

He moved closer. "Arabella, what is it?"

She stared up at him, memorizing every gorgeous line of his angled face, the brightness of his green eyes. She wanted to collect it all to store for when she finally found the bravery to walk away and save them both.

But it wasn't going to be today. Even if that had been the intention.

"Nothing," she said with a shake of her head. "I'm just still trying to get my mind around having a polite conversation with your sister, that's all. No, I came here to—to invite you to supper tonight. My sisters will both be there and I'd love you to join us. And afterward, we could share that big bath I've been dangling before you since we started this."

He nodded. "Supper with your family and that big bath both sound wonderful."

"I suppose I could have sent you a note to invite you," she said, even as she hoped she could manage to get Julia and Evelina to join her for supper. Hoped her staff could put together this last-minute gathering with no trouble.

"I'm glad you came." He caught her hand and drew her closer.

"Are you certain your well, Arabella? You have the strangest look on your face."

She forced herself to smile, to erase whatever he saw. Whatever she couldn't reveal when her head was spinning and her heart was too full of him. "I'm simply planning for our night together. And so I must go to finish all my preparations."

He lifted her hand to his lips and kissed her knuckles. His warm breath sent shivers through her, reminding her that he could make her want in a heartbeat. Wasn't that what she was supposed to do to him?

"Are you sure I can't convince you to stay a little while? Come up to my room?"

She swatted at his chest lightly. "As tempting as that is, I think you must learn to wait, Mr. Windham. I'll make it worthwhile."

"I've never had a doubt about that," he said, and guided her to the foyer.

But even as they said their farewells and she was off and on her way, she was plagued by thoughts of what she had to do. But she would take this one last night. She'd make it worthwhile before she shattered the dreamworld between them and went back to reality.

~

Hours later, it was all arranged. Arabella shouldn't have doubted it, though. Her servants were a wonder and had made certain everything was perfect. And she had never called for her sisters without them being there for her. They had answered in the affirmative without hesitation or even question at the lateness and desperateness of the invitation.

So as she paced her parlor, watching the clock and the door for Silas's arrival, she felt Julia and Evelina watching her.

"Are you truly nervous about a *man*?" Julia asked, the teasing in her tone light.

Arabella stopped pacing and pivoted toward her youngest sister. "Of course not!"

Julia laughed, but Evelina's eyes narrowed. "We've both met him already. It isn't as if you have to worry about our feelings. We both like him."

Julia nodded. "Yes. He's undeniably handsome, I think the most handsome man you've ever had as a lover."

"That's more than true," Arabella said softly.

"And he's well-matched to you," Julia continued. "You're both... both..."

"Fire," Evelina supplied.

Arabella flinched. Although she didn't dispute the description, she wasn't certain it was a positive one. "Perhaps two fires is too much," she said.

"You've never been too much," Evelina said, and crossed to the room to take both her hands. "Never."

Arabella smiled at the support. She needed it, after all. Her sisters believed she was nervous about seeing Silas, and that was true on some level. Whenever she saw him after they were parted she felt a thrill of excitement and anxiousness that seemed to make her entire body thrum. But that wasn't why she paced or worried tonight.

She had to end things with him. Her decision hadn't changed. She got to have this one last night with him and then she'd have to say goodbye. If she couldn't, then the affection that was starting to grow would fully turn to love. Love didn't end well for courtesans, it never had.

Well, not never. But mostly.

"Mr. Windham," Barnaby said from the door with a wide smile for them.

Arabella's heart started to pound as her butler stepped aside and Silas came into the room. Her sisters were already greeting him, welcoming him without hesitation. He smiled at them, but then he looked at her and she felt the air go out of her lungs. How could he do that to her? She had experience with men, she knew how to make them dance on a string and feel like they were in control.

And yet this man moved her.

"Arabella," he said, and came toward her.

He caught her hand, his thumb stroking across the ridges of her knuckles gently. "Silas," she said.

"Oh, kiss him already," Evelina said with a laugh. "We're no proper ladies here."

He glanced toward them with a flash of a wicked grin, then caught Arabella around the waist and tugged her to his chest. "May I?"

She nodded and found herself lifting to him, meeting his lips. He didn't devour her, they had enough decorum to keep from doing that in front of her family, but he certainly claimed her. When he set her aside gently, she felt dizzy from the pressure of his mouth, the taste of his lips.

"Well, that starts my night out very well," he said.

"Would you like a drink, Mr. Windham?" Evelina asked, and moved to the sideboard.

"I wish you two would call me Silas. If you can call your stuffy old duke Harry, I must have the same courtesy."

Evelina tossed a look at him over her shoulder, playful outrage. "Ugh, I'll have you know my Harry is anything but stuffy."

"He *is* a little stuffy, Evie," Julia said, and winked at Silas. "He talks about crop rotations, Silas. You've no idea."

He rolled his eyes theatrically and then threw a smile toward Arabella. "How have you survived him?"

Evelina brought him a whisky with a smile. "Well, he's terribly rich and very generous, of course." She grew a little more serious. "And I believe I care for him more than I've cared for any man I've ever known."

Silas's brow wrinkled a little at that passionate declaration. He sipped his drink and finally sat when the women did the same. "So it is a match of affection?"

Evelina nodded. "Yes. We met at the Donville Masquerade, so it was very passionate as a start. I was just ending my last arrangement and Harry pressed very quickly for a new one. He showered me with gifts and notes. And he made promises, all of which he's kept over our time together since."

Arabella let out her breath. She wanted Evelina to be happy, of course, and there was a great deal of happiness between her and Harry. But sometimes she saw how deeply Eveline cared for the man and she worried. The duke *would* have to marry one day. What would happen to Evie remained to be seen. He made promises, Arabella knew, about keeping her, having her as his true bride even as he fulfilled his obligations.

But without legal standing, could a woman truly expect those promises to be kept?

"And what about you, Julia?" Silas asked. "Do you have a gentleman in mind to be your next protector?"

Julia let out a long sigh. "No one interests me as of yet. I've not the bubbly personality of my sisters, I suppose. All my affiliations have been much more temporary, fleeting. I would like something longer term this time, something with heart to it like Evie and Harry have. So I'm being careful and trying to weigh my options when I go out with friends or my sisters."

"That's very reasonable," Silas said. "I could ask around, see if there's anyone who might fit the bill."

"That would be very kind," Julia said. Then her eyes widened. "Oh, I'd forgotten to tell you, I have gossip!" She looked at Silas apologetically. "You don't mind gossip, do you?"

He leaned forward and waggled his eyebrows at her. "I adore gossip. And there was never a better source of it than the courtesan network."

Julia smiled at him and then turned toward her sisters, hands clasped. "I was out with Bianca Reynolds last night, we went to a play, and we saw Lady Blackburn."

"The Earl of Blackburn's wife?" Evelina asked, her brow knitting slightly. "He's a friend to Harry."

"The very one. She was alone, Blackburn wasn't in sight and then Bianca told me that most scandalous thing. The couple is getting a...*divorce*."

The effect of that startling news on the rest of the room was instant. All three of their mouths dropped open. Divorce was legal, of course, but difficult and expensive and always a terrible disgrace. Arabella couldn't think of the last one she'd heard of.

"A divorce," she breathed. "Why in the world would they do that? Couples of that level can live apart very nicely."

"They say she has a lover, a *titled* lover at that. I've heard that isn't all that rare for her, but this time it sounds like she wants to *marry* him. It's already in motion, apparently, has been for months and somehow Blackburn kept it quiet. But within a few weeks it's likely *everyone* will know."

"Poor man," Evelina said softly. "Oh, that's a shame."

"Indeed," Silas said. "I knew of him in school. He was a decent fellow."

Arabella looked at him. "Where did you go to school?"

"Eton," he said, then laughed. "Oh, all three of you just got the most shocked looks on your faces. Do I seem too much a dolt for that?"

"Too clever for such a place is more likely," Arabella said. "I didn't know you were sent to such a prestigious school."

"Because I'm a bastard?" He shrugged. "I think my father had the idea that I could have the bad blood educated out of me. That I'd get a vocation that he could sniff his nose at, but still support. That I'd stay under his thumb. Instead I played pranks and got in trouble and eventually got kicked out."

"The pranks don't surprise me," Julia said with a shake of her head. "Arabella was also wild with her pranks as a girl."

He turned toward her, face lit up with laughter and interest. Her breath caught at the absolute beauty of him. "Well, I must know more about this," he said.

Arabella shook her head and hoped she didn't sound as breathless as she felt. "They exaggerate."

"You added bitter berries to Miss Jenson's cordials." Evelina said.

Arabella shrugged. "She sold them as curatives when she knew they weren't."

"What about when you climbed up that tree on Hogbellow Lane and convinced Ian Marshall that you were a spirit of the forest watching him?" Julia giggled.

"Well, he was gashing up the trees for no reason and harassing the baby squirrels." Arabella folded her arms. "He deserved a set down."

"He almost pissed himself," Evelina said.

"Sounds like he deserved it." Silas's tone was even, as was his gaze on her face.

"He really did," Julia agreed. "Actually, now that I think of it, Arabella only ever played tricks on people who *did* deserve it."

Arabella shifted. "You make me sound like a heroine not a hoyden, which is utterly ridiculous."

"Not so ridiculous," Evelina said with a gentler smile for her.

Arabella was happily kept from having to respond to that when Barnaby entered the room to announce supper. Arabella rose to lead them into the dining room with her sisters behind her, flanking Silas on either side and telling him tales about her walking fence rails and altering the sheet music at an assembly hall so that the orchestra played nonsense and ruined the dancing.

And he laughed at every story as he slid quite perfectly into her home and her family. Even though she had to pull him away from all of it in just a few hours.

CHAPTER 18

Silas hadn't known quite what to expect when he'd accepted Arabella's invitation to her home, but as he stood having drinks with the ladies in her parlor after supper, he realized he was having one of the finest nights of recent memory.

It was impossible not to enjoy oneself with the Comerford sisters, for they were all witty and intelligent, friendly and kind. And one couldn't help but be mesmerized by their tight bond. They teased each other, but it was always gently. They also noticed the little shifts in each other, anticipated each other's needs and gave without hesitation.

Their love for one another was obvious and he was envious of it, if he were honest with himself. He thought of his afternoon with Phoebe and how she'd told him the family truly wished to repair what had been damaged over decades of loss and pain and competition.

Seeing these three women together, it made him wish he could do that.

"You have the strangest look on your face," Arabella said, slipping up to put her arm through his and rest her chin against his shoulder. "Are you well?"

He nodded. "Very well. I've had a wonderful time tonight."

A little wickedness entered those remarkable blue eyes. "And we haven't even played in the tub yet."

"Naughty little minx," he murmured before he bent his head and kissed her briefly. He felt her shift toward him, lean into the explosive passion they so easily shared.

But this wasn't the place for it, so they parted and her smile grew wider. More beautiful and inviting.

"I'm sorry, Miss Comerford," Barnaby said, suddenly at the parlor door. "There's a situation with Regina."

She blinked. "Now?"

He nodded and she squeezed Silas's hand before she turned away. "I'll be back shortly."

Evelina and Julia exchanged a quick look after she'd gone and Silas laughed. "There's obviously something afoot. You aren't planning to murder me, are you?"

Evelina smiled. "Not tonight, at least. No...well, there's no reason to hide it, I suppose. One of Arabella's housemaids is with child and judging from Barnaby's pale expression, I think she must be ready to give birth."

"She was a lightskirt," Julia said softly. "Arabella found her on the street a few months ago. She offered her a job and a promise she'd help the girl take care of the child, or find the baby a home if that's what she wished to do instead."

Silas looked off toward the door where Arabella had gone. "She so easily takes care of others."

"Yes," Evelina said, her tone suddenly distant. "Sometimes at detriment to herself."

"Though not in this case," Julia said.

"No, of course not." Evelina worried her hands before her. "I should go see if I can help. I want to remind Arabella the name of the midwife I suggested so she can be sent for."

Evelina stepped from the room and that left Silas with Julia. She smiled at him and he returned the expression. "If you'd like to join them, I'm perfectly capable of entertaining myself."

She shook her head. "Oh, gracious no. I've no interest in seeing someone give birth." She shuddered. "I've heard there's blood and screaming. No, I'll stay here and we'll just have a drink and pretend like it's not happening."

"That sounds like a very good plan," he said, and went to refill her drink and his own. "You know you three really are remarkable."

"Are we? I suppose most men are fascinated by the idea of three sisters who are also courtesans." She pulled a face. "Some of them even want to bed us as a group."

"Ugh. That's disturbing," he said.

"I agree." Julia turned up her nose. "None of us have ever continued an affiliation with a man who suggested it."

"You're living here with Arabella now, I think," he said.

She nodded. "Yes. My last arrangement ended a little over a month ago and she welcomed me right back in. That's the power of having this house, of course. We're never under threat."

He looked around. "It's a fine home and you've all made it even more beautiful and welcoming."

"It doesn't bother you that she received it from another lover?" Julia asked, and now she didn't look so sweet or innocent. She looked hawkish and like she was making a measure of him and his future response. It seemed a skill each of the Comerford women possessed.

He set his drink down and met her eyes. He wanted her to see the truth of what he was about to say. "I have nothing but respect for Arabella and what she's built for herself. Jealousy is not in my nature."

"Then you are a singular man. She's had several lovers who tried to demand she get rid of this place, but she always refused." Julia sighed and then shook her head. "It is a good life we've built. Thanks to you, of course."

He cocked his head at that statement. "Thanks to...thanks to me?" he repeated. "What do you mean?"

"Well, you know, of course. That night in Vauxhall Garden. Seeing you with Simone."

"Well, I know about *that*. It was early in her career."

Julia stared at him. "No. She wasn't a courtesan when she saw you. She was seventeen, there with our aunt and father when he was still trying to make a match for her. Seeing you two that night inspired her, I suppose. It was why she ran from our father and into the life."

He drew a sharp breath. Seventeen? He hadn't done that math since reuniting with Arabella, even though he was aware of her age. And he hadn't put together that she had truly been an innocent when she saw him with Simone.

Could what Julia said be true? Was he the cause for Arabella to leave her stable life and run headlong into this? It was one thing to accept and respect it, quite another to have caused it and whatever pains she might have endured to create it.

"Silas?" Julia asked, leaning closer. "Are you well?"

Before he could answer, Evelina and Arabella returned to the room together, their faces bright with excitement. "The baby is certainly coming," Arabella announced. "Regina is comfortably arranged in a room and the midwife is on her way. She is doing very well, though."

"That's good," Julia said, and then glanced at Silas.

The other two women followed her stare and Arabella's expression fell. "What is it?"

He cleared his throat. "I'd like to talk to you alone, Arabella."

Evelina and Arabella exchanged a look and Julia moved toward them, shaking her head as if to say she didn't understand whatever look he couldn't school from his face.

"Well, I should be returning home anyway," Evelina said slowly. "Why don't you come with me, Julia? Harry is not in residence at present, he's busy with other things at his proper estate. I'd be happy for the company."

Julia nodded and then the two women faced him. He heard them say goodnight. He realized he responded, but it didn't seem real. Not when all he could do was stare at Arabella and know what he now knew.

Arabella saw them out and then she returned. She shut the parlor door behind herself and then leaned there, watching him as if she wasn't certain how to behave.

"Silas, it's clear something changed when Evie and I left the room. And now you wish to speak to me alone. So we are alone. Now tell me, what is going on?"

"Your sister…Julia just told me that *I'm* the reason you became a courtesan." He shook his head. "Is that true?"

Arabella stared at Silas, stared at his pale face and guilt-stricken expression and her stomach turned. Not just because he was clearly taking responsibility for her choices, but also because they brought back memories that had nothing to do with him.

She straightened up and lifted her chin. "Don't be ridiculous. Julia sometimes says the silliest things."

"Arabella," he said, sharper now. "She says you were only seventeen in the garden that night. That you weren't a courtesan yet."

"I-I never told you I was. And my age is public knowledge."

"I wasn't doing the math," he said. "You said it was early in your career. I assumed that meant you had already stepped into the life."

She folded her arms. "Well, I did. Just after. What difference does it make, Silas?"

"Because I know how courtesans are made," he snapped. "I saw, albeit briefly, before I was stolen from her arms, what that life did to my mother. And you are stronger than she was, God knows that's true. But don't think for a moment that I don't know that your choice of this path has likely involved fear and pain."

She flinched. He wasn't wrong. There had been kind lovers, but also ones who weren't kind. There had been a surrender of her virginity that had been as gentle as possible thanks to Simone's help, but certainly it hadn't been the beautiful, loving act she'd dreamed of as a girl. There had been loss and judgment, cruelty and sadness over the years she had stepped into her own and accepted all facets of what a courtesan faced.

"I'm sorry that your mother suffered," she managed to croak out. "And that she was harmed by your father. But my experience is very different."

"Not so very different," he said. "You study people, it's your way to protect yourself. And it's mine, too. I see the grief in your eyes sometimes, Arabella. I see the flickers of what you lost."

She pushed off the door and paced across the room, trying to find space between herself and what he was saying. How he was digging into the soul of her and mining facts that she didn't want to share. Not with him, not with anyone.

"You are being ridiculous," she gasped, but she could hear the strain in her voice that belied her words.

"Please," he said. "Look at me and tell me whether I was the one who caused you to choose this path because I smiled at you in the garden like some twisted snake sent to drag you from propriety."

She did face him then, feeling the truth bubble up in her. Strain against her restraints in ways she had never experienced with any other man who had tried to pry it from her. This man, this beautiful man, he hardly even had to pick the locks on her heart and her past and her pain. He was the key, wasn't he?

Even if she didn't want him to be.

"It's not because of you," she finally burst out. "You weren't the villain in my story and you didn't turn me to or from any path. That was my...my father."

His lips parted. She'd told him just the tiniest hints of this, given him the fuzzy edges, but now he would know the whole picture, because she couldn't stop it anymore.

"How?" he asked gently.

She bent her head. "I think you've guessed that he was cruel and callous. But he was also violent. Toward me and toward my sisters. I tried to jump in front of his wrath as often as I could to protect them."

His expression softened. "Because you always do, don't you? Try to stop the bully or the cheat like the way you played pranks on people as a girl."

She shut her eyes. "Only I couldn't change *him* just by mucking up his cordial or pretending to be a forest spirit. He *hated* us for being girls, and he wanted to use us for his own gain as soon as it was socially acceptable."

Silas shifted. "To marry you off, you mean?"

She nodded. "He started when I was hardly more than a child, trying to haggle for me with men four or five times my age."

He flinched and she continued so he wouldn't say something more and break her when she already felt on the edge of tears. "He decided seventeen was the number. The time when he could marry me off without facing judgment. My birthday was the worst day of my life. And when he dragged me to London so I could get my trousseau, I knew I wouldn't come back again. He would sell me to someone just like him or worse."

"Arabella, I'm sorry," Silas said, his voice low and rough. "You must have been terrified."

"I was." Her voice broke and to her horror, she felt a tear she never let herself shed sliding down her cheek. She wiped and it hurriedly, wishing he hadn't seen it when he obviously had. "My aunt, my father's sister, was the only shining light. She tried to reason with him to no avail. So she switched her tactics. She tried to give me some little taste of joy before the inevitable. We went to exhibits and plays and when she heard of my obsession with Vauxhall, she arranged for tickets even though my father grumbled about the expense."

"And you saw me with Simone," he breathed.

She nodded, flashing back to that night just as she often had over the years. To the passion, to the pleasure. To the hope that had flared in her in that moment that she'd realized Simone was a courtesan.

"Yes. I snuck away and went to Simone the next day. I begged her to help me, to train me. To help me escape and regain some autonomy over my body and my future." She moved toward him. "To escape my father, the *real* villain in my story, I stepped onto this path and I've never looked back. And yes, it's been complicated. And yes, there has been pain. But that wasn't your fault, Silas. It wasn't because of you."

There was relief that washed over his features then. "I'm sorry you had to endure that. I know a little about fathers who harm. But what about Evelina and Julia? How did they come to join you?"

"You must see how." Now the tears fell again and she couldn't stop them. "He turned all that energy on them. All that cruelty, and it was even worse. I ached when I read the letters they smuggled out with the help of our aunt. I had no means to save them. And then one day Evelina appeared on my doorstep. She had run just like I had."

"And Julia?" he pressed. "Did she run, as well?"

"No, she had to be saved. She wasn't even seventeen when we realized he had made a match for her with a man in his sixties. A lecher who could overlook her two whore sisters. We rushed to her rescue and stole her from our father. Evie and I tried to keep her from this life. She's so gentle, so romantic, I feared she wouldn't survive it. But she made her choice when she turned eighteen. And so here we are. All three of Albert Comerford's daughters are courtesans. Publicly."

"That must have enraged him," Silas whispered.

She nodded. "Oh, his rage has no bounds when it comes to me.

He believes me the architect of his demise. His vitriol comes in the form of threatening letters twice monthly. Sometimes more when I'm unprotected."

Now his gaze grew sharp. "He threatens you?"

She shrugged even though the thought of the hat box filled to the brim with his threats made her shiver. "It doesn't matter. He can't reach me. It's over. He has no power. And it's meaningless. I feel nothing about it."

Silas stared at her a long moment and then he crossed to her. He took her in his arms so gently that she fought so she wouldn't sag against him. Then he wiped her cheeks, showing her the wetness on his fingers after he had.

"Sweet, it's very clear that isn't true." Then he folded her into his arms and held her.

And with shocking power and unexpected speed, a dam Arabella had been trying to shore up for years…broke. She shook as she began to weep in his arms, all the fear and pain and disappointment and loss rolling out of her in long, agonizing waves as she cried into the shoulder of a man who simply smoothed her hair and let it all come. Let it pour into him like he was strong enough to bear it.

And when her knees gave out, he didn't hesitate. He swept her up and carried her from the parlor, up the stairs, down the hall to her bedroom. She was aware of him putting her on her bed, removing her slippers gently.

She tried to pull herself back together then. He would want to have her. That would be the way he'd comfort her, that was what any other lover in her past would have wanted, if they lasted through the painful story at all.

But to her surprise, he didn't take off her clothing. He didn't take off any of his own except for his boots. Then he joined her on the big bed and drew her up to him. He curled his body around her, cocooning her in the protection of his body heat.

"You've been so strong to carry all this, Arabella," he whispered at last, she had no idea after how long. "Please put it down tonight. Just tonight."

She let out her breath in a shaky sigh and clung tighter to him. When she dared to look up into his face, she found him watching her. In the firelight, he almost glowed, like he was some heroic knight from some medieval story, sent to slay all her dragons.

And she knew in that moment that she wasn't just falling in love with Silas Windham. She was already there. It was too late. No matter what she did next, no matter how she managed whatever was to come, there would be no surviving it. Her heart would be broken.

But not tonight. Tonight she cuddled closer, reveled in the way his arms tightened around her, and let herself drift to sleep. Perhaps the first truly good sleep she'd had since the night she'd run from her father's home and into the life that had led her to Silas.

CHAPTER 19

Silas woke alone in Arabella's big bed. He reached for her, eyes still half-closed, and she wasn't there. With a sigh, he rolled over on his back and stared at the velvet canopy above him.

He'd shared passionate nights with her, of course. Given all his body, and even some of his soul. But nothing had been more powerful to him then the trust she'd shown last night. Her story was painful, her tears were heartbreaking, but somehow she'd let herself give them to him.

And he would never be the same.

He heard movement coming from the room adjacent to the bedchamber and sat up on his elbows a little as the door opened. Arabella stepped through. She was no longer in her clothing from the previous night, but in a silky robe, her hair down around her shoulders.

She looked at him and for a moment there was nothing but vulnerability there on her lovely face. Then she smiled and the mask was back, though perhaps not as firmly as before.

"Good morning," she said. "I didn't mean to wake you."

"You didn't," he said. "I was just waking up all on my own."

"Good." She worried the tie of her robe. "Perhaps you'd like to share that big bath with me this morning?"

He didn't have to be asked twice. He was up and on his feet in an instant, coming around the bed to her. "That is the best offer I've had in a long time."

She held his gaze a moment, desire readable there but little else. Still, her slow smile was pure seduction as she pushed closer to him, reaching up to unbutton his shirt. "I aim to please."

He bent his head and kissed her. Her fingers dug into his chest as she let out a low, shivering sigh of pleasure. There was part of him that wanted to push, to talk more about what he'd uncovered about her past the previous night. But she clearly wanted to regain some control and this was how she would do it.

So he surrendered to her, just as she wished and didn't resist as she drew him into her dressing room without ever parting her lips from his. He tugged the shirt over his head and then gathered her against his chest again, deepening the kiss, gasping as her nails raked gently against his skin.

She wedged a hand between them and stroked his length with her palm. "We should have done this last night," she whispered against his lips.

He pulled back a fraction and looked down into her eyes. "We did exactly what we should have done last night."

She smiled, but it wobbled a fraction. Then she grasped his shoulders and turned him. His eyes widened as she did. Against the back wall of the dressing room was the famous tub she'd been telling him about. It was huge, definitely large enough for two to share comfortably. The inside was brass shined to a gleam and it was currently filled with steaming water with rose petals sprinkled along the surface.

"Well, *this* is what I want to do this morning."

As an answer, he unfastened his trousers and tugged them off. He was already half-hard just from touching her and she gave a satisfied smile as she caught him in hand again and stroked once, twice. Fully hard now. It was just that easy with her.

"Get in," she ordered.

He did so without argument. He wanted to share that tub with her for one, but he also could see the edginess to her. He wasn't going to steal her control.

Not this way, at any rate.

He sank into the perfectly warm water and dunked his head under, slicking back his hair when he resurfaced. She had remained where she was and now she untied her robe and let it fall away to reveal all those gorgeous curves a man could lose himself in forever.

She sashayed forward, putting a little more twitch in her hips as she did so. Then she dipped one foot into the bath, then the other and sank in, facing him in his lap. She caught up the soap and lathered it between her hands. As she did so he cupped her backside and massaged it, rocking her against him without making any effort to take her. He could have. But they had all morning for that.

She let out a little gasp that told him he was loosening her control just like she was loosening his, but she kept eye contact with him as she set her soap away and began to glide the bubbles over his chest.

"It won't work," he whispered as she let her hands go under the water and stroke his stomach muscles, then up his sides. The soap made the slide of them slicker and easier.

"What won't work?"

"I'll never be clean, not really," he said. "My thoughts of you alone are entirely filthy."

She laughed then and it was real, not something put on like a mask to cover herself. He couldn't help but grin at coaxing that from her.

"Well, then we'll be dirty together," she said. "Because I certainly have some very dirty thoughts about you, too."

He let his fingers play along her backside, against the rosette of her bottom and then lower, between her legs where she was hot and ready for him. "I can tell."

She lifted up, taking him inside of her slowly, almost gently. When he was fully seated in her satiny heat, she went back to washing him. He took the soap as she did so and lathered his own hands. They worked together then, teasing in the guise of cleaning, a blur of clenching fingers and heated flesh. And she never looked away. Not once as he memorized her curves and lines.

At last, she cupped his cheeks in her soapy fingers and then her mouth found his. That was when she moved, rocking over him, grinding against him as her breath got shorter and heavier in the quiet of the dressing room. He lifted beneath her, creating waves in the deep tub that sloshed over the edge occasionally.

The grip of her was so good. It didn't matter how many times they did this, every time he was always stunned by how good she felt. Like a homecoming. Her legs were starting to shake and her lips broke from his with a soft moan of pleasure.

"That's not enough," he whispered, and reached between them to circle his thumb around her clitoris as she rode him. "I want more than that."

Her soft sounds became louder and she rode him faster. She arched her back, grinding over him, using him and pleasuring him in the same heavy strokes. When she came, it was volcanic, a sudden rush of gripping heat and pleasure that shot up the length of him. He grasped her hips, leaned his head forward to press his mouth to the sweet hollow between her wet breasts and let her ride out the crisis as she wailed and moaned and at last whimpered his name.

He pushed her from him as the pleasure became too much, sliding her backward on his lap so that he popped free before he came in great gasping gulps that were lost in her mouth when she kissed him.

Their bodies were still tangled for a while afterward, her legs wrapped around him, his fingers stroking out a pattern along her spine as their panting breaths merged and slowed between kisses.

"Breakfast?" she whispered at last.

He chuckled as he leaned up to kiss her damp temple. "Sounds perfect," he said.

They took their time getting ready. She straightened him and tied his cravat, he fastened her even though she had those magical gowns that she could put on and take off without help. The fact she let him felt meaningful in some way.

But in not a very long time, they exited her chamber together and came down not to the formal dining room where he'd broken bread with her sisters the night before, but to a smaller, cozier breakfast room. As he settled himself in and watched her pour them each tea, he really looked at the room.

The rest of her house was made to be seen. The chambers she'd opened to him over the weeks were perfectly decorated and inviting, with bold colors and artwork that reflected her sensual nature and position in life.

But this room was something different. It was private, he thought. Something she perhaps only shared with her sisters. It was full of light and the tea set was mismatched and she looked more at home when she sat at that table than he'd ever seen her.

The door to the room opened and a maid entered. She bobbed out a nod and then said, "Mrs. Barnaby has ham and eggs if that suits."

"Perfect," Arabella said with a kind smile. "How is Regina today?"

"She had the baby around four, Miss Comerford," the maid said. "A boy she named Thomas. They're resting now and she's doing very well."

"Wonderful," Arabella said. "I'll come check in on them later today. I'm sure the staff is taking good care of them."

"The very best." The maid left then.

"Your nature is to take care of others," Silas said, and sipped his tea.

She glanced at him, the little edge of her guard coming up. "I suppose so. Old habits."

"I think there's sweetness under all that wild," he said.

She arched a brow. "If you spread that rumor, Silas Windham, I will never forgive you."

He laughed but he refused to discount the merit of the statement. Not to her or to himself. Seeing her like this, at ease in her surroundings, put him to mind of when he'd found her in her hair cloths weeks ago. There was something so genuine to it all, a piece of her she only shared with those close to her.

If he fit that description in any way, he knew that made him a very lucky man.

They ate for a while, he kept the conversation light. She seemed to need it after they'd gone so deep the night before. They were just finishing up with their food, when Barnaby returned to the breakfast room, his lips turned down and a letter on a tray.

"This just arrived, Miss Comerford."

She looked up and her cheeks paled a little at her butler's expression. She took the letter and read the address. Then her own lips pursed and she set it face down beside her plate.

"Is anything wrong?" Silas asked.

She looked at him, there was a brief hesitation, then she shook her head. "Nothing at all."

He wanted to push, because it was clear the letter troubled her. He thought of what she'd said about her father writing notes of threat and vitriol and wondered if this was one of those. But he could feel her pulling away, putting up walls and distance between them again.

And he found he didn't want that.

"Why don't you come to supper at my house tonight?" he said. Then he cleared his throat and added, "I'm expecting my brothers. You could meet Charlie."

She sucked in a short breath. "Silas, no. That cannot end any better than the last time I met with Lord Reginald."

"I see you with your family," he said, covering her hand with his. "You are…you. Truly yourself. I do want that with my brothers. And

I want what I saw when Phoebe met you. She saw me for who I truly was through your eyes. I want to ask them to do the same. And accept that version of me at last."

She shut her eyes. "They cannot want a person like me around, Silas."

"Then I'll tell them to go to hell. Again." He squeezed her hand and she looked at him. "Please."

She looked almost stricken at the request for a moment, but then she nodded slowly. "Very well. If that's your request, I couldn't turn you down."

He leaned forward and kissed her gently. "Thank you." Then he got up. "I must go make some preparations for the night. Will you come at seven?"

She got up and led him to the foyer. "Yes. Seven. I'll be there."

He kissed her again and then smiled as Barnaby opened the door just as his horse was brought around. As if the man had anticipated his need. What a concept in comparison to the servant who despised him back at his own place.

Still, none of that could trouble him now. Not after last night. Not after her.

So he rode off with a spring to his spirit and a hope in his heart for that night. One he couldn't deny was all about the woman who was waving to him from her front step as he rode away from her.

CHAPTER 20

The moment Silas turned onto the lane leading away from her home, Arabella rushed back inside and into the breakfast room. She broke the seal on the message from her father that had arrived during her meal and read it, her heart pounding.

> *You've gotten away with this long enough. You will pay. C.*

C was for Comerford. Her father hadn't signed any letter as *Father* for years. She'd apparently lost that honorific when she ran from him. No great injury—he'd barely performed the duties associated with that name in the first place.

Still, her hands shook as she read the ugly words over and over. There was very little new about them. The letters always contained anything from veiled to direct threats. Usually he called her a whore, so the lack of that slur was at least something.

And yet there was a chill of fear in her. Something she could normally control, but today it lingered. Perhaps it was because her emotions surrounding the man were so much more powerful at present thanks to her unintended conversation with Silas. She'd given over so much of her past to him. And he'd taken it all with calm and kindness and nothing but support.

She took the letter upstairs and went into her dressing room where the tub she'd shared with Silas was already empty and dried. She smiled at the memories it now contained and then reached to the top shelf of her wardrobe and retrieved the hat box she used to store the vile letters. Why she kept them, she could never say, but she felt compelled to do so regardless. She dropped the newest in amongst the rest and set the box on one of the tables in the big room. She'd put it back later.

She went into her bedroom and smiled at the maid who was making her bed. Smoothing away the evidence that Arabella had spent her night in Silas's arms. Only it couldn't be smoothed. His gift of presence and support would linger. Her recognition that she loved him would probably never quite go away.

"That's why you have to end it," she reminded herself as the maid left her and she was alone.

Oh, how that stung. But it was better for both of them. Silas would leave soon. She needed to move on now before she couldn't stop herself from telling him the truth. From ruining them both with what could never be.

But she'd leave him with the last gift she could. She would go to his supper and meet with his brothers and hopefully plant some seed with them. Help them see that Silas was worthy of their love, exactly as he was.

If she could give him that, it would have to be enough.

Arabella wore her full armor to Silas's house that night. Her best blue gown, the one that matched her eyes and had the cut that accentuated her curves without being too showy. She'd fixed her hair, curling and twisting it, then placed jewels within the locks, both real and paste. She'd rouged her lips lightly to bring them color and curled her eyelashes carefully. She was ready to face an army, an invading force. Or at least a marquess and his brother, who would certainly look at her with judgment.

She smoothed her hands along the silken folds of her gown as her carriage began to slow and turn its way onto Silas's drive. She pushed her shoulders back, lifted her chin, ready to become Arabella Comerford, celebrated courtesan, woman who had raised herself to the storied heights of her profession. Woman who held all the power and could wield it.

Woman who would do anything to protect the man she loved, though that part she would certainly keep to herself. To allow Silas or his family to see that would only cause pain and confusion for all parties.

Her driver came down from the rig and opened the door for her. "Thank you, Ingram," she said with a small smile for him. "And I've no idea how this will go tonight, so stay close, just in case I need to leave in haste."

He inclined his head. "I'll be at the ready, Miss Comerford."

She came up the stairs and the door to the home opened, revealing Poole and his pointed frown. "Miss Comerford," he said, ice in his tone.

"Poole," she said, the same in her own as she looked down her nose at him. Let him remember what she'd said weeks ago. Let him sit in the discomfort of it, just as he deserved.

"Mr. Windham expects you. You'll join him in the parlor." He motioned her up the hall and she followed him into the room.

Silas was by himself, standing at the fire, gazing off into the distance. He appeared distracted, up until the moment she was announced. Then he turned toward her and relief came over his features.

"You are perfectly on time," he said as he crossed to her and took her hands. "And perfect in general—my God, you look lovely."

She leaned up to kiss his cheek. He'd shaved, which only served as a reminder of how important this night was to him. She preferred him scruffy and bed mussed, but here they were.

"When the marquess and Lord Reginald arrive, bring them straight here," Silas said.

Poole gave her one final disapproving glance and then exited the room. She focused all her attention on Silas. "Your sister won't join us?"

His expression fell. "I waited too late to invite her. My brothers could make the time, but she had something else to do. Something to do with her daughter, who is coming out next Season."

She nodded. "So it is just us and them, then."

"I hope one day it will just be an *us*, but yes. For now, us and them."

She leaned up to push a stray lock of hair from his forehead. "You look very formal, Mr. Windham. No one could mistake you for anything but a gentleman."

He snorted a laugh at that observation. "Heaven preserve us. Would you like a drink?"

"Desperately," she said. "And that whisky looks lovely, but why don't you make it madeira? Might as well play at being a lady if you are going to be a gentleman."

"You *are* a lady," he said, and poured her drink. "There could never be any playing about it."

She shook her head. They were both fooling themselves if they believed that. She took a sip of her drink just as Poole reappeared.

"Lord Pentaghast and Lord Reginald," he intoned before he stepped away and let the two men into the room.

Of course, Arabella had met Lord Reginald recently, during their unpleasant encounter in this very parlor after her first night with Silas here. But she hadn't seen the marquess out in Society in many months, perhaps even a year. His illness had thinned him, aged him. He looked far more than fifteen years older than Silas.

"Charles, Reginald," Silas said, extending a hand to each of them in turn. Arabella was pleased that both men took the offering. That was something. Silas faced her now. "May I present Miss Arabella Comerford. Arabella, the Marquess of Pentaghast, and you already know Reggie. I'm sorry, Lord Reginald."

"My lord," she said with a small curtsey to the marquess. "And my lord. A pleasure to see you again."

Reginald appeared uncertain but he returned her nod briefly.

"Would you like a drink, either of you?" Silas asked. "We have the whisky you used to like, Reg. And you were always a brandy man, weren't you, Charlie?"

"Yes on both accounts," the marquess answered for them both. "I think we'll both have a drink, won't we, Reg?"

Arabella let her gaze fall to the middle brother. Just as when she'd first met him, she could sense his irritation with this entire exercise. But he nodded. "Thank you."

As Silas prepared the drinks, Arabella motioned the men to the chairs across from the settee. The marquess raised an eyebrow slightly at her playing of hostess, but he took it and even returned her smile when she gave it as she settled onto the settee.

"I wanted to inquire about your health, my lord," she said. "There has been worry amongst a great many of your friends. You look well tonight, though."

"I look like I feel, which is old," the marquess said with a little laugh. "But I am recovering. The worst has passed, I'm almost sure of it. And I'll survive."

"That is good," Arabella said, and meant it. It was clear Silas had suffered a great deal after the death of his father six years before. She didn't want him to have to go through that again with his brother. Especially given their estrangement.

Silas joined her and the conversation was stiff and awkward. They spoke of nothing of importance and yet all the important topics still hung in the air between them.

When supper was announced, Silas rose and offered her an arm. She looked at him in surprise. They weren't in an arrangement and she certainly did not count as a true lady. But he still treated her like one.

She took his arm and they led the other two gentlemen to the dining room. As they took their seats and the first course was laid before them, it seemed Lord Reginald could no longer hold back his feelings.

"I do wonder why you called us here tonight, Silas," he said. "Our last encounter was anything but pleasant. And given what we requested of you, the fact that you are flaunting your mistress—forgive me, Miss Comerford, but I must speak plainly—could be perceived as an act of pure defiance."

"Reggie," the marquess said softly.

"No. He has dragged you from your rest to do this." There was the slightest crack to Lord Reginald's tone and then he schooled it away. "I truly wish to know the answer so we can determine if everything is a waste of time."

Silas was seated at the head of the table and Arabella was to his right. She was close enough to feel the pulse of his emotions roll through him at that directness. It appeared like anger when one looked at his face, but she knew it wasn't that. Well, not only that. There was still a part of him that was that lonely child, pushed out behind the glass so he could only look in on his family. The boy who'd been stolen from a troubled mother, only to be isolated by a cold father.

"Can't even have a polite supper with me, eh, Reg?" he asked.

She reached over and covered his hand with hers. "Silas," she said.

He looked toward her and that hurt was even more reflected in his green gaze. She squeezed his hand, wishing she could transfer all her own strength to him in this moment. Wishing she could build a shield with her love that would keep him from all harm for the rest of his days.

When she broke her stare from his, she found the marquess and Lord Reginald were not looking at him anymore, but *them*. Her. She slowly removed her hand from his and nodded toward him, encouraging him to speak.

"As you two well know," he began, the anger in his tone metered now, though it was still there. "I've been spending a great deal of time with Arabella. I've met her sisters. She's met Phoebe."

"You introduced a *courtesan* to our sister," the marquess gasped.

"The woman I am spending time with came to my home when our sister was calling. And yes, I introduced them, at her insistence. Because unlike you two, Phoebe can see past the layers of propriety this world has forced upon all of us. Unlike you two, she seems to actually care about my happiness. About who I am, not just who you want me to be."

There was a long moment of silence and the marquess took a long drink before he said, "I know things have not gone well since your return. Our last conversation, especially, ended poorly and for that I'm sorry."

"But you must understand that the reason we have to slog through those layers of propriety is because of Charlie's title," Reginald said. "Our father was not a...he wasn't a good man. Our brother has had to navigate more than one scandal over the years as the truth of him leaked slowly to the *ton*."

Now Arabella stared at Lord Reginald. It had been clear from the beginning that he was the problem in the relationship, more than Phoebe or the marquess. But now she saw through that to the truth.

Reginald was trying to protect Charles. Which left Silas without an agent to protect him. And so she straightened her spine and met the man's gaze evenly.

"My lord, having met you and watched the three of you interact, I may have some insight to this matter. I am not intimately involved with this family. I wasn't raised with the hurts and the regrets, so perhaps I can see things a little more clearly."

"Can you?" Lord Reginald asked, his tone cold. "And what, pray tell, does the country's most shocking Cyprian have to say about it?"

Before Silas could bark or defend, she reached her hand out and covered his once more. She squeezed without looking at him and said, "You only see Silas as the boy who was dragged into your family, against the will of all the children involved. It was difficult for him and I assume it must have been difficult for you. But that wasn't his fault."

"Of course, it wasn't," the marquess said. "And Reg and I, especially, were old enough to behave better toward a sad, confused child who had no idea why he'd been brought there."

"You weren't always awful," Silas said, at last. "There are good memories."

Now Reginald bent his head. "There are. And I do want to create more of those. Damn it, when Phoebe said you'd written that you were coming back straight away, do you know what I felt? *Happiness*, Silas. I was happy I'd get to see you again. Happy we would all be together. I want to be able to see you, to build a relationship as men that we couldn't as boys because our father pitted us against each other. Pushed you out."

Silas's breath caught, wavered. "But you must see that this edict you gave me last week about being who you want me to be *still* pushes me out. You are offering to let me into this family, fully into this family, if I change everything about who I am. If I only make myself palatable to you."

The marquess bent his head at that statement and Arabella could see his shame in it. Lord Reginald was harder to read. She understood why. When one plunked oneself into the role of protector for decades, it was harder to allow for anything but whatever was defined as the protection.

"I didn't mean for that to be the impression," the marquess said.

"Nor I. And of course you may still be you," Reginald hastened to add. "Men gamble, you would still gamble. Men go to the Donville Masquerade, you could still do that. If you want to have a mistress, that's a perfectly acceptable thing to do just…" He trailed off and his cheeks grew a little darker as he seemed to recall Arabella was there.

And she realized, with a start, that *she* had become chief amongst the problems that these men had with Silas. She was infamous and her infamy was what rankled. What brought too many eyes toward Lord Pentaghast and brought out every sense of protection from Lord Reginald in response.

"The problem is me," she supplied softly.

Silas turned toward her. "No. They do not get to—"

"Silas, your brothers are not so incorrect. I *am* the country's most shocking Cyprian. I have worn that mantle with pride and I feel no shame in you saying it, even if that's your intention." She directed that statement toward Reginald now. "Not very well done of you, by the way."

He had the decency to bend his head slightly, but he still said, "But what are we supposed to do? Ignore it while every person who calls to check on my brother's health slyly inquires about you and Silas because you're racing around London, dancing in the middle of presentations or fucking in opera boxes?"

She smiled at Silas now. "We've never fucked in an opera box."

He was controlling his emotions, but his gaze softened as it met hers. "I would enjoy the opera more if we did. A good suggestion."

"*This* is what I mean," Reginald said, and threw his napkin across the table next to his untouched soup. "You want to revel in your dissipation, indulging every worst impulse and she *isn't* helping."

Silas shook his head. "You've no idea how much she helps. How just the fact of being near her makes me feel more myself than I have in all the decades of being your brother."

She pivoted to look at him. His green eyes were flashing with anger, and she might have believed this response was just a way to tweak his brothers. But there was passion to it that had nothing to do with them. That had everything to do with the truth.

If she stayed here, stayed with him, as she had for too long, they would be at an impasse. He would be hurt. And she couldn't allow that.

She pushed her chair back and stood. The men raced to join her out of politeness. She inclined her head toward them. "I think my presence here is only making this worse. I wouldn't want to do that. I'm close to my sisters, I couldn't imagine being anything but. I wouldn't see a loss of such closeness done to Silas, not any more than it already has been."

"No, please don't go," he said.

She managed to look at him without bursting into tears. "Silas, you must discuss this with your brothers without my presence making things more complicated." Her attention shifted to the marquess and Lord Reginald. "And you two must be able to see past whatever judgments you have about who your brother has been bedding and truly look at the man he is. The very good, intelligent, free-spirited man who is more than worthy of your affection without changing even a fraction of who he is. You would both be lucky to have him in your lives."

"I'm sorry this has been unpleasant, Miss Comerford," the marquess said. "I truly am."

"As am I," Lord Reginald agreed.

She looked to Silas again. "Come, walk me out."

She took his hand and he sent a quick look toward his brothers before he let her take him from the room. They hadn't even reached the foyer when Poole was calling for her carriage with a great glee in his tone.

She sighed. "He must have been listening."

"I don't give a damn about the butler," Silas said, catching her arms and forcing her to look at him. "Please don't let them push you out of my house or my life."

She stared up into this face she had come to truly adore. "Silas, we both knew this was temporary. We said it from the beginning. If it's ending anyway, why not give in on this with your brothers? It gives them a point in this argument, gives them a reason to loosen their grip on anything else they demand. I can see they both *want* to do that."

He glanced back at the dining room and there was such a

longing on his face that it broke her heart. "I don't care what they want," he whispered.

She shook her head. "Of course you do. Let me go. Talk to them. Try to work it out. Don't be so bullheaded about an affair that you won't let yourself have what you've wanted since you were a boy."

"It is more than an affair and you know it," he said, his voice broken and his eyes stormy seas.

Her carriage was already arriving at the door and for that she was happy because him saying those words made her heart soar and crash all at once. She cupped his cheeks and leaned up for a kiss. His arms came around her, almost desperate to keep her. But when she pulled back, he allowed it.

"It can't be. And you know it. Good night."

She stepped away then, didn't even hear whatever snide comment Poole made when he helped her into her rig, didn't feel the carriage move when Ingram set them on the road back toward her house. She was numb. That was a good thing because she knew when this pain came, it would be powerful. It would be changing.

How could it be anything but when she'd just walked away from the man she loved?

CHAPTER 21

Silas could hardly hear over the pounding of his heart as he strode back into the dining room after Arabella left. She'd left *him* and it was perfectly clear that it wasn't just for the night or for show. She was ending this and he hadn't felt such a pain in a very long time.

"I'm sorry she felt she had to leave," Charlie said as Silas entered the room.

Silas shook his head. "No, that was the purpose, wasn't it?" He threw himself back in the chair. He couldn't muster enough energy to speak angrily anymore, so his tone was flat, instead. "To drive her away. To take her from me so that you two could dance me all the more on your string."

"Take her away?" Reginald repeated with wide eyes. "Do you know what you sound like?"

"Like a man who loves a woman," Silas shouted.

For a moment that statement hung between them, stunning all three of them equally. He hadn't allowed himself to recognize until now when it was being threatened. When he'd had to watch her walk away and felt like she'd ripped his heart out and put it in the carriage with her.

"You're in love with her," Charlie repeated softly. "What does that mean?"

"I don't know. I've never felt such a thing before. But it's there and I won't apologize for it. Arabella is sunlight streaming into a room where you've only ever had the curtains drawn. She is laughter in the midst of sorrow. She is bright and glorious and when I'm with her, I feel…happy. She makes me happy." He shifted. "The very idea of walking away from that, of not asking her to stay in my life forever, is a pain I cannot describe. And it's one I won't bear, not even to have you two in my life."

"You sound like you're talking about marrying her," Reginald said, his hands gripped on the tabletop.

Silas swallowed. "Yes. If she would have me, I would marry her."

He had no idea if that was possible, of course. He knew that what they shared was real. He knew she cared for him, perhaps even loved him, though he wasn't *certain* of that larger feeling. But she might not agree to linking her life with his. She might push him even further away to protect herself…to protect him.

"If everything you wished for came true," Charlie said carefully. "If you asked her to wed and she agreed, how do you picture that working? What would you have me say when it was brought up in clubs or at parties?"

He shook his head. "I expect you to tell anyone who bothers you about me to fuck off. And if you cannot do that, then roll your eyes and laugh and say something about bastard blood. That's what everyone thinks of me anyway, isn't it? You don't have to claim ownership for anything I do. You can just be bemused by it."

"I *am* bemused by it," Charlie said with a sigh. "And perhaps a little envious that you have always gone your own way, never been constrained by all that goes along with being a son of the Marquess of Pentaghast."

"Oh, trust me, I was more than constrained by that man's name and expectations," Silas said. "But it isn't *his* name anymore, is it?

They aren't *his* expectations. You don't have to be anything you don't want to be, or at least you don't have to live the life he required."

Charlie and Reg looked at each other and it was as if they had never considered that. For a brief moment, Silas wondered about their childhoods with their father. They'd both been grown when he met them, Charlie fifteen years his senior, Reg twelve. But what had Pentaghast done when they were boys to put them so firmly in line that they feared to stray even into their forties and he was dead in the grave for more than half a decade?

Silas leaned forward. "I wouldn't ask you to invite us to your fancy parties, I want nothing to do with that. But why couldn't you invite me and the person I hold dearest to Christmas? Or to the country estate for a week after the Season so we can all play croquette and watch the children swim in the lake? Jesus, you're offering me family but acting like it's a business connection."

There was a long, charged silence and then Charlie cleared his throat. "Perhaps it's all we knew. Perhaps we could all learn something from you on the matter of following your heart."

"I'd be happy to teach you. But not if it means losing my chance with her."

There was a long silence and then Charlie leaned his hands on the table. "I wouldn't take away your happiness. That seems more like our father's way of running things than my own. And perhaps you're right, the change in this family must come from us moving more toward you and away from him than the opposite direction. I'm sorry, Silas."

"You're saying you would accept me?" Silas asked. "And her, if I'm so lucky as to win her?"

"Yes," Charlie said. "I would accept you. And I doubt anyone could do anything but accept her. I think she would demand it and somehow make it the other person's own idea."

"She would at that," Silas said with a chuckle.

He suddenly felt so…light. So free. He could stay here in London and still be who he was. He could start to create a family with the siblings who had once been taught to push him aside. And he would have Arabella. Or at least try his damnedest to win her.

But if Charlie seemed resigned to this arrangement, Reginald now squirmed. There was something troubled to his face and Silas sighed. "You're going to cause me trouble, aren't you?"

Reginald shook his head. "No. I've only ever wanted to protect Charlie. If he agrees to this new arrangement, I would do nothing but what he wishes. What you need. The problem is more that… that…"

"What?" Silas's voice was sharper now. He couldn't help it as his brother's guilty expression created a fear in him that he couldn't quite define. "What is it?"

"I was contacted by a man a few days ago," Reginald said. "His name is Albert Comerford."

It felt like someone had pulled the rug out from under Silas's feet and now he was falling. His ears rung and his hands shook as he managed to choke out, "Arabella's father? You talked to her *father* about her?"

~

Arabella had never trudged in her life, but when she stepped out of her carriage and onto her drive, she almost felt as though she couldn't fully lift her feet.

She'd done the right thing, of course. Setting Silas free, pushing him back toward his family, that was the best course. Now she could focus on forgetting her feelings for the man and he could focus on building the relationship he always should have had with his siblings.

But it didn't feel like the right thing. It felt awful.

"Good evening, Miss Comerford," Barnaby said as she stepped up to the door.

"Good evening, Barnaby. Is Julia at home, then?"

"No, she went out with Miss Reynolds again. She told me she wouldn't be home until late."

There was relief in that fact. She didn't want her sister to read the pain she couldn't hide for much longer. She forced a smile. "Well, then do you think you might have something light sent to my room to eat? And then you are relieved of duties. I'll be in for the night."

If her butler thought it strange that she'd left for a supper engagement but returned early and in need of food, he didn't express it. He merely agreed to the request and left her to her own devices.

She took the opportunity to go into her parlor. The fires weren't lit in the small room, not that she'd expected them to be. She'd been out, after all. Not likely expected back until late, if at all. But the dark suited her and she moved to the sideboard only by the moonlight streaming through the front window. She was pouring herself a drink when she heard a sound from the back corner of the room.

"I wondered how long I'd have to wait."

She froze, for she knew that voice well, even if she hadn't heard it for six years. She swallowed hard, set down her glass and turned toward him slowly. He was nothing but a shadow in the dark, the shape of a demon come to collect her.

"Father," she said, and was proud her voice didn't shake. "I didn't expect you. How rude of my servants not to give you light and refreshment."

"Don't be stupid, you know they aren't aware that I'm here."

She inclined her head. "Of course not. If they were they wouldn't have let you in."

That was her standing order, after all. To keep away the man who regularly threatened her. She was even happier Julia wasn't here. At least the threat was only directed at Arabella for now.

"As if you have the right to lock me out." Her father moved closer and the moonlight hit his face. For a moment, she was ripped back in time to when she was a very little girl with no way to fight him. No way to stop him from hurting her with his words or the back of his hand. When she'd been terrified of him.

She still was, but now she could remind herself that she had power. Or at least she wasn't a child who was entirely weak.

"What do you want?" she asked. "Have you come along to speak your threats in person? I've received them, you needn't bother."

"You've ruined my life," he growled.

She shook her head. "Yes, so you've repeated ad nauseum. But I've been a courtesan for six years, Evelina joined me four years ago, Julia two. Why in the world would you break into my house *now*? I couldn't have freshly damaged you, I've done nothing different."

"I've been working toward a marriage," he said, rubbing his hands together. "The middle daughter of the second son of Viscount Trafford."

She stepped back. "Christ, Father, she cannot be more than two years older than I am. That's disgusting."

"What choice did you leave me?" His face grew red and spittle flew from his mouth as he spoke. "You and your sisters stole any chance I had of furthering myself through your marriages. And then you went and whored yourselves out so blatantly, damaging my name. It took me this long to work on Trafford. To convince him through a variety of means."

"Blackmail him, perhaps?" she asked softly. "He has a secret family, yes?"

He arched a brow. "Seems you have your information, too."

"What in the world would your disgusting bargains with Trafford have to do with me?" she asked.

"A few weeks ago you started up with that Windham bastard. All your scandalous activities started spiraling back to the country. The scandal rags were dripping with the stories of your races and gambling and running around like a fool with him. They named your sisters, they named *me*."

She flinched. Using her own name, trying to tweak her father's fury, it had been her biggest mistake. And now it seemed it was coming back to haunt her.

"And?" she asked coolly, though she had an idea of what happened next.

"Trafford said he was trying to avoid a scandal, not fall back into one. He refused the match, bought off my source of information about his other family. Matched his daughter to some other man before I could protest too publicly. I lost my connection to an increase in my worth because of *you*." He got even closer and she backed up, but there was no more room to move. He had to her pinned against the table. "And it will keep happening. You will keep up what you are, and it will always damage me. But if you're dead, then it ends."

Raw, powerful fear roared through Arabella as she stared into the face of a man who should have loved her, but had only ever hated her even before she ran. A man who looked entirely serious about what he wanted to do.

There was a light knock on the parlor door and they both froze and looked toward it. "Miss Comerford?"

It was Barnaby. When she looked back at her father, she saw he had a gun out now. Pointed toward the thin door and the servant beyond.

"No," she whispered. "Let me." She hoped her voice sounded less shaky when she called out, "Yes?"

He hesitated when she didn't call him in, but then said, "The food has been delivered to your chamber—a few of your favorites."

"Good man," she called back. "You're so kind. Now, please, you and your lovely wife must take the rest of the night off, as I said earlier. I'll lock up before I go up."

"Yes, miss. Goodnight," Barnaby said, his tone lined with confusion. But he didn't try to come in and she heard his footfalls moving away. To safety. At least she could provide that.

"Funny how you'd protect a servant but you'd throw your sisters to the wolves and destroy me." Her father caught her arm and dragged her toward the door, his fingers digging hard into her flesh and his gun pressed against her side. "Now, you're going to write a letter of goodbye, Arabella. And we're going to take care of this."

"Fine," she said. "Fine, I'll do as you like. Let me write it upstairs. I can leave it where someone will see it."

He glared at her as he pulled her into the hall. There the light was fuller and she gasped. He looked twenty years older rather than just six. And his gaze was wild and so cruel.

"If you alert anyone in this house to my presence, if you think you'll get away somehow by tricking me, know that I will kill anyone who comes for you with no hesitation. Your servants, your sisters, your latest lover. I'll shoot any of them without any remorse and let you watch them die."

She nodded, blinking at the tears stinging her eyes. "I won't do anything."

He drew her to the stairs and they staggered up together and into her chamber. She looked past her bed, toward the dressing room. "I'll write it in there," she said, and pulled from his arms.

She went into the other room, ignoring the tub where she'd last been with Silas for the moment. To realize that might be the last time they were ever together in any intimate way was too painful. She would die and he might believe she'd killed herself. Might think it had to do with their supper tonight and the rejection of his family.

God, he would hate them and himself. She had to make sure he didn't believe that. That her sisters knew she wouldn't leave them on purpose. She had to leave clues that her demise had been at this man's hand so she could protect her sisters from any retribution he might seek against them when he wasn't satisfied with only destroying her.

She drew paper from a drawer in her dressing room and stood at the table, staring at that blank vellum for a moment. "What should I say?"

"That you know you're a ruining whore who doesn't deserve to live and that you went to the Thames to kill yourself. Wash away all that disgusting sin. Oh, and add that you're mostly sorry to your dear father."

She shut her eyes and drew a shaky breath. He had no idea that he was playing into her hand. No one she knew or loved would ever believe any of that nonsense.

> *My dearest Evelina and Julia,*
> *This is all too much for me, knowing how I destroyed*
> *you.*

She stared at those words, knowing that sometimes she had truly believed them to be true. Salvation had been so close to destruction for both her sisters. She blinked at tears and continued.

> *And I cannot go on with the guilt any longer. Not in harming you, nor in the humiliation I caused against our innocent father, who only wished to raise us with love and kindness. To free us all from my mistakes, I must end my life. Think of my favorite spot and know that I'm washed away from all the pain. With all my love to you and to Silas, goodbye. Arabella.*

Her father held out a hand for the note and she watched with bated breath as he read it. Would he notice she'd spelled Silas's name wrong? Or that she'd gone on a little too far about his kindness? Would he ask about her favorite spot, a little grove along the Thames that was just across from the house she now stood in? The one she'd now try to convince her father to take her to?

Would they see the clues and find her, either dead or alive? Would they avenge her or save her? Or at least would they understand she hadn't done this out of her own volition if he succeeded?

He handed the letter back and grunted. "Put it where it will be found."

She looked at the hat box on the table where she'd written her note. She hadn't ever put it back after she hid his latest letter inside. If she set it here, surely one of her sisters would wonder at the odd placement when she normally put her things away carefully. They'd open it.

They'd see the threats she'd so often pushed aside and minimized, both to them and to herself. They'd realize what a danger their father truly was.

She folded the paper and set it carefully on top of the box. "Julia wished to borrow the hat within. She'll come looking for it in the morning and find the note."

Another lie, but he seemed to believe it. He caught her arm and began to drag her out of the room and down to the back of the house. "Now, let's go," he said.

"Wait, how will you take me?" she asked, tugging back slightly and feeling the press of the gun in her side become harder. "If you get my carriage, my servants will have to be called. If you have a horse, it will draw attention to have two on it and to ready my mount will take time."

"Oh, you are so interested in making certain your suicide goes well?" he asked.

"I'm interested in making sure you don't kill anyone innocent in your zeal to destroy me." She was trying to catch her breath, but it was getting harder now. "May I suggest that the Thames runs through the park just across from my house? Wouldn't it make more sense that I'd go somewhere close to end myself?"

He glared at her. "You aren't in control of this."

"No. I am certainly sure of that." She glanced down at the gun buried in her side, the barrel bruising her. "Please, if you're going to end this, at least do it quickly and without harming others."

He seemed to accept that and turned her toward her front door. They exited together, looking every bit the happy pair, she supposed, as they stepped out onto the drive and moved their way across the street toward the dark park.

Toward her end, if she couldn't figure out a way out of this. And the fact that she'd never again see her sisters or Silas was the greatest heartbreak she'd ever felt.

CHAPTER 22

"What the hell do you mean you talked to Arabella's father?" Silas asked, jumping to his feet.

"*He* talked to me," Reg insisted. "He found me at my club. And while the man was wild, he seemed to know a great deal about my situation. Apparently news of the behavior you two have been indulging in has reached the countryside. He offered to talk to her, to get her in line."

"In exchange for what?" Silas growled, trying to temper the wild terror that rushed through him. Considering what Arabella had confessed to him the night before, he couldn't imagine her father had any good intentions.

"Money, of course," Reginald insisted. "I gave him fifty pounds to try to talk some sense into her. He wanted to do it this afternoon, but I told him we intended to sup with you, so he seemed to change his mind."

"You told him her schedule?" Silas gasped. "You offered him money to handle her? Do you know what you've done?"

Reginald got up now, shaking his head. "Tried to manage this in a gentlemanly way."

"Her father has been threatening her with physical harm for

years," Silas spit out, running a hand through his hair. "It's only her arrangements with powerful men that have kept her safe. The man blames her for all his woes and has no interest in her well-being. You fool, you've offered her up to him."

Now Charlie was on his feet too and he glanced at Reginald. Their brother looked sick at the facts being laid out before him.

"Do you—do you truly believe he would harm her?" Reginald asked, his tone shaky.

"I don't know. But I know he's said he would. I must go to her, right now."

"And we'll go with you," Charlie insisted.

Reginald faced him. "You'll do no such thing. You're not well enough to ride or physically encounter someone with violence on his mind. I'll go. It's my fault this has been unleashed and I must handle it."

Silas stared at his brother for no longer than a few seconds. While he didn't entirely trust Reg, the fact was that he needed help. Arabella might need help. That overrode any hesitation he might have.

"Will you contact the guard?" he asked Charlie. "I know you don't like the attention—"

"I would never see someone come to harm just to protect myself from scandal, for God's sake. Certainly not someone you love and who obvious cares deeply for you." Charlie shook his head. "I will send for them immediately and have them go straight to Arabella's home. Now go!"

Silas was already rushing from the chamber, Reginald on his heels. They didn't wait for the sneering Poole but went out and straight to the stables. Silas was struggling to put a saddle on his horse when Reggie grabbed his arm.

"You're shaking too hard to ride and I came here in Charlie's carriage. We'll take that."

Silas bit back a breath. Everything in him wished to argue, but they were wasting precious time and the carriage was already prepared, the driver coming up into his seat as Reggie gave him directions and told him to race as hard as he could.

"Very well," Silas said and followed his brother into the vehicle, which then thundered from Silas's gate, rushing toward Arabella's home. He couldn't help but yank the curtain back and continually stare out the window, as if he could will the carriage to go faster.

"I am sorry," Reggie said softly, drawing his attention away from city streaking by.

Silas glared at him. "I don't doubt you had no idea this man would threaten her. But my God, why would you work so hard to get rid of her?"

Reggie let out a long breath and his expression crumpled. "Do you know what Father used to do to Charlie? Long before you came along, long before our mother died?"

"No," Silas said, and then reached up to brace himself on the carriage ceiling as the driver careened around a slower rig. He could hear the curses of the other driver even from inside.

Reg let out a shaky breath. "He beat him. I always tried to intervene, to stop him, but he wouldn't be stopped. And one night he beat him so badly, he couldn't breathe. Broke one of his ribs, I suppose, perhaps even bruised his lungs. Phoebe and I stood with our mother around Charlie's bed and prayed he wouldn't die. Somehow he didn't, but only through a miracle, I think. Seeing his heir nearly die scared the marquess enough that he didn't do it again."

"My God," Silas breathed. "I knew the man was a bastard, a true one, not by blood. But to harm a child?"

"It was disgusting. A dreadful thing to do." Reggie's breath got shaky. "When Charlie lived, I vowed to stand by him. To do everything I could to make his life...easier."

"That's why you're so angry with me," Silas breathed as understanding dawned.

Reg shook his head. "It's foolish, I know. It wasn't your fault you were born to such a man. That he used you as a pawn to hurt your mother. That he fought with all his might to turn all of us against you and to lock you out for his own twisted pleasure. But when you started to go wild, I saw the strain it put on Charlie. Father made sure it put strain on him."

"He made him responsible, I know," Silas sighed. "Charlie used to show up at my old place here in London and try to put me back on the straight and very narrow path. And I always rebuffed him. I had no idea the old man lorded that over him or I would have told the last marquess to go straight to hell, myself."

Reg gave a slight smile. "His old injuries sometimes bother him. Make it hard to breathe. When you left, it happened. And then it started again months ago and your return frightened me. The idea that you would race around just being…you. Untethered."

"I do understand," Silas said. "And I thank you for helping me do that. The last thing I'd want to do is harm Charlie. I came home because the idea of him dying without us coming to some resolution was horrible. I think we all want the same thing."

"To be a family," Reg said with a sigh.

"But we can't do it on the terms our father laid out, you must see that." The carriage turned down the last street leading to Arabella's. "And we can discuss that more after I've ensured the woman I love is safe."

"Absolutely."

As they peeled into the drive, Silas burst from the carriage before it even came to a full stop. He rushed to the front door and began to pound on it, calling Arabella's name. Most of the lights were out, even though it wasn't particularly late, and it took far too long for Barnaby to finally arrive at the door.

When he answered, the butler was not in his usual formal garb, but in a plain linen shirt, no jacket or waistcoat and his hair was slightly mussed.

"Mr. Windham, we weren't expecting you," Barnaby said.

"Is Arabella well?" Silas asked, pushing past him. "Where is she?"

"She's fine, sir," Barnaby said, casting a quick glance at Reginald as he entered the room behind Silas. "But she asked for food to be brought to her chamber less than an hour ago and retired."

Silas was already going up the stairs. "Arabella!" he called out. "Arabella, please answer me!"

Barnaby wedged himself between Silas and his brother as all three men moved up the stairs. "Sir, I don't know what is going on, but you cannot just—"

Silas ignored him and went to her door. Just twelve hours before he'd been lounging in a tub with her here, now the house felt cold and terrifying. Like he could feel something wrong had happened here. He could only pray that intuition was wrong.

"Arabella!" He pounded on the surface but received no answer. When he tried the door, it was locked. Without hesitation he hit it with his shoulder, buckling the wood and letting it fly open as Barnaby continued his protests.

She wasn't in the bedchamber and it didn't appear she ever had been. He was moving toward the door to the dressing room when he was interrupted by the arrival of her sisters. They must have been out together and now they rushed in behind them. At their heels, though considerably slower, was the Duke of Southwater.

"What in the world is going on here?" Evelina asked. "We bring Julia home and find this madness?"

"I'm sorry, Miss Evelina, they pushed their way in and broke Miss Comerford's door," Barnaby said, clenching his hands together. "Shall I call for someone?"

"Please!" Silas gasped out as he looked at Arabella's sisters. "I already have, but there cannot be too many. I have reason to believe that your father might be pursuing Arabella. Here. In London. Right now."

Both the women faltered and Evelina reached behind her to catch Southwater's hand. Her protector took it, but he made no further move to comfort her.

"And she isn't here," Silas continued. "You know she would be bursting out and shouting at me for breaking her door if she were."

Evelina rushed forward. "Our father? What do you know about him?"

"She told me about the letters. The death threats."

Julia's face went pale. "I knew he wrote her horrible things, but… but death threats?"

Southwater's face scrunched in horror. "Threats? Why didn't I know about this?"

Evelina glanced at him. "Arabella always played them off as unimportant. I didn't want to believe they could be anything but."

Silas nodded, but it was Reginald who spoke. "Your father reached out to me a few days ago trying to work out a way to intervene with your sister on my behalf. I had no idea of his true intentions toward her."

Evelina pushed past them all and opened the dressing room door. It was empty and relief flooded Silas for a brief moment. He'd worried, in some part of himself that he hadn't been willing to accept, that Arabella might be dead in that room. That he would find a body.

But the chamber was much as it had been left that morning when they'd bathed together. There was nothing out of place except—

"Why is her hat box on the table?" Evelina whispered, and now Julia pushed into the room.

"She never leaves a thing out of place." Julia stepped up and her voice trembled as she said, "There's a note here."

They took it and read it, first to themselves. When Evelina gasped and Julia let out a broken moan of pain, Silas couldn't wait. He snatched it from them and read it out loud,

My dearest Evelina and Julia,
This is all too much for me, knowing how I destroyed
you. And I cannot go on with the guilt any longer. Not in
harming you, nor in the humiliation I caused against our

innocent father, who only wished to raise us with love and kindness. To free us all from my mistakes, I must end my life. Think of my favorite spot and know that I'm washed away from all the pain. With all my love to you and to Silus, goodbye. Arabella.

He was unsteady on his feet and Reg reached out to catch his elbow. "Suicide?" Silas whispered. "No. Not possible. She would never."

"I agree," Evelina said, though her voice was thick with emotion. "I know she sometimes feels guilt at where my path and Julia's took us, but we've spoken of it often. She would know that losing her would be a far worse thing for us than anything else we've ever done or endured. Someone must have compelled her to do it. Look at how she's spelled your name wrong."

"She wouldn't do that, even in haste?" Reg asked.

"No. Never." Julia paced away. "She's written that name so many times in the years, she could probably do it in the dark with her left hand. It was on purpose. Which means she's trying to send us a message. Let us know this isn't real."

"Let us know she's in danger if she were lucky enough that someone found it." Silas pivoted toward Barnaby. "How long ago did she come home? It couldn't have been long."

"Less than an hour," Barnaby said. "She went into the parlor downstairs. When I came to tell her that the food she asked for had been delivered to her chamber, she refused to open the door to the parlor. I thought it odd. A little while later my wife and I heard her come up and assumed she went to her chamber."

Evelina swallowed hard. "If our father was there, if he was truly of a violent bent, she would have tried to keep Barnaby and the rest of the staff out of it."

"Yes," Silas said. "That wonderful streak of protection in her would have wanted to save him. But she went to the trouble to write this, to leave these clues. So there might still be a chance. If we can find her."

Reg drew the letter from Silas's fingers. "This line is odd: *Think of my favorite spot and know that I'm washed away from all the pain. Why would she be so specific?"*

They were all silent for a moment, the women pondering the answer and then Julia gasped, as if she'd thought of something. "When she received this house from the Duke of Kentwood a few years ago, I remember her saying she was especially happy to have it because it was so close to her favorite place in the world. She meant the park across the street."

Evelina nodded. "Yes, yes! There's a place with a little grove of trees where one can sit and watch the Thames rush by. That could be what she meant by washed away."

"Come on," Silas said, rushing from the room. "Reg and I will go. You stay here and direct the guard when they arrive."

"Like hell we will," Evelina said, and started for the door. "We are coming, Julia and I and Harry."

"I cannot," Southwater said. Gently but still firmly.

Evelina stopped and pivoted back to stare at him. "You—you would not go to help my sister?"

"My reputation, Evelina," he said. "I could not be involved in such a scandalous thing. You shouldn't either. Come with me. We'll get word when it's over."

She drew back, her face twisting. "When it's over? You mean when they find my sister dead?"

He flinched. "Or alive and well. And then we would have involved ourselves for nothing."

Evelina swallowed hard, but then lifted up to kiss his cheek. "You should go. I understand your desire to protect yourself. But I'm going with the rest of them. I'll call on you tomorrow and let you know what has come of it." She glanced back at Silas. "Come on."

She and Julia raced from the room and Silas and his brother followed. As Silas passed the duke, he muttered, "Cowardly fuck."

They made their way out of the house and across the road, dodging carriages and horses in their haste. The park across the way was very dark, but Evelina and Julia seemed to know the way by heart. Of course they would if Arabella had taken them to this "favorite place" over the years. Silas could only hope he wouldn't find her crumpled in that spot.

But he couldn't bear to think that so he kept his mind on hope. And on the love he felt for Arabella that he would never keep inside again if he found her alive and unharmed.

~

Arabella stumbled as she was dragged through the woods by her father. There was a path, but he seemed bent on causing her as much pain and fear as possible, so he dragged her through the brambles instead, tearing her dress and scratching her arms as they went. When she tripped, he didn't hesitate and continued to drag her as she staggered to try to get back to her feet.

"You're not going to make a suicide very realistic if you batter me the whole way," she snapped.

"Well, they won't find you for a good long time, if ever," he said over his shoulder. "The river so rarely gives up its dead."

She swallowed. He couldn't make her drown, he wouldn't be so sloppy as to give her a chance to get away. So he'd likely shoot her and toss her in the current. And he was correct, there would be very little change she'd be found. And even if she were and could somehow be identified, who on the guard would put much effort into determining the cause of her death? She might have a pretty title like courtesan or Cyprian linked to her name, but a whore was a whore was a whore to all of them.

She didn't want to cry. That would give her father too much satisfaction. She bit her lip until she tasted blood and let him take her to the water.

"Is this the place?" he asked. "The grove? The riverside?"

She nodded, for there was no reason to lie anymore. She'd given herself...what? Perhaps an hour from the time she'd found him in her parlor to when he'd shoot her in the head without a thought or a care? Her sisters wouldn't be home before then to determine she was missing. Silas was with his brothers, hopefully settling their relationship in a positive way.

No one would come.

"You know, we loved you, despite it all." One of the tears she so desperately didn't want to shed slid down her cheek. "All three of us wanted to make you happy. To give you what you wanted."

"And yet you all ran away. You traded respectability for scandal without a thought," he snapped, facing her.

He was once again highlighted in pale glow of the moon and he looked like a monster again. She tried to find her father there, but couldn't. It felt like no remnants of any positive part of him remained. He was only this. And it was nearly as heartbreaking as the acceptance of the fact she would die.

"We weren't being offered respectability," she said softly. "*You* made me a whore, Father. *Papa.* You were trying to sell my virginity with just as much zeal as any madame ever has. I ran because I feared the consequences. And so did my sisters. The funny part is that if you had just been a fraction less cruel, we would have all fallen in line. We would have given you just what you wanted and hoped it would be enough. But I look at you now and see it never could have been enough."

He blinked at her. "No...*I'm* the victim. You stole from me. You stole my future."

"You stole mine first," she whispered.

He was silent for a very long time and then he pointed the gun at her. "Then perhaps we go together. Perhaps we both atone for our sins in one fell swoop. I can't fix what you broke. There's nothing left for me. So you die and I die with you and we erase all the damage done."

She couldn't stop the tears now. Couldn't hold off the terror and the regret. Not for the life she'd led that this man so despised, but for the one she wouldn't get to lead. The love she wouldn't get to share with her sisters and with Silas. She'd never get to tell that man that he was everything to her. That she adored him beyond reason and hope and reality. He would *never* know that.

She sank to her knees in the wet grass and stared up at her father beyond the pistol now leveled at her head. "Please don't do this," she said. "You don't have to. You can let me go. Let all of this go. I would give you the money to leave the country if you wanted it. You could take a new name and forget you ever had three daughters."

"Three ungrateful daughters," he said, but she could see the hesitation.

"Three very ungrateful daughters," she corrected herself, trying not to hope that she might be getting through to him. That she might make it out alive. "You could start new. Become someone you want to be instead of what you became when we abandoned you. Please. Please let me do that."

He stared at her a long moment and then he lifted the gun that had drooped momentarily in his fingers. She squeezed her eyes shut, ready for the blast and the darkness that would come after.

But when the blast came, there was no pain, there was no darkness. She heaved backward onto her backside out of instinct and scooted away before she realized she hadn't been shot. Instead her father lay on the shores of the Thames, smoking gun still clutched in his hand.

And he was dead.

CHAPTER 23

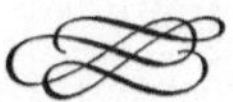

When Silas heard the gunshot as he raced through the thick woods, he began to hear another sound. It took him a moment to realize it was his own voice, howling in pain and horror as he pushed through the brambles and onto the shores of the Thames.

He saw Arabella there, crumpled on the ground and for a moment all he could do was scream her name into the night. But then she turned toward him and he saw, to his shock and relief, that she wasn't harmed.

He threw himself down beside her, gathering her into his arms as she began to sob, her fingers digging into his jacket as she almost tried to claw her way into his coat.

"Shhh," he soothed. "I'm here, I'm here."

"He's—he's dead."

It was Evelina's voice that said it and that brought Silas back to reality. He looked to where the rest of them stared and saw there was a man lying on the shore. A gun smoked in his hand, a hole was in his forehead.

Arabella stopped sobbing and pushed at him, silently asking him to help her up. He did so and she rushed to her sisters, gathering them close as they trembled together.

"He shot himself," she gasped out at last. "He was pointing the gun at me and then he shot himself instead. I was trying to give him a way out, I don't know why he took this one."

They collapsed together then, Silas watching the love that always glowed so brightly between them create a warmth that he knew would carry them through this awful truth. He looked toward his brother and found Reg watching him just as closely.

"I'm very glad she's unharmed," Reg said as he came to Silas and clasped his arm gently.

"At least physically," Silas said.

"Miss Comerford," Reg said, and then shook his head. "Arabella."

She jolted at the use of her name and looked toward Silas's brother. She left her sisters to hold each other and moved to him. "Y-Yes, my lord? I'm so sorry you had to be involved in this, that you were dragged into—"

"I have no regrets in coming to your aid, only in my part in all this, which I'm sure Silas will tell you soon enough. But the guard will be coming, Arabella, and soon."

She blinked, as if she were only just realizing that she would potentially be implicated in this death. That she might be seen as a suspect, even if she hadn't done anything wrong.

Silas slid his arm around her. "We'll get through it," he whispered.

She looked up at him. "I don't want to harm you or your family with all this."

"You misunderstand," Reg said. "I'm not telling you about the guard's arrival to make you see that you're in danger. I need to know what happened, if you can bear to tell it, so that I know how to make it go away. For you. For him, as well. And I suppose for us, too."

"Make it go away?" she repeated.

He smiled. "You've been involved with many powerful men.

Enough that you should know we can make most distasteful things go away with the right pressures and payoffs. And since you were clearly the victim in all this, I think the full weight of the title Pentaghast will have never been used for a better purpose than to ensure you are left unscathed. Please, tell us what happened."

Arabella clung to Silas as she choked out the whole story of her father's arrival, plan to make her death look like a suicide and finally his taking of his own life after she had offered him an escape.

Silas held her tightly, feeling her heart pound with fear and grief with every word. How he wished he could take some of that pain, lift its weight from her shoulders. But he knew from experience that he couldn't. She would have to feel it. The best he could do was be there to hold her through it.

"I understand," Reg said when she was finished. He dug into his pocket and offered her his handkerchief, which she used to wipe her eyes. There was a commotion from above them in the park. "I'll meet them. And I'll be sure they understand what truly happened."

"What will you say that was, my lord?" Julia asked.

"The truth. That Mr. Comerford approached me tonight, very drunk, wanting to get in touch with his daughters to apologize for his long estrangement. And that we discovered him staggering down to the river after he couldn't reach you. We tried to stop him from acting a fool with his revolver, but it went off. Probably accidentally in his state."

"You'll make it appear accidental?" Arabella breathed. "That could never be believed."

"Anything can be believed with enough power and influence. Why don't you four go back to the house now? Go through the other side of the trail. I'll handle it and come up later."

Julia and Evelina each took one of Arabella's scratched and shaking hands and started to take her up the path Reg had indicated. Silas stayed behind for a breath and then reached out his hand toward his brother. "I owe you," he said.

To his surprise, Reggie pulled him in for a brief embrace. "Perhaps no one owes anyone anymore. Perhaps we can just start over."

"I'd like that," Silas said, and then turned away to let his brother manage the consequences while he tried to comfort the woman he loved.

~

After their return to the house, everything had become a blur. Arabella had been aware of Evelina and Julia tending to her, cleaning up her scratches and removing her torn gown to replace it with a nightrail. They'd even gotten the brambles from her hair.

Silas had been there the whole time, watching, mostly silent, sometimes helping. Evelina and Julia had stayed with her a while but eventually they'd gone to their own rooms and Silas joined her on her bed, his arms around her, his body heat the only thing keeping the chill from her bones.

The reality of what had happened was hitting now. Long waves of grief and terror that she knew would last a long time. They might fade eventually. They might soften. But they would be there.

"Would you like to try to eat?" Silas asked softly, his fingers threading through her hair gently. "You didn't have supper or the tray Mrs. Barnaby put together."

"I couldn't eat," she murmured, tracing the edge of his waistcoat with her fingertips. "I will later, I promise."

He pressed a kiss to her temple. "I'll hold you to that."

She let out her breath in a shaky sigh and leaned away so she could look up at him. "When I saw you next, I thought I would be ending this between us. Not that you'd come tromping through the forest to save me."

He stiffened. "I didn't save you. You saved you. And we don't have to talk about the other. Not right now. Not tonight."

She shook her head. "But we must because we don't know what will happen later. Tonight proved that, didn't it?"

He sighed. "I suppose it did."

"Do you know what I was thinking while my father was dragging me to my death?"

"No."

"I thought of my sisters, of course. Of how devastated they'd be if they thought I killed myself. Or if I didn't survive full stop. But there was peace there. We have said all our hearts to each other a great many times. Evelina and Julia know I love them. I know they love me."

He smiled. "They do. It's a wonderful thing."

"And that's why *you* haunted me most. Because you and I have danced around whatever is between us for weeks. And I hated that you wouldn't know that I…I love you."

His eyes went wide. "You love me?"

"I do. And worse than that, I know you love me, too."

There was a softness to his expression at that. And then he laughed, though there was little humor to it. "Worse than that? You don't want me to love you?"

She shook her head. "I do want that. Oh God, the idea that you could love me, that you and I could fit together after so many years of never feeling like we fit at all? That's poetic. That's perfection. That's everything. But that doesn't mean it won't cause pain. That's why I was going to walk away."

He let out his breath in a long sigh. "You think loving you will take away from my life."

"It will." She shrugged. "That's just fact."

"You are sunshine through clouds, Arabella Comerford. You are fizz in champagne. You are ribald laughter at a good but particularly wicked joke. You are beautiful arias sung by a master. You are a good meal after a long fast. *Those* are the things that make the world go round. They make life worth living. If you don't think that you are worth any troubles that might come to pass because I love you, then you don't understand love or me."

She stared at him. "I don't understand love."

"I didn't either." He touched her face. "But I do now. Through your eyes. Won't you please let me teach you through mine? Let me dance with you and flirt shamelessly with you and make love to you at parties behind hedges and marry you over an anvil in Scotland because I have no patience?"

Now the air was gone from her lungs. "You want to *marry* me?"

"Yes. I said I wasn't the kind of man who became someone's protector. Turns out I just misunderstood why." He shook his head. "This is terribly unromantic considering what you went through tonight. But as you pointed out, we don't know what will happen tomorrow. So I can't wait. I *won't* wait to tell you what I want. But you can wait to give me the answer if you need to."

There was a swell of emotion in her. It crested over top of the pain. That was temporary, she knew, but for now it was wonderful. The emotion was love. And it was the knowledge that if she said yes to this man he would brighten her life and hold her fears and give her joy and music and laughter for the rest of her life.

And so Arabella Comerford, who had somehow thought she knew everything, let go of what she believed and said, "Yes."

EPILOGUE

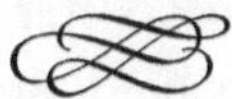

Silas and Arabella had been married for a month before they went to Vauxhall Gardens together.

Much had changed there in the six years since her first arrival when she had been filled with fear and uncertainty. Ownership had changed hands, some of the artwork had been removed. There were different performers and new delicacies being served. Time marched on, as it always did.

Arabella knew that so very well. Because much more had changed for her.

She was Arabella Windham first and foremost. Her happy marriage had indeed happened over an anvil in Scotland, but with her sisters and all of Silas's siblings as witnesses. She welcomed that her family was growing, and she celebrated Silas's delicate steps toward closeness with his brothers and Phoebe.

Her father was dead and buried for almost two months. She didn't fully understand what had made him end himself rather than her, or take her offered alternative to death. When she asked that question out loud, Silas always held her and murmured about madness. That was true, of course, but she thought perhaps it was more, too. Her offer to save him…maybe it had made him regret. Maybe it had made him see, through his haze, just how horrible he'd been and he couldn't bear it.

Whatever the reason, he was no threat to her anymore and so she was learning to grieve for what he was, as well as what she'd always wished he'd been.

Things had changed for her sisters, too. Evelina had told her about Southwater's refusal to help. She could see it had changed their relationship. And even though Evie hadn't said so, Arabella had to believe that the betrayal would eventually end it. When it did, Arabella would open the house she had been gifted all those years ago to her sister so she could have some time to herself before she decided her next steps.

Julia was already gone from that same house now. She'd found her next protector and seemed content enough with his company even though he didn't seem particularly special to Arabella.

Arabella and Silas no longer lived there either. He'd bought her a new townhouse away from the past. A fresh start, they'd said to each other as they happily made love in every room to truly make the place their own.

There was still a place for the past, of course. It was what they visited now as she walked through the twisting paths, music and fireworks at her back, through to the grottos and their hidden delights.

She found him where she'd first seen him all those years ago. But Silas wasn't with a lady, at least not yet. He was sitting on the wall edge, watching her come close, those green eyes dark and filled with sensual purpose. He stood as she reached him and held out a hand.

"Good evening, Mrs. Windham," he said. "I assume you've come here for an assignation with a very wicked gentleman."

She smiled as she stepped into his arms. "I don't think he's half so wicked as he pretends."

"That sounds like a challenge," he murmured as he dropped his lips to hers.

She laughed against him, but she knew, as she had known from the moment she said yes to his proposal, that the worst of the challenges were over. Now was the season for all her joy, all her hope and so much love that she was overcome by it.

EXCERPT OF WHEN THE EARL WAS WICKED

THE COMERFORD COURTESANS BOOK 2
(JANUARY 6, 2026)

Even after five years as a courtesan, Evelina Comerford didn't take comfort in sparkling balls, the wicked masquerades or the erotic dance of the chase. No, she was, at heart, still a simple woman. And tonight since her longtime protector, Harold Talbot, the Duke of Southwater, had left her early, she was indulging in equally simple pleasures.

She'd had a decadent chocolate tart, taken a long, hot bath sweetened with orange essence and now she sat tucked into her bed in a flannel nightrail, reading the latest gothic masterpiece she and her sisters had been sharing. And it was not even nine at night. Bliss.

It wasn't that she didn't enjoy it when Harry stayed with her. She'd been with the duke for nearly two years, his mistress, but certainly more than that. He was the love of her life. She told anyone who asked the same and she knew he loved her, even if he rarely said the words.

They had made promises to each other, and he always treated her gently. There was value in that. She enjoyed his touch, they made love twice weekly at this house and he often stayed and shared breakfast with her. Life was perfectly fine.

Well, perhaps not fine. She set her book aside with a little sigh as thoughts troubled her. The same thoughts that had been bothering her for the last few months. Ever since her beloved older sister, Arabella, had nearly been killed after their estranged father had kidnapped her. That awful night Evelina had begged Harry to help, to go with Arabella's now-husband, Silas, to find her.

Harry had refused. There had been no bending him. He didn't wish to be part of a scandal and he had left her behind when she refused to depart with him. That night had shifted something between them, no matter how much she tried to forget it. To wish it away. To pretend it away.

It was a scar on the otherwise smooth history of their affiliation and it still hurt. Still made her angry even though she tamped both reactions down with all her might and never spoke of them to him or to her sisters. She just had to work harder to overcome those pesky emotions. Harry was, after all, otherwise a good companion and he had made a great deal of promises about her future. Even when he married to make his heirs and spares, he had promised her a life as his beloved companion, one filled with comfort and his affection.

A courtesan didn't just walk away from something like that just because a gentleman didn't rush to her aid every time she requested it. That was foolishness.

There was a light knock on her door and she started from her spiraling thoughts. "Yes?"

"I beg your pardon, Miss Comerford," her maid, Deborah, said as she entered the chamber. "There's been a message delivered, from the Duke of Southwater."

Evelina caught her breath as she set her book aside and rushed to receive the note. It wasn't like Harry to reach out after they'd been together for a night, but he had been a little odd that evening. They'd eaten supper and were supposed to go to the opera, but he had cried off. They'd made love and then he'd left her.

Perhaps something was wrong.

She nodded to Deborah. "I'll ring if the duke intends to return or if I require anything else. Thank you."

Her maid bobbed out a nod and left her. Evelina rushed to the seat before her fire and sank into the comfortable cushion to break the seal on the folded sheets and read whatever was within.

Dear Miss Comerford.

Evelina blinked at the address. Miss Comerford? Harry hadn't addressed her so formally for years. It was always Evelina or perhaps Evie if he was a bit in his cups. Her heart raced and she had to force herself to read the next line as the sense of impending doom filled her.

I cannot express to you my appreciation of our time spent together these last two years. You have been a fine companion. However, these sorts of arrangements always have their end and I'm afraid that is where we have arrived.

Now Evelina couldn't breathe at all as she stared at Harry's even, careful hand and those hateful shocking words written in it.

The home I have let for you will remain available to you for the next month so that you may take your time in vacating it. And I have arranged for my solicitor to settle you with one thousand pounds, to be delivered in four payments of two-hundred fifty pounds a month for four months. This should provide for any gap in protector you may find, as well as provide you with an investment for your future. Please accept it, along with my thanks for the time we have shared.

Yours Respectfully,
Southwater

Evelina couldn't stop staring at the words swimming before her eyes, blurring in and out as she tried to make sense of them. But she couldn't.

She stood and staggered to her door, pulling her bell with a shaking hand. Deborah reappeared in what could have been only a moment but felt like a lifetime.

"Yes, Miss-" Her servant stopped. "Oh, Miss Comerford, you are pale as paper. Please let me help you, I fear you'll fall over."

She caught Evelina's elbow and helped her back to her seat at the fire. Evelina tried to find her breath to speak.

"My-my sisters," she gasped out. "I need you to send for my sisters. Tell them I'm-I'm well, not ill, but I need them to come to me. Now. Please."

There must have been something in Evelina's face, because her maid didn't ask questions or say anything else, but rushed from the room to do as she was told. She knew Arabella and Julia would come to her side right away, assuming they were each home when her message arrived. Since neither lived very far away, they would likely be with her soon.

So all she could do was wait, reading and re-reading Harry's words, trying to find an explanation in two short paragraphs that ended two years of partnership and, she had believed, affection. But she could find nothing. She folded and unfolded the letter, as if reopening it would change what was to be found inside. She rubbed her eyes in the hopes she would wake from this nightmare. But the letter remained unchanged, as did her shock and horror at its contents.

She was startled when there was a knock on her door again. When she glanced at the clock, she realized nearly an hour had passed since she received this horrid news. She hadn't even reached the door when it flew open and Arabella and Julia rushed in together, faces pale with worry.

"Oh, Evie," Julia said as she tugged Evelina in for a hug. "You look terrible. What is it? What's happened?"

Evelina opened and closed her mouth, trying to find words and coming up mute instead. She extended a shaking hand at last and gave over the letter that had blown up her world and all her future and paced to the window so she wouldn't have to see her sisters' expressions when they read it.

"Poxy bastard!" Arabella gasped out after a moment's silence.

Evelina did turn then, watched as Arabella threw the letter aside, her blue eyes bright with righteous anger. Her older sister had always been like that. Certain and ready to go to war if she felt someone needed it.

Arabella was coming toward her as Julia bent to retrieve the discarded letter and read it again, her face as pale as Evelina's felt.

"I don't understand," Julia said softly. "Harry loves you. He loves you."

Those words pierced Evelina's breaking heart and she bent over just as Arabella reached her. Her sister shored her up as she let out a long, pained wail that echoed in the room.

"How could he love me, have ever loved me, and end things this way?" she sobbed. "How? How could this happen?"

She sank down then into the settee, Arabella's arms coming around her, Julia rushing to flank her on the opposite side as she sobbed out her confusion and heartbreak and the loss of every dream she had apparently foolishly allowed herself to have.

Every dream that had been ripped away in a few cold words from a man whose heart she had so deeply misjudged.

Pre-Order When the Earl Was Wicked at retailers everywhere now! Available for download on January 6, 2026!

ALSO BY JESS MICHAELS

The Comerford Courtesans

Once Upon a Courtesan

When the Earl Was Wicked (January 6, 2026)

The Trouble With Seduction (April 7, 2026)

About An Earl

The Wallflower List

The Hellion's Secret

The Accidental Countess

The Courtesan's Protector

The Lady Once Known As

Theirs

Their Marchioness

Their Duchess

Their Countess

Their Bride

Their Viscountess

The Kent's Row Duchesses

No Dukes Allowed

Not Another Duke

Not the Duke You Marry

The 1797 Club

The Daring Duke

Her Favorite Duke

The Broken Duke

The Silent Duke

The Duke of Nothing

The Undercover Duke

The Duke of Hearts

The Duke Who Lied

The Duke of Desire

The Last Duke

To see a complete listing of Jess Michaels' titles, please visit:

http://www.authorjessmichaels.com/books

ABOUT THE AUTHOR

USA Today Bestselling author Jess Michaels likes geeky stuff, Vanilla Coke Zero, anything coconut, cheese and her dog, Elton. She is lucky enough to be married to her favorite person in the world and lives in Oregon settled between the ocean and the mountains.

When she's not out birding or rewatching Bob's Burgers over and over and over (she's a Tina), she writes historical romances with smoking hot characters and emotional stories. She has written for numerous publishers and is now fully indie.

Jess loves to hear from fans! So please feel free to contact her at Jess@AuthorJessMichaels.com.

Jess Michaels offers a free book to members of her newsletter, so sign up on her website:
http://www.AuthorJessMichaels.com/

facebook.com/JessMichaelsBks
instagram.com/JessMichaelsBks
bookbub.com/authors/jess-michaels